# I AM
# THE STORM

## MONIQUE SINGLETON

## By Monique Singleton

*To the storms.*

Vinci Books

vinci-books.com

Published by Vinci Books Ltd in 2025

1

Copyright © Monique Singleton 2022

The publisher and the author have made every effort to obtain permissions for any third party material used in this book and to comply with copyright law. Any queries in this respect should be brought to the attention of the publisher and any omissions will be corrected in future editions.
A CIP catalogue record for this book is available from the British Library.
Paperback ISBN: 9781036705176

*The Devil whispered in my ear:*
*'You're not strong enough to withstand the storm.'*

*Today I answered:*
*'I AM the storm.'*

## Chapter One

THE RAIN CAME DOWN in sheets, obscuring us from their view.

No one would see or hear us.

Not before it was too late.

For them.

Navigating the fence was easy.

Long ago it might have been electrified, but today it wasn't. Jonah cut the mesh, and I held it back as our five-man team entered the factory compound.

The crumbling buildings and roads covered an area of more than two square miles. In times gone by, this would have been a loud, busy place. Now it was empty and abandoned.

The hard wind echoed in the empty buildings, creating a hollow, haunting cry. while the incessant deluge hammered on the tin roof of the lower building and dripped loudly from crumbling gutters onto broken concrete floors. All the buildings—but one—were dark and foreboding, their cavernous empty hallways dark as hollow eye sockets in a skull.

We hugged the shadows, moving stealthily from doorway to doorway. Sly took point, followed by Jonah, two more of Ebony's crew and I made up the rear.

The lit building was up ahead to the right. Our destination was within its walls.

We had a date with some very bad people.

We shouldn't be here.

With my father on our tail, we should lie low, but we figured life was short and we had a job to do. Our quest was never more real than now. The escalating violence between the fanatics on both fundamental sides cost more and more innocent people their lives and their livelihoods. Fundamental Christians targeted innocent Muslims, and fanatical Muslims returned the favour. Like in every war, the greatest damage was collateral. Innocent people died. Not the zealots.

We couldn't go after the Christian kingpins now we were in their crosshairs, so we turned our attention to the soldiers. More accurately, to the recruiters.

Ebony fed us with information on new endeavours the ever-creative recruiters were fabricating to gather as many lost souls as possible and turn them into killing machines.

We'd noticed a clear increase in recruitment over the past month. They needed new meat to sacrifice to the cause. The recruitment efforts were becoming more brazen and had moved from individual enrolment to mass events. The dark web was full of them. And that led us here, to an abandoned factory on this miserable night in the pouring rain.

Sly held up his hand and we dropped into a crouching position. There was movement up ahead.

It was too early for the would-be recruits. They had

been told to come at midnight, now—two hours earlier—only the recruiters and their thugs were in the compound. You could debate whether the recruits were innocents, but maybe we weren't too late to save some of them.

I could always hope.

We crouched in the shadow of a heavily damaged building. Bullet holes showed its most recent use as target practice. The windows and doors were broken, glass shards littered the floor and made it difficult for us to avoid cuts as we knelt on the debris.

Three shadows passed ten metres from us. They made no attempt to conceal themselves, secure in the knowledge that no one knew what they were up to. No one who shouldn't be there.

Jonah glanced my way and looked mildly disappointed when I shook my head. Not yet, my big friend. Patience.

Two minutes after the men disappeared into the dark, we moved into the shadows behind the lit building. Sly took out a small camera on an extension and slipped it through a break in the windowpane. He scrutinised the image on the hand-held and shook his head. No one there. We continued along the side of the massive factory hall and slipped through a dark recess into the building where a few camping lights set out a path in the dark. Sly sent his companions onwards to circle the entrance while Jonah and I pushed further into the bowels of the ruins, following the trail of lights.

Seven people stood in the centre of the cleared area. One woman and six men. Heated words echoed in the empty space as the Asian woman and the man we identified as the leader argued over who would approach the recruits. The rest stood by silently, waiting for an outcome. Finally, the woman threw up her hands and stomped off back through the hall to the exit, followed by her adversary's derogatory laughter.

My phone vibrated in my pocket, the agreed sign everyone was in position. We'd decided earlier to get in and out as quickly and quietly as possible. We would terminate the recruiters with minimal bloodshed and take their bodies with us to dispose of at a different location. The recruits had to come here and find an empty building without a sign of a struggle. One thing we did not want, was to make martyrs of the bad guys and push the recruits further into the Establishment's arms. We figured the would-be soldiers would leave in disappointment, hopefully disillusioned. The woman leaving didn't help. We would have to catch up with her later if she was still on the premises.

No loose ends.

The group dispersed, three moving to the opposite side of the clearing, one coming our way and the other two fanning out to the sides. I saw Jonah slink away after the man on the left, Sly tiger-crawled to where the guy on the right stood lighting a cigarette. That left me to take the one approaching, the would-be leader.

He was a tall man, rough looking, thin in a wiry manner. His cheekbones were pronounced with the skin stretched over what in this light looked almost like skeletal features. His frame was sinewy, but the manner in which he walked belied the first impression of a weak man. He wouldn't be a push over.

He passed where I was hugged the shadows, completely unaware of my presence, his attention on his phone.

Again, I felt the vibration in my pocket. I counted to ten, the determined amount of time before we all sprang into action at once. On ten, I moved up behind him, my garrotte taunt between my hands. A muffled sound caused him to stop and turn his head towards the right. I saw his body tense and quickly slid the thin piano wire over his head and pulled back. His body fell back onto me, unbalanced by the suddenness of the attack, his hands pulling at the thin wire that cut off his oxygen. I pulled harder as he scrambled to get his footing and, in a reflex, tried to grab me. I sidestepped, holding on to the handles and pulled even harder. The gurgling sound he made resonated in the quite building and seemed like a shout. In reality it was a whisper as the life ebbed out of him.

He stopped struggling and I gave another hard yank on the garrotte, breaking his neck with the sudden change in direction. He was dead.

I pulled the corpse out of the path of lights into the darkness.

To both sides of me I heard the soft sounds of something heavy being dragged over the concrete floor.

Three vibrations indicated my companions inside had taken care of their targets. Four additional answering vibrations filled the quota. Only the woman left.

We waited in absolute silence. Straining our ears to hear any sound. Nothing.

I picked up the body, threw him over my shoulder and started down the building, avoiding the lights, but following that general direction out into the open air of the night. Jonah joined me and I could only just make out Sly in the dark distance, we were making our way to the vehicles the recruiters had arrived in. The others were already there.

The bodies were unceremoniously dumped in the back of the cars.

There was no sign of the woman. We assumed she had left.

I felt relived. There was still some part of me that was reluctant to harm a woman, even if she was the enemy.

Sly and the others each took a car and left the compound. Jonah and I made our way back to the hole in the fence. Our own vehicles were located two blocks from the fence and needed to be retrieved.

'That went well,' Jonah commented.

I nodded. It had been a quick mission. One that the Establishment would feel. They lost six of their recruiters and a large number of would-be recruits in one sweep. It would be a blow. We had no doubt they would know who was responsible. It was too much of a coincidence after my father's visit.

Jonah crawled through the fence and stood upright making room for me to struggle through the small opening. Bending my knees, I ducked my head and held the wire to the side.

A sharp pain in the centre of my back and a second in my side pushed the breath out of me as I stumbled through the fence and fell at Jonah's feet. He was already pushing back through the mesh to confront a man brandishing the bloody knife I'd felt. Jonah rushed him—oblivious of the weapon—and tackled him to the ground. They rolled in the slick mud, both trying to get the upper hand. Jonah held onto the attacker's wrists, twisting viciously in an attempt to dislodge the knife. But the man was strong and pushed back.

I struggled to my feet, blood gushing from the deep wounds the hunting knife had inflicted.

I was almost upright when another figure brandishing a machete came out of the dark behind the fighters.

The Asian woman we had seen earlier raised the big weapon above her head, aiming for the big man's neck as he struggled with her companion. I dove back through the hole, rolled on the ground and jumped up behind her. With one hand on her neck and the other on her head, I quickly snapped her neck.

Her companion wasn't faring any better. Jonah let go of his wrist and chopped into the upper arm holding the knife. A loud crack announced another broken bone. Jonah caught the knife before it hit the ground and in one fluid movement brought it up in between the man's ribs, effectively stopping his heart.

We looked around, all senses attuned to any sounds of more unexpected company, both breathing heavily.

I was badly shaken. My hearts beat rapidly and out of sync, pushing massive amounts of adrenaline through my veins.

We scanned the area, our backs to each other in defence.

'No one,' Jonah whispered.

'Let's get out of here.'

'Hell, yeah.'

We shuffled towards the hole in the fence, one stood guard while the other slipped through. I figured we were far enough away from where the recruits would be, so we left the bodies. We made our way to the vehicles and drove off into the darkness.

My pulses were still raging.

I berated myself.

Our complacency almost got us killed.

## Chapter Two

'WE'RE SCREWED.'

'I wouldn't put it that black and white,' Jonah tried to lighten the sentiment.

'You wouldn't? And how would you describe our current predicament?' Ebony shot back, her stare daring him to contradict her.

'We have challenges?' he tried.

Ebony brought her hands up to her face, rubbed her eyes and sighed. She plucked at a strand of hair that had escaped her cap, sighed again, and looked at the ever-smiling Jonah.

'Okay,' she said exasperated. 'Let me summarise this. Make sure I have the right perspective.'

Jonah and I nodded. It seemed the safe thing to do.

Ebony turned and walked to the three moveable white-boards arranged in a semi-circle near the computer set-up. She picked up several markers in different colours and beckoned us over. Naturally, we complied. Failure would not go down well in her current mood.

She began to write on the central whiteboard, then turned to face us.

Why did I always have the feeling I was back in the school benches when she was like this? I felt disproportionately intimidated by the tiny five-foot-two computer wizard in front of me. I glanced at Jonah and saw he wasn't much better off. Not even with his six-foot-six, two-forty pound frame.

'Right,' she started.

We were all ears.

'Your dad,' she pointed to me. 'The self-proclaimed Christian God, is now aware that you've joined forces with the big man.' She pointed to Jonah. I nodded. She turned and wrote it on the central board.

'He declared war on you.'

'Technically yes, but I suppose we did that earlier...' I stopped talking. Her stare was so intense it almost made me stutter. 'Yes. Right. Not the time for semantics.' I felt the blush rise and cover my cheeks as I averted my gaze.

'You think?'

I refrained from answering. Jonah stayed silent. He didn't even gloat.

'He doesn't know about me yet,' she continued. We both shook our heads vigorously and she wrote the statement down in a new list on the right-hand board.

'Your family has technology that can transport them to wherever they want including cross-dimensional.' Again, the centre board.

'We don't have a way to trace them or be forewarned.' Centre board. 'They are also the driving force behind the Establishment.' Again. 'The Establishment basically has control over the Christian Church.'

I was about to say something when she added, 'and the

other major religions as well.' I nodded. My input no longer needed.

'Your dad will have informed the Establishment so basically we're at war with them too.' It was starting to sound very bleak.

'It's just the three of us,' She continued to write, not bothering to look at us.

'Not just us,' Jonah dared to contradict. 'There's the archbishop as well.'

'Archbishop Benedict.' She stated, turning to him with a cold stare. Jonah nodded enthusiastically.

'The guy you think is our ally, who you haven't heard from since you visited him months ago?' she commented with an edge.

'Well. Yes. But I'm sure he's on our side,' he stammered.

Another big sigh from Ebony. 'Shall we put him down as a maybe then?' Jonah nodded sheepishly. Benedict was added to the left-hand board under our names.

'Let's continue, shall we?' When neither of us commented, she picked up her narrative.

'Thanks to your archbishop, the big man's picture is hanging on every cop-station wall.' Jonah was about to say something but decided just in time to keep his mouth shut.

'And you,' she pointed to me again. 'Are quickly coming into the spotlight of the anti-terrorism squad.'

I was taken back. 'Say what? When did that happen?'

'Anti-terrorism has had their beady eyes on your mosque for a while,' she explained. 'They're probing your background along with the other "persons of interest".'

Shit. Not what I wanted to hear. That would put an even shorter deadline on whatever we could find at the mosque.

'And to top it all off,' Ebony continued. 'I still haven't

deciphered the contents of the hard drive you downloaded.' That really bugged her. Maybe more than all the other things.

She added all the comments to the boards. Our "good guys" list on the left board was pathetically short and the plusses on the right-hand board were even worse. The one list that stood out was the shit list. The centre board. Our challenges.

If you put it that way, it really was depressing.

She took a step back and studied the overview, then turned to us.

'We're screwed.'

We didn't contradict her that time.

# Chapter Three

'SO HOW DID THEY FIND YOU?' I asked Jonah.

He glanced at me, his eyes dark and unfathomable. 'Not important,' he declared and went back to unpacking his duffel bag.

'It is actually,' I countered. 'We need to know, so we can avoid making the same mistake again'

He stood up straight and gave me his best intimidating stare. Under normal circumstances, it would unnerve even the strongest of men. Me, I was used to it. It didn't have any more effect on me than mild amusement. After all our months together, surely he didn't think it still worked?

'Where did they grab you?' I tried a different avenue.

His stare continued. I returned it with a smile.

'You're not going to give up on this, are you?' he asked. I shook my head.

'At the beach,' he answered sullenly, turning back to his bag.

I waited. There were loads of questions I could have

asked, but he knew them already. It was a waiting game now.

He finally finished unpacking and moved to the living room of his new apartment. I followed and walked to the kitchen, taking the groceries we'd picked up on the way here.

San Diego was nice. The town had a distinctive Mexican vibe, and it was more laid-back than San Francisco or L.A. The few people we'd met up to now seemed friendly. More open. Jonah had definitely already made an impact on the ladies in the apartment complex. With his big frame, powerful aura, and the mischievous glint in his eyes, he was undoubtably already the topic of pool-side conversations.

We thought it prudent to move him to a new location after the debacle in San Francisco. We weren't sure whether his previous address had been compromised, but we couldn't take the risk. There were too many people hunting him. I had to stay put in the Golden Gate City, my job at the mosque wasn't done yet. San Diego was Ebony's suggestion. Far enough from Frisco and on the beach somewhere.

I wanted to know how my brother Michael found my partner.

Jonah poured two mugs of coffee from the ever-present coffeemaker and handed me one. We made ourselves comfortable in the lounge chairs and sipped the black gold.

'I was surfing,' Jonah finally divulged. 'At twilight. The beach always emptied around six and I figured I would be inconspicuous then.'

I looked at him in surprise, my eyebrows raised. Inconspicuous? How in hell did he think he could ever be anything close to low-key? He wasn't built for it.

'Let's face it Jonah,' I answered him. 'You will stand out wherever you are.'

He smiled and cocked his head. 'You know what I mean.'

I did, but a bit of banter lightened the mood.

'Anyway,' he continued. 'They were waiting for me when I walked back over the beach. Two of them approached me from the side, one in front and another came up behind me. They boxed me in.'

'Did you recognise them at all?'

'No. Never seen them before. Though I did pinpoint them as your people.' There was a slight reproach in his tone. I let it go—for now.

'They made it clear they would take me, voluntarily or not. There were still a few people around and I didn't want anyone to get hurt, so I complied, and they took me to a van in the parking lot. They made me get in the back, and that was where I saw Michael.' The hatred was back in his hard glare. Well, I had the same sentiment for my sibling. No discussion there.

'I was about to wipe the smile off his face when everything went black.'

I thought about it for a few minutes. Michael must have known where to look. It couldn't have been a chance encounter. That would be too much of a coincidence. There was more. There had to be.

'How did he know where to find you?' I asked in general, not expecting an answer.

'How the hell would I know?' Jonah avoided my gaze. 'Maybe it was just a case of being in the right place at the right time.'

I cocked my head and observed my partner. The question had been a rhetorical one, no more than me thinking out loud. Why had he taken it so personally?

'I don't believe in coincidence,' I continued, eager to find out what he was hiding.

He glared at me. My answering smile didn't help to improve his mood.

'What are you implying?' He spat out the words. 'That it was my fault?'

'I'm not implying anything.'

I continued to observe his fidgeting. He stood up and walked back to the kitchen to replenish his coffee. He stayed there, his back to the kitchen counter. The big man felt my eyes on him and looked up. There was a mixture of anger and self-reproach in his features. I waited him out.

'I just went surfing,' he finally broke the silence.

'How often did you do that?'

'Few times a week. Always in the evening and on quiet beaches.'

'Was there a pattern? To your visits?'

He shook his head and took another sip.

'Was there anything different that day?'

'No. Nothing. Look Gabe, I've been racking my brain trying to find out how they found me. I have no idea.'

I nodded. Aggravating him further wouldn't get answers. We would have to approach the conundrum in a different manner.

'Okay,' I said in a more conciliatory tone. 'Let's backtrack and see if we can find any clues.'

He moved back to the living room and sat down opposite me.

'We have to assume they were staking out the beach,' I began. Jonah nodded.

'There are loads of beaches. Was there anything special about this one that made you go there?'

'Just the peace and quiet. The waves are okay, not as good as in other places. But it's almost deserted. I thought that would be safe.'

'You'd think. Right?'

I peered into my coffee cup. Nope. No answers there either. There was something nagging at the back of my mind.

'I know we can't hide your size, but I thought with all the changes, it would be difficult to recognise you,' I mused.

He nodded as well.

'Yeah. My own mother wouldn't recognise me clean-shaven with this blond hair,' he laughed.

'Not to mention with the tats gone,' I added.

The atmosphere in the room changed immediately. I looked up at him. His brow was creased, the eyes hooded. What had I said? I rewound the last thirty seconds. The tatts. Could that be what had such an impact?

The nagging voice slowly made its way to my conscious-ness to form the question I didn't really want to ask. 'When you surf,' I asked. 'You wear the wet suit, right?' The wet suit covered the tattoos. A necessity because the usual camouflage foundation washed off in the water.

He stared at me. 'Yeah. Of course.'

We were silent. I held his gaze, he couldn't. Not a good sign.

'Most of the time,' he added sullenly.

'Most of the time?' I couldn't keep the reproach out of my tone.

'Okay. Once. I didn't wear it just once. There was no one at the beach. I checked. It was deserted.'

'Fuck.'

He didn't react. The self-reproach was enough.

'Someone must have seen you,' I said quite redundantly. He refrained from his usual sarcastic replies.

'How long after that surf did they grab you?'

'Two days. I didn't go back to the beach the next day.'

'Well, at least we know.' It wouldn't help to rub in how reckless he had been, he knew. 'Let's just be grateful they didn't follow you back to the apartment. They could have found your laptop and made the connection with the mosque or Ebony.'

# Chapter Four

'HAVE YOU HEARD FROM THE ARCHBISHOP?' I asked Jonah.

'No.' He shook his head. 'Should I contact him? We agreed to radio silence until Benedict was ready to contact us. I'm cautious we could call at a bad time. He has to decide when.'

'Yeah, but I'd still like to know how things are going on that front.'

'Me too. But we can't run the risk of exposing him.'

He had a point; however, the inactivity was getting to me.

'Frankly, we need another way into the Establishment. The Islamic angle is slow and laborious. Not to mention dangerous. I'm not sure I'm fooling everyone. Besides, things are getting heated, and we need to decide how far we want to go. They're radicalising fast and I don't want to get caught in the crossfire if Anti-terrorism is in the picture.'

'Radicalising, in what way?'

'It's all talk for the moment, but I don't think that will

last long. They're getting restless. Some of the recruits are impatient. They've been brainwashed so completely they can't wait to die for the cause. It's frightening.' My brow creased and I felt the familiar block of concrete that nestled in my gut at the thought of the mosque.

'And all of it is Musa?'

'Musa and Ibrahim mostly. The other imam is more moderate, I doubt that he's part of it all. But the rest compensate for that more than enough. It's a powder keg. One I don't particularly want to be caught up in when it explodes.'

Jonah mused over that for a moment then added, 'I still don't want to push Benedict.'

Reluctantly, I had to agree with him.

To be completely honest; I was ready to jump ship on this scam.

I guess I'd been naive in my expectations. I imagined an exciting—very short—undercover operation. A thrilling cat-and-mouse game, reminiscent of the movies and TV programs. It wasn't. We'd been immersed in this scam for four months. Four long months of living a pretend life twenty-four-seven. I lived and breathed my persona on a daily basis, only occasionally punctured by a short stay at a conference out of town or when I really managed to escape. Even there, I had to be careful most of the time. The stress of constantly toeing the line and pretending to be what I was not, was seriously getting to me.

It was also very boring. The long waits. The endless hours of pretending to pray. I was on automatic pilot most of the time. No emotions, no thoughts. Nothing.

All except the dread I experienced every time I walked through the doors of the white mosque. It was supposed to be a place of worship. A safe haven in the midst of the chaos that was life. It was, most of the time. Just not when I was there, at least not for me.

Even the daily prayers were constricting and weighed heavily on my shoulders. Any and every minute I was inside the mosque, I expected to be unmasked as the fraud I was. I felt eyes on me that were most likely not there and interpreted strange glances as hostile. The walls were pressing in on me and I desperately wanted to get out.

'We persevere,' Jonah pulled me out of my reverie.

I nodded.

I was committed. We'd started this thing, and we had to finish it. There was no going back anyway. It's not like I could just go back home. An "oops" wouldn't do it this time. All ties were completely and irrevocably broken, torn, smashed and pulverised.

I had no choice.

LATER THAT NIGHT, once again in San Francisco, I came back from an exquisite dinner in a small neighbourhood restaurant I'd found near my studio. I knew the owner from the mosque, and we were on friendly terms. The sixty-year-old man was warm and inviting, a change from the usual crowd I mixed with there.

The food was fantastic and the company soothing. I felt slightly more at peace than earlier that day when I spoke to Jonah.

I yearned for a stiff drink, or two, or three. But that was absolutely impossible until I got back to my secret stash in the studio apartment. As the devout Muslim, I was not allowed alcohol.

I held the lobby door open for my neighbour and

murmured the mandatory greetings. She smiled at me from behind the veil.

At the door to my apartment, a strange tingle started at the base of my skull. It immediately put me on high alert I took a close look at the door, the almost invisible hair I'd put there earlier was still in place. Thank you, Hollywood, for your sometimes silly burglary-alarm ideas.

I put the key in the lock and turned it to open the door. The studio was dark. Exactly as I had left it. Well, maybe not exactly. There was something here, or someone. My sensitive ears picked up a very light breathing other than my own. How the hell? The door hadn't been opened, and my studio was on the sixth floor. Not exactly accessible from outside.

I carefully walked into the space, my senses on high alert. I was sure someone was there, just had no idea who and where.

A whiff of perfume identified the intruder and explained how she had gotten there.

I switched on the light and turned to the comfortable chair opposite the small sofa. An amused Aaliyah sported a wry smile. 'Hello Gabriel. You took your time.'

'What are you doing here?' I asked bluntly, not happy with her presence.

She laughed. That didn't help my mood much.

'Just thought I'd drop in,' she answered in an exaggerated friendly tone. Who did she think she was fooling?

'Well, you can drop out again.' I turned from her and went to the small kitchen. I took a glass from the cupboard —just the one, I was making a point here—and rummaged in the bottom cupboard behind the garbage bags to find the bottle of vodka I kept there. It was gone.

I turned around. Aaliyah held up a glass of her own and

toasted me. The bottle of vodka stood next to her chair. By the measure of content remaining, she'd been here a while.

I don't know what angered me most, that she'd been rummaging around in my possessions or that she'd been drinking my secret stash.

'Hope you don't mind.' Her singsong voice increased my anger. 'You took so long, and I was thirsty. Besides you owed me a drink.'

'How do you figure that?' My anger was barely contained.

'The incident in the mosque.' She cocked her head. When I didn't answer she added, 'in the computer room.'

'What about it?'

'I told you which drive, and I didn't rat you out. So, in my books, you owe me.'

'I don't owe you anything,' I said curtly. I moved forward and retrieved the bottle of booze, ignoring the glass she held out for a refill.

'You disappoint me,' she remarked in mock indignation. 'A good Muslim values hospitality as a virtue. But then, you're just playing a game, aren't you?'

I looked up at her smiling face. 'It's not a game.'

'Then what is it?'

'I told you.'

'You mumbled something about a conspiracy, our fathers working together and more of that nonsense.'

I refrained from answering her. She was pushing my buttons and doing a good job about it too. My anger was barely contained, and her laughter still didn't help.

'Besides,' she surprised me. 'I'm not here for you.' Aaliyah emptied the last drops from her glass, put it down on the small side table next to the chair and stood up.

'What?' I couldn't help myself.

She looked down at me in a mixture of humour and disdain. 'I'm not here for you.'

I stayed silent.

'Your friend,' she continued. I shrugged my confusion. 'The big guy. Jonah.'

'What about him?'

'I'd like to see him again,' she said in a completely innocent tone.

'What the fuck?' I was astounded. 'You break into my apartment to get a date with Jonah?'

She shrugged and smiled.

'You've got to be kidding me?'

Aaliyah shook her head, her smile still plastered to her lips and amusement in her violet eyes.

'What do I look like? A fucking dating club?'

'Might be a new vocation for you,' she remarked dryly. 'Now that you've left your father's employ.'

With that she walked to the door and opened it. She turned back. 'Tell him I said hi,' she said in a husky and very sexy voice.

'Shouldn't you transport out. Someone might see you,' I remarked, desperate to have the last word. 'Someone from the mosque is watching me.'

She laughed again.

'Yes. Someone is. Me.'

With that, she left.

No way was I going to tell Jonah about her visit.

He wouldn't stop laughing.

## Chapter Five

'I FOUND something on the disks you copied.'

Ebony had brought us together in a Teams meeting to discuss the next steps.

I was at a coffee shop in downtown San Francisco. It was packed. The noise of the clientele drowned out any possible listeners to my side of the conversation. The pods in my ears relayed my friend's messages and the avatars on the screen meant nothing to anyone.

I loved the hectic closeness of people in the coffee shop. It was so in contrast with the quiet serenity of the mosque and made me feel alive again. I'm a people's person. I don't do well on my own for long spells and the forced solitude of my office and one-man studio was getting to me.

'You need to plant information in the mosque?' Ebony brought me out of my reverie.

'What kind of information?' I asked.

'A document. I found a scan of a delivery schedule in the data. My program duplicated it and made some minute changes in the information. If you get that into the mosque without them knowing, they should go for the mission.'

'What mission?'

'We're going to hijack a shipment of weapons that's coming to the port later this week. It's destined for the mosque.'

'What kind?'

'PKM's mostly. Some cases of FN MAG 58's and a few rocket launchers. All in all, a full container.'

'That's some serious firepower,' Jonah remarked.

No one commented on that. I wondered what the guns were for? Was Ibrahim planning a terrorist attack? Or did they intend to sell them on the streets? Whatever reason they had; it would not be a nice one.

'So, we intercept the shipment?' I queried.

'Yes,' Jonah joined in. Seems they'd spoken about it already. It emphasised my isolation.

I talked over my feelings, banishing them to the background. 'I swap the original document for a new one and then the shipment comes to us instead of to them?'

'That's the idea.'

'Then what?' I asked. A nagging feeling eating away at me.

'What do you mean?' Jonah asked.

'What do we do with the products?'

'We use them if we need to,' Ebony interjected.

I didn't like the direction this was going.

'What's eating you?' she asked.

'Won't we just be another player in the battle. Making it even worse? I mean how are people supposed to know the difference between us and them.'

'I'm not advocating we actively join the fight.' Ebony explained. 'I just want us to be prepared if this ever gets really out of hand. We might need to intervene in some way.'

'By stockpiling weapons?' I whispered, unwilling to let it go.

She was silent.

'By removing them from the equation,' Jonah joined in the discussion. 'Anything we can take away will help. We have to do that. Get them off the streets. At least it's better than what we're doing now. Just sitting on our ass and waiting for whatever massacre is coming.'

I understood his thought process, but it still didn't sit well with me.

'Why do you think they'll go for it?' I asked. 'I mean, they have the electronic version, what makes you think they have a paper one?'

'You yourself said that Musa is a-technical. It stands to reason he will work from printed copies.'

'You hope.'

'I can doctor the mail from the side of the sender. Make sure they send a confirmation with the new data. But if they compare that with a paper one, we'll have a problem.' Ebony considered.

'Doesn't that still leave any copies on their server? I mean, that's where you got it from.'

'It does, but I have that covered. I'll tag along a virus that will make the necessary adaptations to the original communications.'

'You can do that?'

She didn't answer me. I suppose it was a rhetorical question. Ebony could do anything.

'We have to coordinate it,' she continued. 'Time is of the essence.'

There were still too many parameters we couldn't control, but I would have to trust her perfectionism. She would have thought of everything. Still, I couldn't stop myself.

'What if someone memorised the information in the mail?'

After a few seconds of very painful silence where I honestly almost logged off in shame, she answered me in a tone that resembled a mother talking to a small child.

'The coordinates in the new version are only minutely different from the original. Just enough to send them to us and not to their original destination. The chance that the changes will be detected is infinitesimally small. Looking at the possible results, and the alternative impact if we don't do anything, I think we should take the risk.'

I nodded, then realised they couldn't see me with my video off. 'You're right. We have to try.'

'So we agree this is the way forward?' she stated resolutely.

'We do.' I imagined I heard a sigh of relief.

'What happens when the suppliers come to the new coordinates?' I asked.

'Don't worry about that,' Ebony answered. 'I'll take care of that part.'

Ebony was an enigma. Just when I thought I knew her, she turned around and amazed me again. Tackling the gunrunners wasn't without risk. I had the distinct feeling she and her team weren't going to pose as the rightful owners of the weapons. They had an alternative plan. This would not end well for the suppliers.

'What's to stop them from just ordering new weapons?' Jonah asked. He had been thinking along the same lines as me.

27

'Let's just say, the suppliers will be unavailable.' Ebony closed the discussion.

Almost.

'Can I come?' Jonah asked. I guess sitting on his hands was getting to him too.

'We'll talk about that later,' Ebony declared resolutely. There was no doubt who was running this show. How had that happened? I smiled at the thought of our tiny, but very formidable ally.

'I'm sending you the document by courier with some contracts for dummy projects,' she continued. 'Then you have to find a way to substitute it for any print they might have made. Make sure you do it soon, the handover of the guns is staged for Friday. Let me know when you plan to do it, so I can coordinate the digital replacement for the same time window.'

'I will,' I answered more confidently than I felt.

'Good. Speak to you both soon.' With that she terminated the meeting.

Now all I had to do was find a way to achieve my end of the plan.

I SETTLED on Wednesday after midnight.

Musa was at a convention with Ibrahim and some of the elders. That left only Abdullah holding the fort. Up till now I hadn't seen the friendly imam in any of the fundamentalist meetings. He seemed to be the legitimate front to the whole mosque scam. A truly devout Muslim, Abdullah preached lenience and compassion. He was a breath of fresh air compared to the other two.

He also lived outside the mosque grounds with his wife and young family, unlike bachelor Ibrahim who had a small apartment on the grounds. The mosque would be empty after last prayers, except for the guard. There was a security system, one I knew all details of because I had audited it, so I could circumvent what was in place. Posing as an IT security expert had its perks.

It shouldn't have been a problem.

It was.

# Chapter Six

'YOU'RE A TRAITOR,'

Not the first time I'd heard that. It was actually getting tedious.

Ibrahim trained the gun on where he imagined my heart was. His grip was confident, strong. A bullet probably wouldn't kill me, but I had no intention of finding out. Besides. I had a job to do here. He was in my way. I cursed my complacency. He should have been out. Yeah, and I should have checked.

'What?' I answered in my best version of astounding outrage. 'A traitor? What the hell do you mean?' I tried to portray what I hoped was anger at an unfounded accusation.

He laughed at my dramatics. Maybe I wasn't as convincing as I thought. Bummer.

'Cut the crap, Karief. Your pathetic act won't save you now. You might have been able to pull the wool over Musa's eyes, but I always knew there was something wrong with you.' He looked so smug.

'You have no idea,' I answered. There was no use in keeping up the ruse. Not anymore. I would have to kill him and just hope he was the only one who'd seen through my obviously sub-par acting. Only issue with my reasoning was that he had the gun.

He motioned for me to move out from behind Musa's desk. I complied, there was little else I could do, he had the upper hand at the moment. In the meantime, I racked my brain to find a way out of this without the gun going off and preferably without me getting hurt.

It wasn't looking good.

The larger space at the centre of the room might even offer me more opportunities. I kept my eyes on him as long as possible as I moved to the side, then into the centre of the office space.

'Stop right there,' he ordered. I obeyed.

I recalled details about Ibrahim from the briefing Ebony gave us at the start of the scam. He was a proficient fighter, a black belt in some kind of martial arts. Great. Just the kind of extra hurdle I needed right now.

An unexpected hard blow to the back of my knees sent me crashing to the floor. He jumped onto my back and grabbed my right wrist which he pulled up painfully over my back much further towards my neck than it should go. His knee on my lower back prevented me from pushing my body upwards and freeing my painful appendage. My legs hammered the floor uselessly in a futile attempt to free myself. He pushed my arm higher and a sharp stab of pain in the shoulder joint took my breath away as it disjointed from the socket. I closed my eyes in utter agony and stifled a scream that pushed its way up my throat.

I felt him grab my other hand and tie-wrap them together painfully. A reluctant grunt escaped my mouth as he punched me viciously in the kidney. I doubled up as much as his weight on my body would let me.

His bulk lifted and he grabbed me by the hair, forcing me up on my knees. My wounded arm hung uselessly from its mangled shoulder.

Ibrahim walked around and stood in front of me, an ugly sneer on his lips and utter disdain on his face.

I took a deep breath as I tried to block out the agony that ravaged through my body. My vision was blurred, and I could feel both my hearts beating out of sync. I had to get a grip on myself. This was no time to faint.

I forced the bile in my mouth down back to my stomach, took another deep breath and tried to slow the rapid thumping of my hearts. I closed my eyes, extended my spine and breathed through my nose, taking the air in and concentrating on following its journey into my lungs. I felt the cold as my lungs filled and expanded. The concentration calmed me. I switched my deliberation to my hearts. In my head I counted slowly, trying to get the frantic pumping down to that cadence. Eventually It worked and I felt the blood move through my veins in a more disciplined manner.

Control flowed back into my body, and I got a grip on the pain. I pushed it to the background as my mother taught me to long ago. My meditation techniques kicked in and I compartmentalised the agony. My spine straightened more, I pushed myself up off my slumped posture and lifted my head to look at my captor.

'Back to the land of the living, are you?' he taunted me.

I refrained from answering.

Ibrahim sat on one knee, two metres opposite me. The vicious grin on his face brought out the real nature of the Imam.

'Who sent you?' he asked.

Again, I stayed silent.

'Who was it?'

My silence wasn't appreciated. He slapped my head with the back of his right hand and sent me reeling. I landed on my damaged shoulder, the pain pushing the breath out of my lungs. Unwanted tears stung in my closed eyes as I struggled to stay conscious. I rolled back onto my knees and agonisingly slowly righted my torso. My eyes opened and I stared into my tormentor's grinning face. A low growl pushed at the back of my throat.

'You will tell me what I want to know,' he taunted me. 'Not too quickly, I hope. I want to savour every moment of your pain.'

I pushed the agony back and watched his eyes.

He laughed, stood up and walked to the wall of cupboards. He opened one and took something from the back of a plank. I watched his every move, frantically trying to think of a way out of the predicament I was in. My last hopes were dashed as he turned back and brandished what I could only call a massive "Rambo" knife. The light bounced off the twenty-five-centimetre blade emphasising the sharp cutting edge and the serrated opposite side.

Ibrahim held the weapon with obvious proficiency. I couldn't keep my eyes from the blade that rivalled Jonah's axe in bloodcurdling intimidation.

Ibrahim circled me with the knife. I forced myself to stay in the exact same posture as he moved out of my sight to stand behind me. My nerves were screaming at me to do something—anything—to get out of the hopeless situation I was in. Would this be my final moment? Was this, after all we had been through, where I would die? At the hands of a psychopath in yet another scam?

I felt him move closer. He placed his feet on either side

of my knees, his right knee pushed between my shoulder blades as he grabbed my hair and pulled my head backwards. I struggled, but there was nothing I could do. He had me incapacitated. The knife came closer to my throat, and I followed its trajectory from the corner of my eye. The sharp edge was placed on the skin at the bottom of my neck, just above my wounded shoulder and Ibrahim scraped it over the skin up to my chin. I felt the skin pull and stretch and tried in vain to arch my head away from the blade. Ibrahim held onto my head and pushed it into the knife. The sharp edge dented my skin from the underside of my chin over my jugular and into the hairline of the back of my head.

The tie wraps cut into my wrists as I frantically tried to free myself. My shoulder screamed out in protest when I twisted my upper body to get away from the more imminent threat of the knife.

There was nothing I could do. I was completely defenceless.

Suddenly the pressure eased, and Ibrahim let go of my head. He moved from behind my back and took up position again in front of me.

I didn't dare to breath. I was rooted into the same posture he left me in. Slowly I realised the immediate peril had abated. I opened my eyes and stared at my executioner.

'You're stronger than I thought,' he commented. 'I expected you to have shit your pants by now.' He laughed. I remained silent. What I wanted to say wouldn't be helpful to my still hazardous position.

'I will get what I need,' he continued. 'You will spill your guts, before I do the honours.' He laughed again at his own twisted sense of humour. Well, excuse me if I missed the wit.

34

'I always knew there was something off with you,' he continued. 'You were just too…well, too squeaky clean.'

'Like you?' I had to add.

He smiled. 'Yes, like us.'

'I researched you. Intensely,' he said. 'That's some sophisticated image building you have.' I was silent.

'Whoever made your internet history is good, very good. I'm looking forward to looking him up, after our talk.' I sent silent glares his way. 'You will tell me his name. It will be a shame to have to kill someone of such clear proficiency. But sacrifices have to be made for the cause.'

'You can drop the cause nonsense,' I interjected. 'You're no more a devout Muslim than I am.'

'True. I just act a lot better than you. And I'm the one with the knife, in case you hadn't noticed. You are going to die, the only control you have is how long it will take. Quick and clean, or prolonged and in agony.'

No way would I give up anything. For once, I was grateful for my violent upbringing. I had a high tolerance for pain. Higher than most. A necessity to survive within my family. It made me reasonably confident I could hold out long enough so I wouldn't say anything important. He would kill me before I did that.

'You will talk. My mentors taught me the art of interrogation. I excelled at it.' I bet he did. The carefully polished veneer of his alter ego was completely gone. What was left, was the cold reality of the sociopath.

'I will skin and dismember you, bit by bit,' he continued. 'Just enough to keep you alive for as long as I want. And that will be way past your last coherent thoughts.'

'Just get it over with, will you?' I answered. 'Or are you going to talk me to death?'

Maybe taunting him into hurting me more than he intended was the way to go.

He squashed that avenue when he laughed at my attempts. 'Oh no. You will not force my hand. I will savour every minute of what I am going to do to you. Starting now.'

His sudden movement was unexpected and caught me by surprise. The serrated side of his knife sliced into the skin just above my left eye before I could react. I felt the immediate flow of blood from the jagged cut as it obscured the sight in my eye. The intense pain of the ragged edge hit me a second later. I cried out and moved my head back involuntarily.

I pulled myself together again, steeling myself for the next attack. This was just the beginning.

Nothing happened.

I looked up at Ibrahim. The surprise on his face was unanticipated. He was staring at me, then at the knife. I realised the colour of my blood had floored him.

'Who are you?' he asked.

He surprised me and I registered the "who" not the expected "what".

'Which family are you from? Surely not ours?'

What? I didn't see that coming.

He knew?

He knew!

Ibrahim put the knife back on the ground and moved closer. I stared at him, refusing to answer. My mind was running a-mile-a-minute trying to find a way out of this changed situation. I berated myself for not realising the effect my purple blood could have if he was initiated into the Establishment.

A massive blow to the side of my head stopped any further contemplations as the world went black.

I woke to the sound of multiple voices. The fog in my head wouldn't let me recognise them just yet. I kept my eyes closed and willed myself to waken my painful body, checking each limb as I went along. A stab of pain in my shoulder informed me it was still dislocated. The sting of new reattached skin above my eye told me I hadn't been out for longer than twenty minutes. The bruise behind my right ear told me where Ibrahim had knocked me out.

I took in my surroundings. Ibrahim had moved me. I was no longer in Musa's office. I didn't recognise my new location. Through the eyelashes of my almost closed right eye, I saw furniture, a sofa, table, chairs. It looked like an apartment.

I lay on my left side curled in an almost foetus position. My left eye was glued shut with the blood from the ragged cut. Other than that, and the aforementioned shoulder, I was in reasonable shape.

There were more people in the room. They stood to my right about two metres from where I lay in the centre of the room.

The conversations were animated. Through the fog I made out one female and two male voices. One of the males was Ibrahim. He was in a heated argument with the female. She sounded familiar, but my mind was still too muddled to recognise her. The second man joined in the discussion but was silenced by a hard comment from Ibrahim.

I opened my right eye just a sliver and saw the figures up to their knees. Looking up would necessitate moving my head and I didn't want to alert them to my new conscious state.

It was enough. Ibrahim's long white robe placed him to the far right. Mustapha's signature high-top expensive trainers gave him away. He stood to Ibrahim's left. Sandwiched between the two men I recognised the woman's dark red leather boots and the intricately decorated knife in the sheath strapped to her calf.

'You will not hurt him,' Aaliyah stated resolutely. 'You have no idea what the backlash will be.'

'I will do as I please,' Ibrahim retorted angrily. 'I do not take orders from you.'

'You will. My father will hear of this…'

'I do not answer to your father,' Ibrahim interrupted her. 'I will contact Bashir. He will be ecstatic when I tell him I have his enemy's son here in my grasp. When I offer him Gabriel's head, he will know how committed I am.'

'No. You will not kill him.'

'Shut your mouth, woman. You have no say in this.'

'She is Lord Arand's daughter,' Mustapha attempted. 'Please Ibrahim. Don't antagonise her.'

'I don't care whose daughter or wife she is,' the psycho continued his ranting. 'She is a female. I do not answer to women.'

I opened my eyelid. The three were so engulfed in their argument that they had no eyes for me. I observed the volatile dispute from my position on the floor. Ibrahim was at his most intimidating, towering over Aaliyah and attempting to push her into submission. Aaliyah was not impressed, quite the opposite. Her face was red with rage and her body poised for action. Mustapha took a step backwards as far as the restricted space would allow.

Ibrahim turned and grabbed the hunting knife again, brandishing it cruelly.

'Now get out of my way, or I will offer your brother two heads he yearns for. Gabriel's and yours.'

I held my breath. The tension in the room was tangible. Mustapha's eyes were open wide and fixated on the cruel blade in his companion's hand. His mouth opened, but no sound emanated.

After what seemed like hours, Aaliyah averted her eyes and took a step backwards; out of Ibrahim's direct path to me. My hearts sank. She was surrendering me to Ibrahim's knife.

The pseudo-Imam smiled viciously with his perceived success, his hand brandishing the weapon at chest height. He took a step forward to pass Aaliyah.

I held my breath.

Aaliyah turned her body sideways from the approaching killer and swivelled on the ball of her feet as her hands went to the hilt of the knife in Ibrahim's hand. At the end of her swivel, she turned the blade inwards and pushed it squarely in the centre of the oncoming man's chest, expertly using his momentum against him. She pulled the knife out and continued her step forward where she slashed the ragged side of the blade over the astounded Mustapha's throat, silencing the cry that was about to escape his lips. Both bodies dropped to the floor before she stepped back and stopped moving.

My own eyes were spread open wide. Like them, I did not see that one coming. I stared at my saviour, unable to comprehend why she had done this. She stared back at me with a mixture of anger and resignation.

I didn't dare move. I had no idea what would happen after this unexpected turn of events.

Aaliyah quickly slashed the right underarm of both bodies and removed the ticket-to-heavens, which she pocketed. She then pushed the knife into Ibrahim's dead hand and walked up to me. My reluctant liberator roughly turned me over and cut the tie wraps from my wrists with her own blade. I let out a grunt when the weight of my released right arm pulled at my damaged shoulder.

Aaliyah's hands probed my shoulder crudely and elicited a scream as she found the dislocated humeral head.

'Brace yourself,' she said quite redundantly, then pulled and twisted my arm hard before I could answer or prepare. Through the burst of pain, I felt and heard my bones realign with a loud pop. I screamed into my left hand, stifling the sound as much as possible. Bright lights popped at the edges of my tightly closed eyes as I struggled to keep control of my body.

Aaliyah let go of me and I slumped to the floor, my left hand held on to my throbbing appendage. I ignored the tears that streamed down my cheeks. I'd experienced a lot of pain in my day, but this was of a completely different order.

'Pull yourself together, Gabriel,' she said coldly. 'We have to get out of here.'

I pushed myself up on my knees again and tentatively placed one foot on the ground. Aaliyah hooked her arm under my left shoulder and hauled me up onto my feet. My knees buckled as she propelled me forwards, towards the door.

'What about the security?' I pointed out.

'Shit.' She changed direction and sat me down in the nearest chair. 'Wait here.' And with that she was gone.

I used the time to push the pain back into the special compartment in my mind, effectively redirecting my energy. I hoped my tendons would heal as quickly as the cuts and bruises in my skin. Concentrating on the flow of my blood I felt the pull of muscles as they settled back into their appropriate positions.

'I need to get back to Musa's office,' I stated when she came back.

'Fuck that.'

'I need to. No discussion.' I stared her down.

She grabbed my arm hard and pulled me to the door. We traversed the dark mosque, me clinging to the walls. I noticed that she didn't even try to avoid the cameras. That struck me as strange, but I deduced she must have disabled them while she was taking care of the security guy.

I pushed open the door to Musa's office and flicked on the light. Aaliyah stayed outside.

'Hurry,' she pushed me as she moved into the hallway.

Hesitatingly, I moved to the desk to continue my task. I had to finish the job I was here to do. I pulled the document from the secret pocket in the lining of my robe and carefully placed it in-between the head Imam's daily notes and to-do list. The ripped scrap of paper was put back into the drawer and I walked towards the door just as it opened, and Aaliyah slipped back into the room.

She was mad. Very, very mad.

'Come on.' She gestured me to follow her. On unsteady legs I slipped through the door out into the hallway after my reluctant saviour. She navigated the corridors. We left the mosque through a back door in the woman's entrance hall and hurried in a half crouch over the edge of the parking lot towards the back street where we could disappear in the badly lit corridors.

I registered the direction she was going. She steered me in a round-a-bout manner away from the mosque and the bloodbath we'd left behind, in the general direction of the studio where I lived.

'You really stink at undercover work, Gabriel. It's a miracle you're still alive as it is.'

Great. Reproach. Exactly what I needed.

'Yeah, well screw you,' I answered angrily using my key to open the door and pushing forward into the entrance of my building.

'Is that your idea of gratitude for saving your life?' she called after me.

I turned. 'Thank you,' I bowed in an exaggerated demonstration of flair. 'Now, fuck off.' I was past mad.

She laughed. Not what I expected. I turned and made my way up to my studio. I left the door of my small domain open so she could follow and headed straight towards a bag I kept hidden underneath the bed, my second secret stash, one she hadn't found during her last visit. I brought out a full bottle of Jose Curedo Tequila. I walked back to the kitchenette and pulled a glass from one of the upper cupboards and poured in a generous measure.

Aaliyah stood in the centre of the room observing me. I handed her the glass, then turned back to the sofa and dropped into the soft plush, the bottle at my lips. I drank heavily, relishing the burn of the fifty-five percent alcohol as it made its way down my throat.

The pain in my shoulder receded to a dull ache. The bruise behind my ear was still tender but would be gone by the morning. Nothing was visible anymore of the cut above my eye. My healing was improving. Every wound only a memory within record time. Another benefit of my prolonged stay in this dimension.

Aaliyah pulled a chair from the table and sat opposite me. She sipped her drink.

'Quite a mess.' She finally broke the silence.

I nodded. Any comment would have been superfluous. I had no idea how to continue after what happened tonight.

'What will happen when they find the bodies?' I asked no one in particular, not expecting an answer. 'Will they be able to pin it on you or me?'

She shrugged. 'I fixed security. If no-one knew you were there tonight, you should be okay. They didn't expect me.'

'Where do we go from here?' Another redundant question. One neither of us had an answer to.

We drank our liquor in silence. The only sound the soft whirring of the traffic outside the building. This part of the city never slept and the hum was a constant. In a strange way it was comforting. A link to life going on, no matter what.

We were silent.

I raised my eyes and looked at Aaliyah. 'Thank you for helping me. For saving me,' I said with more emotion than I intended.

She nodded.

After another bout of silence, I asked what had been bothering me most, 'why did you stop him from killing me?'

She sniffed and looked me right in the eye.

'I don't know.'

I waited.

'I really don't know. I just couldn't let that butcher carve you up. He would have gone to town on you.'

The shivers ran up my spine. 'Yeah. No doubt about that.' Just the thought of what I escaped from was enough to make me glad I wasn't on my feet. My legs felt like jelly.

'I would have been history if you hadn't come in.'

She nodded. 'How did it happen?'

'I've been racking my brain to think what I did wrong,' I answered, as much to myself as to Aaliyah. 'There shouldn't have been anyone there. I made sure I was out of range of the cameras, so the security wasn't compromised, or so I thought. It's a hole in their security. Stupid really, they failed to secure the woman's entrance. How's that for misogyny?'

I stared at the copper-coloured liquid in the bottle. What should have been a simple information plant turned into a big mess with possible long-term repercussions.

'Is your position there blown now?' I asked looking up.

She shrugged. 'It should be okay. I wiped the security computers thoroughly and shut off the cameras.' She paused. 'What about you? Did anyone know you were going to be in the mosque tonight?'

I shook my head. 'No. I wasn't supposed to be there. They think I'm at a security conference in Las Vegas. I was careful to make sure the security guard didn't see me.'

'He isn't a problem anymore.' Aaliyah sounded hollow. The security man's death was needless. It shouldn't have happened. It rested heavily on my shoulders too, like Mustapha. The guy might have been radicalising, but he was just a lost soul. Not like Ibrahim. Aaliyah actually did the world a favour with that one.

'Are you going back to the mosque?' She asked me.

I shrugged. 'I'm not sure I can.'

'Give me your phone number. Go to the conference. Make sure you're seen there and then wait for my message,' she said. 'I'll let you know if it's safe.' I gave her the number of my burner phone and refrained from asking for hers. If she wanted to, she would give it to me. She didn't.

'So what do we do now?' I asked.

'There is no "we".' She was resolute. 'Tonight was a one-time thing. I bailed your ass out of trouble, and you owe me. Other than that, I want nothing to do with you or your quest.'

'Clear. I'm not sure what I can do now that I'm persona non-grata back home, but I do owe you.'

'You were non-grata a long time ago.'

I smiled and nodded.

Aaliyah drank the last remnants of her Tequila and stood up. She walked to the door and let herself out. There was nothing more to say.

I turned out the lights with the remote and stared at the skyline from my perch on the sofa. The coloured neon lights blinked as they always had, but now they seemed invasive and irritated me. How could the world just pretend things were as they should be? How could humans be so naive that they didn't see the scams in front of them? Why did they continue to believe?

What had shocked me most was that Mustapha had been caught up in what was about to have made him a co-conspirator to murder—mine—and that he had been relatively okay with that.

I drank the last residue of my tequila, grabbed my always-packed suitcase, my computer and the car keys.

Pulling the door shut behind me, I set off for Las Vegas.

# Chapter Seven

'SHE WHAT?' Jonah was never one to hold his opinions to himself.

I refrained from answering.

We were in one of Ebony's many homes. This one was a penthouse apartment at the Venetian in Las Vegas.

My cover was the aforementioned security conference. The event was vast, making use of the complete exhibition facilities of both the Venetian and the Palazzo, with most of the Palazzo suits reserved for conference visitors. The whole place lived and breathed IT Security for a whole week.

That made it so ridiculous that we were able to be there in complete anonymity. You'd think the measures would be in line with the subject of the conference, but nothing was further from the truth. It served us well, though. The three of us were lounging in the big plush sofa enjoying the view over the strip, without even a smidgeon of anxiety that we would be identified in the hugh mass of people. Another added benefit was that the organisers put a ban on paparazzi and any other news crews because of the secretive nature of new security measures on show.

The suite wasn't strictly the penthouse. The top level of the Venetian was famously taken by St Mark's Square with its canals and gondolas. But this floor was so luxurious it rivalled even that landmark.

My own room was a standard one. Still very luxurious, but it would fit in this place at least four times.

'Why?' Ebony asked.

'I asked her the same thing. She said she didn't know. She just felt she had to intervene.'

'There has to be more to it than that,' Jonah pressed.

'Jonah, I told you; I don't know. Maybe it's a "Them-and-Us" thing. I have no idea.' He was getting on my nerves again.

'But you let her follow you home.' He wouldn't let it go.

'I didn't have to, she knew where I lived, she's been spying on me for the imams. Besides, that wasn't a secret. I moved there exactly for that reason, in case anyone looked into me.' My tone became heated. The incident the day before had rattled me more than I was willing to concede. For the first time in my very long life, I'd felt completely helpless. Even my father's surprise visit hadn't scared me as much as my near-death at the hands of Ibrahim.

'You should have been more careful,' he continued.

'Jonah. I really don't need your criticism right now.' I tried to keep my rising anger in check.

It wasn't working.

'Well then you shouldn't have screwed up.' Jonah just couldn't stop himself.

I stood up so suddenly I spilled my coffee on the plush grey rug, and quickly made my way out of the room on to the balcony.

Jonah's words sounded far away, and I tried to block them. A sharp stabbing pain caused me to close my eyes and pinch the bridge of my nose. I willed myself to relax, concentrating on my breath and the accelerated thumping of my hearts.

'Breathe,' I told myself. 'Breathe.' I counted slowly. One…Two….three. Inhaling on the count, holding my breath and then slowly exhaling. Again. And again. Finally, my hearts slowed. The thumping in my ears diminished and the pain in my head eased. I opened my eyes, walked to the balcony rail and placed my hands on the cold marble. I concentrated on the neon lights of the city that never sleeps. So many people out there totally oblivious to what was going on around them. So many hapless believers whose world would be shattered when the scam-of-all-scams was revealed.

The enormity of it all struck me there, on the balcony of a ridiculously expensive, cliche apartment in the city of sin. It was appropriate.

What we were doing was the gamble of the century. There were three of us. Four if you added Aaliyah, though that was still a stretch. Three of us against the most powerful conspiracy of all time.

Okay, we had Ebony's teams. That helped. But you get the idea. We were grossly out-numbered, out armed, and out of our league.

But we did have Ebs. Our own personal wizard. Who she really was and which side she was on, was still debatable for me. Don't get me wrong. I really appreciated her being on our team. I just hadn't figured out what she was yet, and what she got out of all this. Something in the back of my mind kept reminding me she was a businesswoman. She had no ties to religion. There had to be something she wanted out of all this. One way or the other, her help would have a price tag.

I heard Jonah's footsteps behind me. He stepped up to the guard rail, a mug of coffee in his right hand and a mini bottle of whisky in the other. He poured the liquor into the steaming coffee and handed it to me.

'Thought you could do with something a bit stronger.'

I nodded, a strained half-smile on my lips, and accepted the mug. 'Thanks.'

'You going to be okay?'

'I'm not sure,' I answered truthfully.

I sipped at the hot beverage and felt it scorch a line down my throat, the heat of the drink as much the culprit as the whisky. I welcomed the burn. It made me feel alive.

'It got to you, huh?'

'That's an understatement.' I took another sip.

I turned to face my partner in crime. 'I've been in a lot of fights,' I continued. 'Won most, lost a few.'

'I know,' he interrupted me with a smile.

I chuckled. He still thought he won that first one.

'Anyway. I've been beaten up before. Bones broken, the whole lot. Mostly, care of my brothers. But never in my whole life have I ever been so completely helpless as yesterday. I was laying there, trussed up like a turkey, staring at Ibrahim's knife. There was nothing I could do to stop what was inevitable, just shudder at the serrated edge of the weapon and the pure hatred in my executioner's eyes.'

I took another sip, both of my hands around the mug to keep it steady. 'I felt powerless to save myself. I couldn't even fight or move. There was nothing. Just that knife coming to cut my throat, or probably even to cut my head off.'

'No coming back from that.'

I looked at Jonah. He was deadly serious, no more banter there.

'No,' I agreed. 'That would have been it. If, that is, my father decided not to reincarnate me. And seeing as we're not on speaking terms, he just might do that.'

Another sip.

'What got to me most. What I see when I close my eyes, is his face. The hatred. And worse than that, the excitement and anticipation. The elation at the thought of what he was about to do to me.'

'He was a psychopath.'

'Yeah, he was.'

'There are hundreds of them, maybe even thousands, on both sides.'

His words gave me goosebumps, but he was right.

'It's why we're doing this,' Jonah stated.

He squeezed my shoulder and smiled. 'Take your time. But not too much. We need to get this thing back on track.'

'I'm not sure I can go back there, Jonah.'

'We'll see.'

He walked back to the room, and I turned to stare at the skyline again.

It took half an hour of silent reverie, after which I was calm enough to re-join the others.

## Chapter Eight

EBONY AND SLY were setting up a bank of whiteboards in the familiar semi-circle. She pulled a folder with screen-prints from a briefcase to the side of the desk and hung them on the three boards with magnets. With a marker she added text from a tablet she carried.

'Time to get to work, guys,' Ebony stated.

I swallowed the last drops of my fortified coffee and put the mug on the sideboard, turning around to fully face the whiteboards. Jonah switched off the massive TV and stood against the desk, all attention on our tiny computer wizard.

'The team managed to decipher most of the data you obtained from the mosque,' she started the serious part of our stay here in this Mecca of overindulgence.

There was a knock at the suite door and Sly let in three of Ebony's team. Two young girls, one Asian with hair down past her waist, one as dark as Sly, and a rather nerdy looking Caucasian boy of no more than sixteen. They carried a collection of lap-tops and moved with clear familiarity to the whiteboard set-up. One of the girls and the guy joined me on the sofa and the other one, the one with the long braids, took up station next to Ebony.

'The team,' Ebony announced. No names were given.

Ebony always worked on a need-to-know basis, and we clearly didn't need to know. It worked both ways, with her team completely unaware of our real identities. Though looking at the subject, that would probably be more difficult to hide.

All three nodded.

'What do we call them?' Jonah asked.

'You don't.' Okay, that effectively shut up my big friend. I laughed silently. Ebony had certainly set the tone of the meeting.

'As I was saying, we deciphered most of the content. It was interesting to say the least. With the parameters you gave us, Ed.' We were back to the "code" names. 'We categorised the information from the download and what we already knew, into three compartments. This meeting is to start organising the data and to perform a fit-gap for what we need to further our goals.' She was all expert now. I'd never seen her this way and was in awe at the transformation. This wasn't just a computer wizard talking. She was an accomplished businesswoman chairing a team of experts.

Ebony nodded to the girl next to her. She addressed the data on her tablet and moved to the left to stand between the whiteboards.

'The data can be divided into three specific topics, as Lady E indicated.' She turned back to the whiteboards to write the topics at the top of the boards in clear capital letters.

She wrote "Islam" on the left whiteboard. 'The first is

data specific to the Islamic side of the organisation.' Then moved to the middle one and wrote "The Establishment". On the right she wrote "Christianity."

Turning back to us, the girl continued her briefing. 'From what we know; the Establishment is a common theme in both of the religions, though deeply hidden under layers of authorisations and access restrictions. Only the initiated are allowed access to the specific data we acquired. For the mosque that was Musa, Ibrahim and someone we cannot place at the moment called Afan. He's quite the anomaly, reference is made to him in a lot of the documents, but we haven't been able to find any personal data with which we could identify him in any way. He's what we'll call a "ghost" for now.' She wrote the names on the left whiteboard.

'The information we found in the data from the mosque about the Establishment is a very one-sided story, as to be expected. We have the basis but need to fill in the gaps.'

'That's what you can help us with, Ed,' Ebony joined in.

Everyone looked at me. I got a very noticeable tingle in my spine. How much could I divulge? There were still some things I wanted to keep to myself.

I nodded slowly. I would have to comply, just edit it here and there. Yes, I know. I'm not a very trusting person. I guess I go by my own example. Kind of sobering.

The girl with the braids continued her narrative. 'We found mention of the Establishment as far back as the Islamic Golden Age, between the eighth century and the fourteen hundreds. It was a time of exceptional cultural, economic and scientific advancement for the Islamic world. The Establishment comes into the picture near the end of the Golden Age. The Abbasid Caliphate collapsed under the Mongol invasions and the siege of Bagdad in twelve-fifty-eight. It may be a coincidence. One of the gaps we have at the moment.'

Ebony looked to me.

'Not a coincidence,' I answered the unspoken question. 'The Islamic religion was strong. It offered no way in for our world other that occasional raids and turncoats. Arand needed to break that strength before he could get a hold on the dogma. He backed the Mongols with technology that was unheard of before then. That ultimately brought down the caliphate and with it the Golden Age. It also offered a steady supply of souls for him to harvest. Around that time, my father and Arand had still joined forces to conquer this dimension.'

'What did they do before that?' Jonah asked. 'How did they get their labour before they started using the religions?'

'Basically, they just killed humans and took their souls. It was very barbaric and very direct. The battles were extensive and bloody on both sides. But it garnered too much attention, so they had to think of a different tactic. Arand had been studying the human religions and together he and my father devised the plan to break into the dogmas and organise a much steadier flow of souls without endangering their own people.'

'We found reference to strange mystical creatures in the old scriptures,' Ebony added, corroborating my story. 'And something like teleporting.'

'Yes. Those would be the first contacts.'

'So that was when you first contacted humans to work together?'

'Yes. We wanted to stay out of the spotlight.'

'How did you find the first allies?'

'The concept of another dimension or aliens was

completely foreign to humans at that time, though there were some broad-minded people around. Branded as heretics by their own kind, they offered us a way into humanity. The persecution they faced from their own religions made them the ideal partners for my father and Arand.' It was strange to explain my history to humans. But I guess it was a shared one in many ways.

'The Establishment started off in Islam. At the same time as the decline of the Islamic Golden Age, the Christians identified the lapse in strength and saw their chance to push Islam back out of Europe. They launched the Crusades to counter the weakening Islam Caliphate. My father saw this as the ultimate chance to gain his own slice of the market. Up till then he and Arand had worked as partners and my family shared in the souls harvested from the Islamic faith. They worked out a status quo. Both understanding that the opposing parties on earth could work to their combined benefit.'

It all sounded so clinical. So cold. Exactly the way I'd been brought up. Humans were a commodity. Much like your cattle; raised for a specific function, to supply you with a needed resource.

It was difficult to come to terms with this way of thinking now I'd been on Earth for a while, and considered some of you my friends.

'They came to an understanding. Arand stayed with Islam, and my family took Christianity.'

'And that was when the Establishment was born?'

'More or less. As I said, it started with recruitment of the heretics. They needed a secret organisation to be able to stay safe.'

'Anyone not toeing the line with either dogma was

quickly hunted down and faced torture and certain death,' the girl with the braids picked up the conversation. 'The Inquisition in Christianity and a similar manhunt in Islam necessitated other-minded people to go deep underground. We know from Christian history that many secret societies were formed around that time. They were hunted down and most eradicated by the Inquisition.'

'Along with many innocents,' Ebony added. The atmosphere was understandably becoming heated and very uncomfortable for me.

'What allowed the Establishment to continue? How come they weren't unmasked and eradicated?' Jonah asked.

'They took a different approach,' I answered. 'Instead of going underground, they hid in plain sight. They joined the churches. Made their way up the ladder in the hierarchy and made themselves indispensable. Even joining in the persecution of other "heretics". They were beyond suspicion.'

'And this was your father's doing?'

'Yes and no. He steered them. But ultimately it was their argument with the Church and their greed that fed their need to retaliate. What better way than to use that very same institution that spurned them to forward their own agendas.'

'It's nothing new in humanity,' Jonah added.

'No, it isn't. And greed is not reserved to humanity. My kind is just as susceptible.'

'One thing has bothered me for a long time,' the big man remarked. 'You said earlier that religion was already institutionalised when your kind came here.' I nodded. 'And we just heard that it was a human invention.'

I waited.

'At what time did your Establishment take over religion completely?'

'We didn't.'

He looked surprised.

'We haven't replaced religion.' I continued. 'The Establishment grew as an entity alongside the dogmas. What was already there when we came, is still present.'

'But the Establishment has dug into religion like a cancer.' Jonah's voice had taken on the deep dark tone I associated with my volatile partner's rising anger. His heavy brows hooded his eyes as he stared at me. The tingles up my spine took on a more pronounced presence. Not a pleasant feeling.

'They are no longer separate.'

I weighed my words carefully. 'You're right. They have infiltrated many parts of the Christian Church.'

'And the Islamic church,' Ebony interjected.

'All major dogmas,' I added. 'The Establishment has grown exponentially stronger with each recruit's advancement in their own respective religion. With the strategic expertise and occasional technological assistance of my world, and the humanly inherent greed and lust for power, they infiltrated all levels of the religions. Forever looking for chances to corrupt even more men in power.'

'So you agree? All religion is corrupt.'

'No. Not all. Just the parts that are of use to my father and Arand. The secret status of the Establishment is exactly what prevents it from being the prevalent force within any religion.'

Jonah scrunched his brow and raised an eyebrow in question.

'The Establishment spans all religions. That in itself is completely contradictory to most dogmas. They all profess to be the one true faith. Acknowledging the interconnection the Establishment represents would tax even the most open-minded of church leaders. For this, and because of the foundation of their goals, the Establishment must stay under the radar. Any new recruits are fully vetted to make sure they can be trusted with the secrets. And even then, their knowledge is purely on a need-to-know basis. Only a select few know the real details.'

'The Ventus-Dei?'

'Yes.'

'The Establishment must hide behind the original religion. For this they need to keep it intact.'

'A smoke screen?' Jonah stated.

'No. More than a smoke screen. You are right. The Establishment is a cancer. It feeds off its host, corrupting those it comes in close contact with. But unlike some cancers, it is contained. Its very existence depends on a controlled growth, a controlled presence. Your religions, the real parts, are just as pure or corrupt as they were before we came. Just as real. If what you had before we arrived was genuine, then it still is.'

I fully expected him to contradict me again. He didn't. I saw a change in his demeanour. The anger fought with something else. Confusion, hope. He didn't want to believe everything was cancerous. He needed to have that sliver of hope that there was still good in the institution of religion.

I joined him in hoping there would be.

Not in religion—in humanity.

...But I had my doubts.

The three of us stood in front of the white boards. Ebony's team had left after they completed the presentation.

'What's our next step?' Ebony asked as we studied the content.

I shrugged. Jonah was silent as well.

'Anything from Benedict?'

'No,' Jonah answered her. 'I don't want to endanger him by initiating contact.'

'If he's been approached by the Establishment, they'll be watching his every move,' I added. 'We have to give him time to gain their trust.'

'So, he's out, for the moment.'

We both nodded. We desperately needed a man on the inside, but we couldn't force it. Benedict was our only chance.

'Then Christianity is out of our scope for now?' Ebony stated the obvious.

I knew where this was going to and dreaded the outcome.

'So, back to Islam.'

'This ghost Pigtails was talking about,' Jonah thought out loud. 'Any ideas on him?'

'He's important.' Ebony moved to the notes on the Islam whiteboard. 'That we know, because of the way he's featured in the communications. There was reverence there.'

'But no lead to who he actually is?'

'Maybe we're missing something here.'

We all concentrated on the documents and notes on the board.

Everything I looked at came back to Musa and Afan. I tried desperately to steer away from them because I knew what it would mean for me. But I didn't see any alternatives. The tingle expanded up my spine to become a dull ache at the base of my skull.

'What about Aaliyah?' Ebony asked as she turned to me.

'What about her?' Another stab in my brain.

'Couldn't you ask her about Afan?'

I didn't like the way Ebony looked at me.

'I can't contact her. She has my burner number, but I don't have hers.'

'We have to wait until she contacts you?'

I shrugged.

'She has no reason to help us,' I tried to change the line of thought here.

'She saved you,' Jonah joined in.

'Yes. And I owe her for that.'

'So, owe her some more.' Jonah sounded irritated.

'That's easy for you to say,' I bit back. 'It's not your neck this is piling up on. You seem to forget that her family has always been my enemy.'

'You changed,' Ebony chimed in. 'Maybe she has.'

I tried a different tactic. 'Who's to say that she isn't this Afan?'

'Chances are very slim,' Ebony stated. 'To start with, Afan's referenced in the male form. You know "he" and "his". Furthermore, in some communications he's attributed the same characteristics and importance as the prophets. In Islam, that is reserved to men. Women play an important role, definitely, but not in the magnitude they describe for this guy. It's a man. Of that, I'm sure. Besides, if she was Afan, why would she have saved you? And killed Ibrahim and the other guy?'

'I don't know. Maybe she was just sick of him. Ibrahim was very irreverent of her. Belittled her.'

'Well, there you are. With the reverence awarded to Afan, his discourtesy wouldn't have been accepted. No. She definitely isn't Afan.'

I conceded to her reasoning. She was right. Aaliyah wasn't Afan, but I still didn't trust her.

'So, talk to her,' Jonah pushed. He was getting on my nerves again.

'Why don't you, you'd have more of a chance of getting her to confide in you?' I blurted out in my anger.

'What do you mean?' Ebony asked, her eyebrow raised in confusion as she looked first at me, then at Jonah.

The big man shrugged.

'Never mind,' I tried.

'What?'

I looked at the big man. 'She wants your number,' I finally coughed up with a sigh.

'She what?' Jonah's laugh said it all. He wasn't even bothered by the puzzled look he got from Ebony.

'She wants to see Jonah.' I glanced at Ebony as I explained my outburst. She was taking this surprisingly well.

'Go on a date?' he asked.

'Something like that,' I murmured.

Ebony observed my uncomfortable stammer. I shrugged, hoping it portrayed a "What can I do about it" attitude.

'Were you going to tell me?' Jonah asked.

'No.' I answered resolutely. 'It seemed inappropriate.' I glanced at Ebony, hoping for some verification from her side. Instead, she just shrugged her shoulders. I wasn't sure about the relationship between these two and to be honest didn't want to get caught up in any threat to whatever might be.

'It could give us a way in,' she said to my surprise. 'When she makes contact, give her the big man's number. Maybe he can persuade her to help us a bit more.'

She was definitely pragmatic about the whole thing. She

had a point too. Aaliyah's infatuation for Jonah might make her more susceptible to our cause. I shrugged. I guess if Ebony was okay with it, who was I to disagree?

Then she dropped the bomb.

'In the meantime, you'll have to go back to the mosque.'

A big block of concrete nestled itself in my gut.

Back to the mosque?

Shit.

Just the thought of it sent stabs of anxiety into my brain. My hearts picked up their tempo and I was nearing what resembles your hyper ventilating. I couldn't breathe properly. Gulping in shallow gasps and clenching my hands to stop them from shaking. I desperately wanted to hold on to some form of dignity here, but that stupid voice at the back of my head informed me I was losing it fast.

I sat down in the chair behind me and put my head in my hands, all pretence gone. Thankfully both my teammates refrained from further comments and waited it out.

With eyes closed tightly shut, I willed my hearts to slow down and beat in rhythm again. I concentrated on my breathing. Agonisingly slowly, my breaths deepened, and my pulses took on their normal cadence. The painful stabs in my brain dulled to a background ache and I carefully opened my eyes.

This was so not like me. I never panicked.

I felt a hand on my shoulder and Ebony offered me a stiff drink. I took it gratefully and downed the liquor in one go. She re-filled the glass and set the bottle next to me. I wasn't tasting it, just gulping the stuff to numb my nerves.

Finally, I sat back in the chair, my body again under control.

They were right. I would have to go back. It was our only option at the moment, if my cover wasn't blown. We had no idea if—or when—Aaliyah would contact me. And our assumption that she might be more receptive to Jonah wasn't much more than unsubstantiated hope.

That left Musa. The imam was still our best short-term bet to find a link to the Establishment.

I nodded, not trusting myself to say it out loud yet.

'Let's talk about it later,' Ebony came to the rescue. 'We need to eat.'

# Chapter Nine

AALIYAH SENT me an SMS two days later. It was short and concise. "You're still welcome."

I thanked her in a return SMS and followed that up with a second text with Jonah's number. I refrained from naming him. She would understand. Why else would I send her a phone number.

Sure enough, ten minutes later, Jonah's burner phone rang. He picked it up, showed me the number and swiped the green image upwards accepting the call. He moved away on to the balcony.

'She wants to meet,' he declared when he came back five minutes later.

I nodded. What else was there to do?

'We settled on a walk on the beach in San Diego,' he continued. 'Seemed neutral.'

'Yeah. Good idea.' I shrugged. It still felt wrong. I wasn't sure why, but there was something definitely awry with the whole situation.

'How's Ebs with all this?' I asked, then immediately

regretted my impulsive question when Jonah gave me the dark look. 'I know,' I added hastily. 'It's none of my business.'

'No. It isn't,' he answered, a bit mollified by my apologetic tone. 'But to answer anyway; she's okay with it.'

I kept my mouth shut, not sure what I could say.

'She knows this is a lead. She can deal with that. Besides, it's not like we're exclusive or anything like that.'

That surprised me. I thought their relationship was deeper than that. Obviously not.

'She'll be okay,' he added.

'When will you meet Aaliyah?' I asked, trying to change the subject.

'Tomorrow. I'm moving out of here anyway. Las Vegas is getting on my nerves. Ebony's staying for a few days, to wrap up some business.'

He cocked his head at me, gauging my reaction.

'I guess I'll be leaving too,' I finally acknowledged the unspoken question.

'Back to Frisco?'

'Yes. Back to the studio.'

And the mosque.

# Chapter Ten

THE NORMALLY INVITING white walls of the mosque seemed threatening and sinister to me as I stood across the road rallying my nerves. My sleepless nights since deciding to come back hadn't helped relieve the tension and I wasn't sure I could go through with it.

I'd convinced myself there was no other way but had to go through the reasons again just to get my body in motion. The billowing robe hid my shaking frame, and I hoped the trembles would abate before I walked in the door.

I had to pull myself together, think of why I was doing this—why we were doing this. I swallowed the bile in my mouth, admonished myself for my cowardice and took my prayer mat from the back seat of the car. I closed the door and took the first step towards the mosque.

Breathing deeply, I righted my spine and quickly breached the short distance to the entrance of the familiar house of prayer. I noticed that each step was easier. I'd resigned myself to whatever would happen. Ibrahim wasn't there anymore so I reasoned my biggest threat was gone.

Walking to the threshold, the memory of my last visit almost made me panic, but I forced my flight reflex to the background.

Imam Abdullah stood next to the door, greeting the believers. He smiled unhesitatingly to me. 'Karief, good to see you again.'

'You too, Imam,' I answered, adding the traditional greeting and bowing my head. 'I have heard about the terrible loss the mosque has endured,' I continued, my face showing the necessary pain and sorrow. 'I was shocked. No words can express my heartache.'

'Thank you, Karief. It hit us all hard. We are in mourning for our lost brothers. And for the senseless violence that cost them their lives.'

I bowed again in acknowledgement. And to hide my guilt. Imam Abdullah was a kind, peaceful man. I felt terrible deceiving him. In all our investigations, he still came up clean. There was no reason to think he was part of the extremist agenda the mosque had. We were sure he was blissfully unaware.

I moved into the cool interior of the mosque and made my way to the prayer room. I unfolded my mat and, for the coming hour, went through the motions.

Surprisingly, the repetition and atmosphere actually calmed me. That, and the realisation that what I was doing was as much for Abdullah as for us. He was the real religion, not Musa or Ibrahim. Extracting the cancer that was the Establishment would ultimately benefit him and all the good people here as well.

An hour later I bowed for the final time and rolled up the prayer mat. I tucked it under my arm and made my way to the doorway.

What was left of the old group was huddled together in

our regular spot outside the mosque. I walked towards them, not doing so would be suspicious. After the normal greetings and nods, silence fell over the company. All eyes were averted. We just stood there. Not saying anything. The silence as oppressive as any words we could have said.

From the corner of my eye, I saw Musa walking towards us. He joined the silent group, and we all mumbled the required greetings.

'You have heard?' I knew he was talking to me.

I nodded. 'I did. It was on the news. It is terrible.'

All present nodded their agreement and silence befell us again.

'Could I speak with you please, Karief?' The Imam asked.

'Of course, Imam Musa.'

The rest of our little group took that as a hint to leave.

I figured that offence was the best defence and started off the conversation. 'What happened?'

He looked at me, his eyes boring into mine. I stood my ground and cocked my head in an unspoken question of what was bothering him.

'You were in Los Angeles?'

'Las Vegas. For a security conference.'

'Of course.' I was certain he'd remembered where I was. He was testing me.

'And you heard from whom?'

'It was all over the news,' I answered.

'You did not call.'

'What would I have said?' I turned the question around. 'In the interest of security, I decided against calling.'

'Security?'

'I only had the information from the news. I thought a face-to-face would be better.'

'True. You never know who might be listening in.'

I nodded.

'What happened?' I repeated my previous question.

He seemed satisfied with my answers and proceeded to fill me in on what he called a cowardly attack on god-fearing innocents.

'They came in the night. At least four of them. They murdered the security guard. Ibrahim and Mustapha must have surprised them, and a fight ensued. Both of our brothers were murdered. They executed them. Mutilating the bodies and performing sacrilege on their remains.'

Along with all the bullshit, it registered with me that they thought more than two people were responsible for this.

'Do you know who they were?'

'The Christian Militia,' he answered.

My brow creased in genuine question. 'I have never heard of them before.'

'We hadn't either. But they declared their culpability.'

'Who are they?'

'A splinter group. Very violent. Fanatics. We think they wanted to desecrate the mosque, kill anyone here, then burn it down. The police found traces of fire accelerators.'

'They shot them?'

'No, they tortured them with fire and knives. Then decapitated Mustapha and placed his head in the prayer room.'

I displayed the expected shock. It wasn't that difficult, I was stunned. Not at the lies he was propagating; at the way he was using this to his own advantage. Ibrahim and Mustapha's death would be used as the ultimate recruit-ment; a clear incentive why zealots were needed to counter the barbarism of the Christian terrorists. He conveniently forgot to mention that both of the dead men were plotting their own terrorist attacks aimed at innocents.

'That was not on the news,' I proclaimed.

'No, we asked that they keep this out of the media. Their families are suffering enough already without the terrible details.' His words were delivered with the utmost sincerity, his eyes downcast at precisely the right moment. He certainly was a class-A liar. Should have been an actor. This was an Oscar-worthy performance.

More importantly, the way he was still trying to recruit me for his terrorist activities by calling on my feeling of repulsion, told me he didn't suspect my involvement in the killings. That was a relief.

Now it was my turn to act. The relief I felt in my whole body couldn't be visible on the exterior. I had to portray my abhorrence at this terrible barbaric act on my brothers.

'Do the police have any leads?' I asked.

'Forget the police.' Musa declared. 'They are useless. And we all know how Islamophobic they are. The Christian terrorists are doing what they lack the balls to do.'

I nodded my agreement, as was expected. My pseudo-loathing revelling his acting prowess.

'Then what?' I asked.

'We take it into our own hands.' He watched me closely.

I cocked my head in question.

'We exact our revenge on the enemy.'

'Do we know who these murderers are?' I asked, the surprise real now.

'No. But we will smoke them out. We will lure them into a trap and kill them in the same way they murdered our brothers.' His zeal was palatable.

'How?'

'By mirroring their violence. We kill their people. Make them our voice.'

'Innocent people?' I was truly aghast.

'There are no innocents on their side. Only the enemy.'

The silence was oppressing. I truly did not know what to say. I couldn't join in a terrorist attack. I couldn't kill innocent people. That was a step too far. I knew this was a test. I had to pass it to stand a chance of accomplishing our goal and moving closer to the inner circle.

'I…I don't know what to say,' I stammered, deciding this would be the best tactic. Surprise, uncertainty.

'What do you feel?' He changed his tactics.

'I feel…I feel anger. Rage at the infidels that murdered our friends, our brothers.'

'You want to avenge them.'

'I do. I want to punish those responsible.'

'For these atrocities.' He continued to push.

I nodded.

'For the pain they have inflicted on Ibrahim's wife, his children, his parents.'

Family? Ebony's research had shown he was single. No wife, no girlfriend, no children, father unknown, his mother a crack addict.

'On his family. Mustapha's family. His young wife, she is pregnant. The child will grow up without a father,' Musa continued.

Man, he was piling it on. I played my part, the apparent anger increasing with every word he uttered.

'If the murderers were here before you, what would you do?'

'I would kill them.' I finally uttered the words he wanted to hear.

He smiled and placed his hand on my shoulder. 'You are a true son of the cause.'

'You are what we need to protect our loved ones, and our faith. You will be contacted soon. Your zealousness will earn you a place in paradise.'

The first reference to an afterlife.

'It is time for you to take your rightful place at my side in this war on the infidels. Together we will reap the rewards of our actions. You and I.' It was a strange sentence.

I nodded and bowed my head in the correct devotion he expected.

Musa changed the subject.

'Your company. It is doing well?'

'It is.'

'You are a wealthy man.'

'I cannot complain. I guess you could say I am successful.'

'And you like the luxury this brings you?'

'Where are we going with this, Imam?' I asked, my surprise showing. 'Do you disapprove of my success?'

'There is nothing wrong with a man enjoying his success, wealth and status,' he answered, smiling. 'I myself enjoy the pleasure money brings me. We are, after all, all seeking recognition and status. Both spiritually and monetarily.'

I nodded, unsure what he expected of me.

Musa squeezed my shoulder. 'I will show you a way to balance both of these. To serve Allah and reap your own just rewards at the same time. You will be successful here and in the afterlife.' He smiled. 'How does that sound?'

'Good,' I answered, more honestly than he could ever know. 'Very good.'

He smiled and nodded his head.

I bowed mine and we said our goodbyes.

As I walked to my car, I realised this was the breakthrough we'd been looking for.

Musa was recruiting me to his own inner circle.

The deaths of Ibrahim and Mustapha punched a hole in his business.

He needed new blood. New recruits.

Me.

## Chapter Eleven

'AALIYAH SAID Afan is someone from your dimension.' Jonah's recounting of his walk with Aaliyah froze the blood in my veins yet again.

'That complicates things.' I interrupted his narrative, my nerves screaming at me again.

'Why?' His tone was accusatory, 'What's wrong now?'

'If he's from home, then he'll be able to recognise me.'

'You don't look anything like you did when you came here?'

Ebony joined the conversation, trying to calm us, I think. 'Would anyone expect you there?'

I tried to temper my anger. Not sure if it worked. Jonah's brooding face stared at me from the Teams app on the laptop. As a balance, Ebony looked friendlier, though just as serious.

'Aaliyah did,' I answered.

'Yes, but that was months ago,' Jonah countered, interrupting me.

'Two months.'

He shrugged an "I told you so".

How couldn't he see this?

'You do look very different from when we first met,' Ebony tried. 'Your thick beard hides most of your face, your hair is much longer. If you started wearing glasses, something with thick rims, it could camouflage your features even more.'

'It's not just my face. I felt Aaliyah's presence, the same happened when Michael came to the loft. There's a vibe I picked up. What if they do the same? Then I'm fucked.'

'Don't be such a drama queen,' Jonah was as blunt and insulting as always. 'Nothing will happen. Who says he'll be at the mosque anyway?'

I swallowed my retort. It wouldn't help. When Jonah was in this kind of mood, nothing would sway him. He was stubborn as a bull.

The silence was laden with reproach. His to me, and visa-versa. I flatly refused to be the first to say anything, adamant he should apologise. Instead, he continued his tale about Aaliyah as though no interruption had happened.

'Anyway. Aaliyah said this guy is someone from her brother's inner circle. She said something about an enforcer. What was that again? A Hecta... Hacta... something like that.'

'Hashta,' I interrupted.

'Yeah. That's it. Whatever.'

He dismissed it so easily. My brain, in the meantime, was doing overtime trying to think how the hell I could get out of this city, preferably even out of this dimension.

A Hashta? Here on earth? And not only that, potentially in the mosque. Any false ideas I fostered of success had just been dashed. Dashed, slashed and stamped out. This was the worst possible development. The voice inside my head screamed at me to run. Run before this Afan found me. Run while I was ahead. As in; still alive.

'If there's a Hashta involved we need to get as far distanced from the mosque as possible. They are legendary fighters, torturers. Sadistic bastards,' I interjected.

No one reacted to my warning. Jonah continued as though I hadn't said anything.

'He's not a frequent visitor of the mosque, just comes by every now and then. And if he does, he hardly speaks to anyone other than Musa. Aaliyah hates his guts. Calls him a misogynistic bastard. But that's her description of most men from her home. I understand though, they seem to be in constant conflict with her.'

Doesn't help. Not reassured in the least. He's a Hashta. I still wanted to run.

'She thinks he visits all of the mosques. He's probably the link between all the recruiting groups. Sounds like the man we need to speak to.'

Speak to? I wanted to scream at him. This was the kind of man we should kill on site.

'It fits with what we were hypothesising earlier,' Ebony chimed in. 'We said there had to be a link between all the small groups. Something to consolidate them all into the Establishment. Only thing is how do we get near him.'

'Gabriel will have to.'

'What?' I broke my self-imposed silence.

Jonah gave me his famous stare again. It didn't help. He was way less intimidating than the idea of facing off to a real life Hashta. Didn't even come close. Not in the same league with the monsters that haunted my dreams since childhood.

'You make contact with this Afan guy and lure him out of there, then we can ambush him somewhere and get all the info we need to finally bring down the Establishment.'

'What part of what I said earlier didn't you get?' I was astounded.

'All of it. It was just the babbling of a coward. You agreed to this undercover thing.' Jonah was deliberately trying to rile me.

Help came from Ebony. 'Can it. Jonah. This isn't helping.'

Instead of letting her do her magic, I went and made it even worse. 'Don't hold your breath, Ebony. He's incapable of understanding what this is about.'

'Are you insinuating I'm less than you?' He was getting mad. Well, join the club. I was about to say something back when the connection was broken.

I tried to restore the link but got a message that the meeting had been cancelled by the organiser. Ebony. She'd put an end to our bickering.

I stared at the screen.

Dread pushed the anger back and replaced it.

I'd never felt so alone in my whole, long life.

Now what the fuck was I going to do without their help? A thought occurred to me. Even with them around, there wasn't really much difference. I was the one who had to go to the mosque. Their help wouldn't change that. I was alone in this either way.

I would have to face my fears.

Or seriously run away from all of this, including our quest.

It was tempting. Very, very tempting.

Two hours later, I was still in the same spot, staring at the view from my dark studio apartment. I was no closer to a solution. The realisation that I had no choice if I was committed to bring the Establishment down, pushed me into a deep depression.

# Chapter Twelve

I KNEW IT WAS HIM.

The absolute terror that gripped me validated my suspicions.

The man Musa was greeting warmly was Afan, the Hashta.

I felt it in every fibre of my body.

I knew.

Musa took his hand in both of his and bowed his head in a level of reverence I'd never seen in the man. The patronising smile on Afan's lips was lost on the Imam. I tried not to stare, but I couldn't take my eyes off the man. He was tall and heavily built like a warrior. His skin was darker than mine, his hair pitch black, streaked with a strange completely white patch over his right eyebrow. Several ceremonial scars adorned his cheeks. A well-tended black beard couldn't hide the tight, vicious mouth with its thin lips.

What caught my attention most was the empty socket where his right eye should have been. The scars that puckered the edges of the dip in his face enhanced the violent manner in which he'd lost his oculus. The result was astounding. It gave him an even more foreboding and intimidating aura. Probably the reason why he didn't have an eye patch. Hasta were renown for wearing their battle scars like medals. Finally, the black tunic emphasised his appearance as he dominated all attention.

Musa and the rest approached him with utmost deference. They moved quickly out of his way as he walked across the parking lot in front of the mosque and approached the entrance. From my position inside the prayer room, I could see his advance through the ceiling-high window up until almost two metres before he reached the door. I followed his movements from the corner of my eye, trying to stay my nerves and continue with the fake absolutions. The urge to stare at him was almost overpowering. Just before he took the three steps into the building, he stopped suddenly and looked directly at me, or so it seemed to me. My breath stalled.

I forced my body to continue the absolutions of my prayers. I bent my head and slowly sank to my knees in the next position as expected. I imagined I felt his eyes on me, that he knew one from his dimension was right there. From the corner of my eye, I saw him cock his head, then shake it and move out of sight.

That, frankly, scared me even more. I couldn't see him anymore. There was nothing I could do, I had absolutely no control over what would happen next. So, I just continued to go through the motions of the prayer, in tune with the others in the room.

Nothing happened. No one burst through the doors. The peaceful atmosphere of the prayer room and the men inside was not disturbed.

My hearing strained to pick up anything from outside

the room, to no avail. There was nothing other than the normal sounds of the mosque. My frayed nerves slowly relaxed, the block of concrete in my gut relented and I dared to breathe deeply. Maybe I had imagined it all. Maybe it was something else that had caught his eye.

What I did know, was that I wasn't going to hang around any longer than I had to.

I almost made it.

AS I STOOD on the step outside the entrance to the mosque, I heard someone call out my name. My fake name.

'Karief!'

I stopped in my tracks and slowly turned to where the sound originated from. Musa beckoned me back into the mosque.

'Please join us,' he said. 'There is something you need to hear, and someone I want you to meet.'

Oh fuck.

That was the last thing I wanted to do. I swallowed the bile threatening to make me throw up and somehow managed to smile and walk back into what I perceived as my possible demise. This was it. The day I had been dreading. I would die in a sea of pain at the hands of Bashir's henchman.

A sense of destiny came over me and I held my head up higher. What would happen, would happen. At least I would keep my dignity. Why the hell that seemed so important to me at that time, I do not know. But the result was that I walked tall and self-assured.

Musa led me into the smaller meeting room and pointed me to a spot at the back of the room. Others there nodded to me in recognition as I settled in the assigned place. I looked around at the men in the room. There were seven of us there. Men I recognised from the group that had gathered with Ibrahim so many weeks before. They did their best to look calm, some succeeding better than others. There was a definite tension in the air, mixed with excitement and anticipation. I stood back against the wall and waited for whatever was going to happen.

The Imam took up a position to the right of the man I'd identified as Afan. He scanned the room, his gaze penetrating and unsettling as it landed on each of the men present. He came to me, and I steeled myself to stay as calm and normal as expected from a like-minded soul. I returned the stare for a moment, then dropped my eyes as required. He moved on to the man next to me. Finally allowing me to let out my pent-up breath.

After what seemed like a long time, the man in black nodded to Musa who addressed the congregated recruits.

'This is a monumental day for us, brothers. Today, we push back against the infidels who are murdering our brothers and our children. Today, we take back control.'

The men around me nodded their agreement. I joined them. Blending in.

'This man,' Musa gestured to their visitor. 'Will show us the way to extract revenge and obtain eternal paradise for those lost.'

The man nodded, his gaze again moving over those before him. He was extremely intimidating. Many around me shuddered under his stare. The man next to me fidgeted and looked down, unable to hold his gaze.

'We are experiencing difficult times, brothers,' the man began. I realised Musa had cleverly circumvented naming our visitor.

'Our brethren worldwide are persecuted, tortured,

murdered. Why? Because of their faith. Because they believe in a better world. Religious persecution is nothing new. We have seen this for centuries. But now it is escalating. With the atrocities perpetrated on us by the Christian fundamentalists we have moved into a new era. One where the hideousness of the religious persecution is the basis for organised genocide of our people.' He paused to let his words register. From the corner of my eye, I saw my fellow recruits nodding their agreement as emotions soured.

'It seems as though we are helpless against this violence,' he continued, asserting eye contact with every word. 'What can we do? We are not soldiers. We are not warriors. We are family men. Men who work to provide a better life for our children. We are but small cogs in this big world. How can we make a difference?'

He was good, whoever he was. I recognised the manipulation of the master recruiters, which convinced me this was without a shadow of a doubt one of my people.

'You can make an impact. You can help push back the infidel. You can make a difference to how many of our kin die at the hands of the unbelievers. You can make this world better for your children. For your family.'

His tone changed to a more rallying cadence.

'We are fighting back. For every bomb they detonate, we will plant two of our own. Every Muslim life that is lost will be avenged with two lives of the infidels. They target our wives and children. They do not dare confront men. They are cowards. We are not. We will find our revenge not in the murder of innocents, we target the soldiers of the enemy. We confront their strength, and we persevere.'

'How? You may ask. How can I be instrumental in stopping this barbarity? How can we make this world safe again for our families?'

He paused for effect. Even if his words didn't have the desired reaction on me, I made sure I mirrored that of my neighbours. He was scrutinising his audience as much as I was observing him. I had to make sure I didn't stand out.

'There are multiple ways people can assist the cause,' he continued. 'Some fight on the front line. We teach them how to fight and how to build weapons that exact our revenge, to be our swords of justice.'

He made eye contact with everyone individually. Some looked away under his intense stare. I held my own.

'Of course, not all of you will be able to pick up arms.' I heard a soft collective sigh of relief. No matter how zealous they were, actually fighting and maybe even dying was probably more invasive than they had imagined for themselves.

'We need soldiers, but we also need recruiters.' He let that land.

'You can find volunteers. Others who will join our just cause, and who will fight. This is an important task. A dangerous one. You will have to work covertly. Find and approach those who have potential. Groom them to pick up arms. It is not an easy task. You will have to be alert. It takes skill to identify who is a real zealot from those who are no more than hangers-on. We will teach you how to recognise the correct candidate and how to evade any suspicion on yourselves.'

Lots of nods. This was much more acceptable for most of the men here. They were reluctant to have their own lives on the line.

The man in black brought them back to earth on that. 'Do not underestimate what this means to you or how dangerous this role is. You must stay under the radar. Your enemies are not only the government and the police, but also the Christian fundamentalists. They will try to find you. They will try to harm you. Secrecy is your most important ally. You cannot even tell your loved ones. It would endanger them and you.'

He continued his recruitment, making direct contact with each and every one of the men in the room. The atmosphere in the room quickly escalated to one of conspiracy.

They felt special.

Chosen.

An hour later, they wrapped up the assemblage.

'Thank you all for coming to this monumental meeting,' Musa addressed us. 'You will be contacted in the coming days to go to the camp. Make your preparations. But remember, you cannot share this with anyone, not even your family. You must tell your wife and your children that you are going to a religious retreat. Under no circumstances can you divulge the road you are about to embark on. Loose lips cost lives. Keep yourselves and your families safe.'

Slowly the men started to make their way towards the door. I was about to join them when Musa added a last sentence. 'Karief, Mohammed, please stay here with us for a few minutes more.'

My heart sank. Shit. Had the Hashta recognised me after all? A big block of something heavy nestled in my gut again. Electricity ran up my spine and I had to force my body to stay where I was. A sharp pain stabbed my skull in anticipation of what I dreaded would happen.

My brain screamed at me to run. They were on to me! The only chance I had was to flee for my life. Staying there was absolute suicide.

I agreed, but the window of escape quickly passed as the

others left. I glanced at Mohammed. He seemed as surprised as I was. We stayed put.

I clenched my shaking hands behind my back. The pounding of my hearts increased exponentially as the man beside Musa stood up and approached us.

'Musa tells me you two are ready for the next step.'

I cocked my head in question and looked from the mystery man to Musa and back.

'You both have potential to be much more than mere recruiters,' he continued. I tried to look at him without shaking, but his proximity made it very difficult. I was sure he was from my dimension. I could feel it. And if I could, I deduced he could too. So why was he toying with me?

A thought occurred to me. I knew it was him because I'd been warned someone from home would be here. Adding the information we had to his presence; this was the logical conclusion. But what information did he have? As far as I knew, Musa and the rest were unaware of my double identity. The Establishment was still under the impression that our rebellious attention was focussed on the Christian church. He had no reason to expect anyone—and especially me—would be here. None of them did.

That strengthened me and pushed the nerves to the background. I observed him closely.

His attention to me was no more—or less—than to Mohammed. He did his best to intimidate both of us in equal amounts. Mohammed shrunk slightly under the aggressive scrutiny. Outwardly, I remained exactly as I was. Internally, the realisation that my situation was not as dire as I expected, gave me the strength to look him in the eyes. Or should I say, eye.

Up close, the scars around his empty eye socket were puckered and red. They were old but had healed badly.

Strange, his healing abilities should rival my own here on earth. That led me to the conclusion that this wound had been inflicted at home. He wore it as a trophy. Something he seemed proud of. And he used it to its full potential.

His remaining eye was dark, the pupil black and the iris deep brown. I recognised the tell-tale violet hue that faintly shone though the coloured contact lens he wore. Another confirmation of his origin.

'You.' He focussed his attention on me. 'Kalief?' I nodded and bowed my head slightly. Just enough to be polite, too little to send a message that his intimidation was working. The edges of his thin lips curled marginally in vicious amusement. I held his gaze, giving him further amusement.

'Musa tells me you have the heart of a lion.'

I refrained from comment. None was expected.

'You have heart for the cause,' he continued unperturbed. 'You wish to make a difference.'

I nodded my head once.

'But you are no fool. You are also a businessman.'

Where was he going with this? I waited him out. Gave him the silence back in kind.

'You're a shrewd man. Not easily intimidated. I like that.' The smile was broader now.

The silence continued. That stupid voice in the back of my mind started nagging me again that I was pushing my luck. The realisation that he knew nothing about me was making me cocky and potentially overconfident.

'How can I help?' I broke the silence, implicitly conceding to his supremacy and taking his attention from the game of power we were playing.

He smiled his understanding. He had won this first battle of wills. I didn't want to alert him to who I was, but this was a man who appreciated strength. I had to portray that to be interesting to him and possibly get closer to our goal.

'Your business. It is in security, yes?'

'IT security. Yes.'

The smile intensified. Intimidation made way for a conspiratory aura.

'That is good.' He nodded his appreciation to Musa as well, then turned back to me. 'The companies you work for. They are big companies?'

'Some are Fortune five-hundred, others a bit smaller. But overall, the big companies.' I desperately tried to remember the names of the companies Ebony had mentioned were part of the cover story.

'How is that possible?'

My brow creased. I didn't understand what he meant.

'How is it possible that an Islamic company is allowed to do the security for major US companies? Didn't they screen you?'

'Of course they did,' I retorted, irritated at his insinuations. 'My company is well respected in our line of work. We have good references and sail through every probe.'

'How?' The suspicion was back again.

'How? Because of our spotless reputation.' Something occurred to me. A lifeline I grabbed hold of. 'And because my company is a US based company with British management.'

His turn to look surprised.

'My nationality,' I explained. 'I am British.'

He looked confused.

'I do not form a threat because I am an ally. Or so they think. I moved with my family to the UK as a child. My time in my home country is deemed to be too short to have been radicalised. It has to be. In my line of work any discrepancies are immediately apparent. I screen security for a living. I make sure the deepest secrets of companies and countries are safe. That can only happen if my own reputation is spotless.'

'But you are a Muslim.'

'I am. And they know that. I use it to my advantage in my business pitches. As a Muslim I am ideally suited to point out where there could be additional threats from Islamic terrorists.'

'But that would make you a traitor.' His tone was hard and dangerous.

'If it were true, then yes.' I gambled on my line of thought. 'This is America. Perception is everything. As long as I portray what they expect to see, they are convinced. To them, I am the consummate western businessman. I drive a Porche. I go on holiday to jet-set locations. On the outside, I'm a playboy. I do the things they expect from their own people, not what they see with the sheiks they do business within the Middle East. Even there, I stay in my persona. I am seen as one of them. It is an identity I cultivate carefully, because it is beneficial to me. Now it will be beneficial to us.'

The man chuckled softly. I hoped to hell it was at the businesses I worked with and not because he saw right through me.

He slapped my arm and laughed, releasing me from the dread that had returned. I breathed a silent sigh of relief.

'We need a list of the companies,' he continued, all business again. I nodded. I'd have to get Ebony to create more background in line with the lie I had just spun. They would investigate what I said. I knew they would. They were thorough. Well, so was Ebony.

'I will get you a list,' I answered. 'By the end of next week.' That was a disappointment.

'Why so long?' Musa asked.

'I will categorise the companies and what my business has done for them. That takes time. Plus, I have a business trip coming up tomorrow. I will be away until next week Friday.' I fabricated the lie as I went along, frantically trying to buy time.

'Where are you going?' The man asked.

'Albuquerque. An international security firm based there has contracted me and my team to do a deep probe into their processes and security to achieve international recognition and certifications. It is imperative for their business. I will do the initial intake.'

He raised an eyebrow. 'And this will give you insight to their weaknesses?'

'It will.' I smiled myself. 'And I will report back on them.'

'Good man.' He turned to Musa. 'I like this one. He is an asset.'

'What do the infidels call you? Karief is an Islamic name.'

'Kal.'

'Well, Kal. Looks like we will be working together.'

Oh shit. Not too closely, I hope. Any lapse on my part would be immediately picked up by this man.

'I am Afan,' he volunteered, validating what I already knew. I nodded. Not sure what else I should do.

Afan turned to Mohammed. He repeated part of the interrogation he had put me under. Mohammed had a shipping company. His standing in the community and squeaky-clean reputation was a magnet for Afan and his cause.

'Your company will be able to help us move cargo,' he

announced. Mohammed nodded enthusiastically. He was way more impressed by the Hashta than I was. The intimidation tactics Afan used had Mohammed in all states trying to please the frightening visitor.

'You both will assist us in our cause. You will earn a place in heaven as well as here on Earth.' Earth? Strange choice of words. Unless like me, you knew he wasn't from around here.

'I guarantee that if you commit to what I am going to tell you, you will reap eternal rewards.' He let that sink in. 'You will live forever in paradise.'

Apprehension filled me now that this could be it. What we were waiting for. What we had worked for all these long months.

'Come,' he led Mohammed and me to a door at the side of the room. We followed him to a small antechamber where a table for four had been set up.

The smells coming from the food on the table were intoxicating. Spicy, deep scents that immediately worked on my digestion. My stomach growled softly in anticipation.

We took the allotted seats and sat down, moving our chairs to the fully laden table.

Talk during dinner was shallow and the subjects superficial. Musa took the lead and spoke about the financial challenges that faced the mosque. He praised the donations made by the congregation as the reason why this particular mosque was doing so well. The location, within the affluent part of San Francisco, no doubt played a big role in the finances. People here had money and willingly contributed.

From there, talk moved to families and finally, at the end of the meal, after the table had been cleared and fresh tea poured, to business.

'This meeting today will change your life,' Musa started.

I nursed the glass of tea, secretly wishing it was vodka or something else alcoholic. Keeping up appearances for such a long time was taking its toll on me. I had been in the mosque now for more than five hours and was exhausted by the combination of angst and wariness.

'You will forget what you have been taught and embrace the new truth.'

Mohammed leant forward, infatuated with what was being said. I stayed put, my back to the chair and the glass of tea in my hand.

Afan watched our every move while Musa explained the real reason for all this elaborate recruitment.

'Within our world there is more than you know.'

I hung on to his words with bated breath. How far would he go?

'What would you say if we could guarantee that some Islamic souls get a direct route to the afterlife? To heaven?'

Heaven? Not what I would call it, but I kept my thoughts to myself.

I nodded to urge him onwards. Mohammed and I glanced at each other. Not sure where all this was going. I saw uncertainty in his eyes, but also anticipation and excitement.

'A direct ticket,' Afan took over. 'A ticket to heaven.'

I pretended to be glued to his narrative. Not a stretch, my excitement was genuine. Just not for the same reasons as Mohammed.

'There is such a thing.' Afan paused for effect. I looked surprised, as expected.

Mohammed took it one step further. 'That is our faith. That is our ticket to heaven.' He stated resolutely.

Afan leaned forward and touched his arm in a gesture of brotherhood.

'Yes, brother. Our faith ensures some of us eventually find a place in paradise.' He smiled at us both, then sat back in the chair, an air of authority oozing off him.

'But there is another way. A way to make sure. To help our brethren. Those who maybe have not led a pious life. Those who joined us later in life. Who succumbed to temptation before they joined our faith.'

'How is that possible?' Mohammed asked.

'There are those amongst us that can identify these repentant sinners so that Izrail, the angel of death, can take their souls to heaven when they die.'

He paused for effect. Again, Mohammed and I glanced at each other in surprise.

I must admit Afan was milking the whole thing like a pro. His manipulations worked a treat on Mohammed and his acting rivalled mine. I smiled internally at the thought that I was manipulating him even more than he was us.

'Who are these people?' I asked. 'How can they identify the repentant?'

'Those here around you.' Afan waved his hand to encompass all of the people in the room. 'Your Imam, me. And...' he paused again. 'You can become a recruiter of souls like us. Like the elders of Islam that you admire and strive to resemble.'

'Us?'

He nodded. Mohammed leant forward, captivated by the lies Afan spun.

'How?'

He had him. It was obvious. This was the reason Afan was here, to recruit the super recruiters. To initiate them in the kidnapping of the souls. Only they didn't know. At least not immediately. Afan played on the religious fervour of Mohammed and, he hoped, me.

'And in recruiting souls,' he pushed the final reward. 'You will earn yourself a place of honour in Paradise. You will be revered as the devout Muslim you are. Rewarded for your tireless assistance to your brethren.'

If you put it that way, it sounded enticing.

Mohammed beamed. I nodded my agreement.

'You will be well rewarded for your work. You will be awarded the respect and wealth you deserve. Both here and in the afterlife.'

'Here?' I asked.

Afan smiled. His thin lips pulled in a caricature of friendliness. He picked up on what I wanted him to. My perceived greed.

'Yes. Here. I knew that would appeal to you as a businessman,' he answered.

I cocked my head in agreement. We both knew the devout part was not the main driver. Mohammed's business sense kicked in and he sat back, observing Afan and Musa more closely.

'There is a need for souls in the afterlife.' Afan let that sink in.

'We,' again he included Musa and us. 'We can supply them. Souls who yearn for paradise.'

'And how do we supply these?' I asked carefully. 'Surely not by killing people?'

'No. No of course not.' Musa was quick to jump in. 'We do not hurt anyone. All we do is make sure the souls of those who die go directly to paradise. We guarantee Izrail can find the soul of the believer as soon as it departs the body.' He paused.

'Continue, please,' I urged him onwards. 'How does Izrail find these souls above all others?'

'We mark them.'

'With what?'

'With a substance that he can identify.'

Okay, not very transparent, but I let that pass.

'And that is a substance that does not harm the believers?'

'It doesn't not. It is undetectable, except for Izrail.'

'How do you administer it?' I asked.

'That is something we will reveal to you later on.' Afan smiled at my curiosity.

'Will you both join in our cause?' Musa pushed home the real goal of this meeting.

'Yes,' Mohammed exclaimed enthusiastically. I just nodded. Afan watched me closely. Gauging my reaction.

'Musa will initiate you in the details, Mohammed,' he addressed his new partner in crime. 'Please follow him and he will explain how you can become a master recruiter and save these souls.'

Goosebumps had returned. Had I pushed my surprise too far? Why wasn't I included in this training?'

Musa and Mohammed stood, bowed slightly to Afan and left the room.

No one had indicated I follow Musa, so I stayed put, anxiety once again building.

Afan stood up and walked to the table where he poured two glasses of the ever-present tea. He offered one and sat down again opposite me.

'You are a technical expert, Karief?' He asked out of the blue.

I nodded.

'Then surely you would appreciate the technology behind identifying the souls. There are many ways to tag a person so that certain data is exposed if something happens to them.'

'Like RFID?' I asked incredulously.

'Like nano technology.'

'Nano technology?' I stroked my beard in thought. Pretending to ponder what he had just told me.

'Izrail can pick up the presence of nanotech?'

'Something like that.'

'Are you telling me that Paradise is a technologically advanced concept?'

'More advanced than you could imagine.' He smiled again. That pompous, arrogant, wicked smile.

'There are theories,' I started carefully, mincing my words. 'They claim that paradise, heaven and the gods are aliens. Are you telling me this is true?'

'I am.'

'But what of Islam?' I acted shocked.

'Islam is real. It is a gift from the aliens to our people. A gift that ensures eternal life in paradise.'

'If?'

He cocked his head. 'If we supply them with souls.'

'What do they do with the souls?' I asked cautiously, gauging it was what he would expect.

'That is of no concern to you. Know that they are in paradise.'

Yeah, I thought, paradise doesn't apply to them. Just to their owners.

'And you want us to administer the nanotech to the believers?'

'I want you to recruit believers. Young men who are willing to fight for Islam.'

'And die?'

No answer, just that smirk.

'Then we will administer the nanotech, and their soul will be recognised when they die.'

After a short silence I asked what he expected.

'And what is in it for us?' I made sure I included him in all this.

'You will be guaranteed a place of respect and opulence after your death. You will live forever in paradise in the luxury that you deserve. The more recruits you supply, the more luxury you will be rewarded with.'

I pretended to think about it for a few moments, slowly drinking my tea and creating an air of greed.

'You mentioned wealth here as well as in the afterlife.'

'Yes, Karief. I did.'

I waited.

'There is an organisation within Islam. A group of like-minded scholars and leaders. They control the recruitment and who is invited to our inner circle. You would be initiated into this upper echelon. There you will partake in the rewards of your work.'

'All for recruiting souls?'

'No. We require more from you. With your company we can infiltrate security at key enemies of Islam and our acolytes can lay waste to the infidels. That will be your main value to our cause. No secrets will be safe from us because of you. That, my friend will guarantee you a seat in the Establishment.'

I held my breath.

When he finally said the word out loud it almost stopped my hearts. The Establishment. The acknowledgement that what we were seeking was there. The Jihad was a front for the Establishment. This was the proof. Not just that, Afan's mere presence here, recruiting the believers, demonstrated the involvement of Arand's clan in the terrorism the jihad preached.

Our quest just became very real.

'Do not agree to join us lightly, Karief. We expect much from you,' Afan cautioned.

'If you do not come through,' he continued in his monologue. 'You will regret it. You, your family, your friends. We demand absolute loyalty. The Establishment is foremost in your fealty. Higher even than your imam. Than your family.'

'We are your new family. We take care of those who deserve it. We punish those who are not. What you do for us is your ticket to heroism. We are the conquerors, the champions. And you will reap the rewards that are due to you.'

# Chapter Thirteen

'I GOT out of there as soon as I could.'

Ebony, Jonah and I were in a safe house in Nevada. After my flight to Albuquerque and subsequent check-in to the hotel. I'd hightailed it out of the back door in a car Ebony organised. She'd convinced me that I had to go through the motions of my hastily concocted story. I'd mentioned New Mexico, so I had to go there. Her team was putting together the details of the smokescreen and digital proof. Just in case anyone was looking. I was sure there was. No way Afan would just trust me. He and his team would be scouring the Internet to find out if I was speaking the truth.

I'd suggested I just disappear. Get the hell out of Dodge, as it were. But Ebony persuaded me to delay my escape for a moment and play along with the ruse.

And that brought me here. To a small ranch house in the middle of nowhere, somewhere in Nevada near the border with New Mexico. The driver was one of Ebony's crew. I didn't know her, but she had the same characteristics. Silent, intense, and professional.

The trip was a quiet one. After the first few sentences to inform me we would be going to the desert, we fell into silence. I turned to the window and looked out at the scenery.

During the long drive, the shrub made way for red sand and rock as we crossed the county line between New Mexico and Nevada. In itself the scenery was beautiful, though the barren desert made me think of home. The sunset was beautiful, colouring the rugged mountains deep red adding to an unexpected stab of homesickness.

I fell into a restless sleep and woke when the driver gently nudged me. 'We're here.'

The house was clearly lived in.

Worn, but clean, comfortable furniture dated from decades ago. It was a homely place that was clearly loved. There were family photos of a couple with teenage children. A few showed sport activities with proud parents and children holding trophies of some sort. The atmosphere here was one of a happy family. Where they were I didn't know. I deduced Ebony had asked them to temporarily vacate the premises. They would no doubt return, just as happy and a bit wealthier.

'You did well, Gabe,' Ebony congratulated me as we sipped coffee. 'You stayed calm.'

'I was scared out of my mind.'

'Nothing happened.' Jonah was his normal sympathetic self. I decided to ignore him.

'Zip it, Jonah.' Ebony came to my aid.

The big man morosely did as he was told.

'This is a breakthrough,' she continued. 'The link between the Jihad and the Establishment is exactly as we expected. And we also know for certain that your dimension is behind all of it.'

'The biggest win,' I explained. 'Is that we have the link that the Establishment is involved and that it is the same organisation that is behind the Christian scam.'

I felt good. I'd come through and our assumptions and been validated.

'It is,' Ebony answered. My heart sank. There was a "but" there. One I didn't want to know. One so bad she was careful how she broached the subject. Shit. I knew what was coming.

'There's no proof.' Jonah's direct and contentious approach brought it home. 'Nothing we can use anyway.'

'But we know now.' I tried half-heartedly. I knew they were right. The realisation had plagued me during the flight and the drive to the safe house.

'Yes. We know. But that's not enough.'

'Not unless we want to go back to our previous way of working,' Jonah chimed in. He glanced at the big axe against the wall.

'We've spoken about that, Jonah,' Ebony said. 'We want to bring down the Establishment, not just some of the players.'

'We could do both.'

'Not without calling attention to ourselves.'

'We'll blame it on the Christian Fundamentalists.' He had an answer.

'That would make us no better than them,' I chimed in desolately.

'Not true. We target the bad ones, not innocents.'

I refrained from answering him. He was out for a fight. Whatever I said would only antagonise him more. The lack of action on his part was getting to him again. He was going stir-crazy, and he didn't do that well. I understood his predicament. He was cooped up in one of Ebony's many houses. He didn't dare go back to the beach or do anything he usually would to let off steam. Thankfully the house had a full gym and by the look of his buffed-up physique, he'd been using that a lot.

But he was a loose projectile. He needed to do something to get rid of all the energy building up inside. Pressure was never a good idea with the big man.

'We could do both.' He stated resolutely, needing the final word.

Whatever. He wasn't my problem at the moment, I had bigger fish to fry. Afan.

'You have to keep up the undercover operation,' Ebony uttered the dreaded words I already knew.

'I'm not sure what we can do to get proof,' I tried dismally.

'We need to have something either digital or on paper that links them. Something we can make public. Just our word against theirs will not persuade anyone. The truth here is too strange to believe without solid testimony and irrefutable proof to back us up.'

'Yes, but how?'

'Stop moaning Gabe, and just get on with it,' Jonah barged in. 'You're looking for excuses.'

He was right, but I wasn't about to agree with him. I was stalling. On the other hand, I was at a loss as to what would satisfy the burden of proof.

I still regarded my escape from Afan as a close call. I'd fooled him for now, but it was just a matter of time before I slipped up. The man was formidable. And, judging by his battle scars and the position he held, he was no fool. He'd been around for a while, had seen it all. Well, maybe not us, but you get the gist.

'If it makes you feel better,' there was a patronising tone to his voice. 'We can take out this Afan guy.'

I liked his suggestion, but he was grossly underestimating the threat.

'Afan is not like anything you have ever seen before,' I cautioned him.

He shrugged.

'He's a trained assassin. I think the closest you could come here on Earth is a combination of a ninja, a SEAL and a psychopath.'

'All the more reason to take him out.'

'He's been around for thousands of years, Jonah. Don't underestimate the threat he poses.'

'He's lost an eye. That gives him a weak spot.'

'I expect that wound was inflicted a long time ago, and that he's been able to adapt to it easily,' I answered. 'Don't make the mistake of underestimating him. The man is a legend.'

'I can hold my own,' Jonah was turning it personal. 'I can take him. Besides, I like a challenge. It'll be a welcome change to the pathetic so-called warriors we've encountered up to now.'

My big friend definitely didn't have a lack of self-confidence. In this case it might just be his undoing.

'I'm sure you can, Jonah,' Ebony intervened. 'But even so, if we take him on, we need to make sure we have a fail-safe plan.'

'I do. Lure him to me and I'll chop his head off.' I admired Jonah's confidence, but he wasn't realistic. If it had been so easy, Afan would have died long ago.

'I was thinking of more of a plan than that,' Ebony

smiled her answer. 'A few more details, here and there.' She became serious again. 'And we need to get proof of some kind from him before he is dispatched.'

'We could tape an interrogation,' I suggested.

'Yes. That would be an option. But I'm thinking more of a real-time streaming. We need to make sure that the Establishment can't claim it's all fake. So, a bit more thought will be needed here.'

I nodded.

'We're only going to have one chance at this. We have to make sure we have all the details worked out and everything is ready.'

I knew she was right, but the amount of preparations signalled a delay. It would take time. Time I would have to sit out. I wasn't sure I could handle that.

I might not have a choice.

'Are we looking at exposing all of it?' I asked. 'The Establishment, the families and all?' I didn't mention what was really eating at me. I was anxious that I would have to be exposed as well. The concept of aliens would need proof if it was to hold its own.

'We will have Afan. We can use him for the exposure of the parallel dimension,' Jonah answered me. I was surprised. It was actually a good non-violent option. Then he went and spoiled it. 'His body, the purple blood and two hearts will convince people that aliens are among us.'

'It will also get the full force of the army on our neck if we don't do it right,' Ebony tempered his enthusiasm. 'Some subtlety is needed here, big man. You can't just go in swinging the axe. No matter how much he deserves it.'

He was about to give an answer but thought the better of it as he observed Ebony's raised eyebrow. Instead, he smiled.

'So, now we need to decide on the next steps.'

I nodded reluctantly. There wasn't anything else I could do.

It occurred to me how much I'd changed in the past two years. My earlier me would have run like hell from the threats that faced us. But hey, the old me would never have dedicated himself to anything worthwhile. And that was what this was. Worthwhile. For the first time in my life, I had a cause I believed in. I'd committed to this, so I had to see it through. And if that meant risking my life—again— then so be it.

I felt good with myself. Another first.

Ebony smiled. She'd observed my internal struggle and identified that I'd come out with the intended resolve.

'You okay with this, Gabe?'

'Yes,' I answered resolutely. 'Let's do this.'

Jonah raised an eyebrow and cocked his head, blissfully unaware of the discussion I had just had with my more cowardly side.

'We have to think of something that will convince Afan to join us somewhere remote. I think we should use the leverage we have. The security company.'

'It will take some preparation.'

'I know.' The dread threatened to come back, but I pushed it away. This was my time to do something worthwhile and I wasn't about to let nerves block that.

We got down to business. 'They will be tracing the information I gave them,' I started. 'That makes that a good place to start.' I turned to Ebony. 'Do you have contacts in Albuquerque that could be the front for the operation?'

'I can get them.' Of course she could.

'We need to make that—or one of the other companies —so interesting that Afan would want to get in on the details. He probably has a passing knowledge of technology, so I will have to be careful. But count on a backfill by real technology experts. It has to be fool proof. Then we can lure him away from San Francisco and carry out the second part of the plan. The exposure.'

Jonah joined in the planning, as happy as I was that we were making concrete steps forward. It gave our purpose a boost. It also distracted me from the real danger I was putting myself in. My resolve was strong, but a bit of distraction was welcome. Nightmares of the Hashta would no doubt continue to haunt my sleeping hours. That was a given. So, I might as well do something good with them.

'We need to know more about this Afan, and the Hashta in general,' Jonah surprised me. 'We need to be prepared.'

I nodded, not sure what to say about this turnaround.

'You said he was the equivalent of a Ninja, SEAL and more, all rolled up in one. What exactly is he proficient in?'

'Anything that will kill, especially cutting weapons. The curved sword is their favourite weapon, and they are renowned for using a small, very sharp knife to torture their prisoners. They basically skin them alive.'

Shivers ran up my spine again. I'd have to get used to it.

'Not a nice guy.'

'That's the understatement of the year.'

I continued. 'If he is Bashir's right-hand man, then he's earned Bashir's respect. That means he is foremost in his kind. An experienced and respected Hashta. The way they achieve notoriety within the ranks of psychos, is by being the best—or in this case—the worst. He's sadistic. Won't think twice about killing. Makes no distinction between men, women or children. The Hashta are the stuff of nightmares where I come from. Not just because of the legends, but also because of the attack they mounted on my family during one of the times my father fell out with Arand.'

I swallowed hard. 'They killed two of my uncles, their wives, three cousins and ten of their staff. They hung the skinned remains of the children on the door to the compound to make a point.'

We were silent. For me, the memories were vivid. If I closed my eyes, I could still see the terrible sight of my former cousins. Two small girls—one a mere baby—and a teenage boy. All had been alive when they were flayed, like their father and mother who were crucified on stakes opposite where the butchery had taken place.

'It was a statement,' I continued softly. 'One that registered. After that my father sought out Arand and negotiated a truce. The family was supposed to be safe in the compound. The Hashta had made it perfectly clear that was not the case.' I retreated into myself. Eager to stop the memories there.

'There's more?' Ebony whispered.

I sighed and pulled myself back to the present. 'My father made my brothers and me take down the children and...' I swallowed hard. 'And reunite them with their skins. I still have nightmares.'

Even Jonah was dumb struck. There was nothing to say. It finally dawned on him what we were up against.

Silence.

'And this truce is still in place?' he finally asked.

'It must be. At least it was last time I was there. I think Aaliyah would have informed us if it wasn't. That would mean war. And that's bad for business. With all the recruiting that's going on and our assumption that they are working together, they would need the truce.'

'Do they trust each other?'

'No. My father still hates Arand with a vengeance. It's a business partnership, one that's beneficial to them now. As soon as the monetary benefits fail to outweigh the hate, things will explode. It's a volatile scenario. My father never forgets a transgression, and what happened to his brothers and their families will be avenged.'

'Can we use that to our advantage?' Jonah asked.

'Difficult, because we can't really show our cards.'

'Might be something to keep in mind when we expose everything,' Ebony suggested. 'Like if you exposed the Islam side, then Arand may take it personally.'

'Yes, that's possible, but what about Aaliyah?'

'Good question.' I mused over the conundrum. 'I'm confused about her place in all of this. She seems very disenchanted with her family, and she has helped, even though reluctantly. But whether that is enough to stand by us, I'm not sure.' I turned to Jonah. He'd had more contact with Aaliyah than I during the past month. I hadn't run into her at the mosque, that didn't mean she wasn't there, but our paths hadn't crossed after that fateful night when she saved me.

'Difficult,' the big man answered the unspoken question. 'She's complicated. Her loyalty to her father is being put to the test because of what is happening. She knows it's wrong. But I don't think she's ready yet to disown her family.'

'Can you convince her?' I asked hopefully.

'I expect it's not my commitment to the cause that she's after,' he replied with a raised eyebrow and smile.

I glanced at Ebony, but she was calm under the thinly veiled innuendos.

'Well, at some point, we will need to find out where she stands.' I closed the subject of Aaliyah.

There was a knock on the door to the living room and

Sly came in, carrying a collection of brown paper bags from which emanated the most fantastic oriental smells. Dinner was served. It formed a great distraction and allowed us to order our thoughts before we continued planning our next steps.

After dinner we sat down to order the actions.

We built a list and awarded each entry an owner, with Ebony and her team doing all the substantial digital work needed to front our plan.

Jonah was put to work training Ebony's muscle team and gathering the necessary hardware. I would go back to the mosque and deepen the relationship with Afan.

On paper it looked good.

Logical and doable.

My nerves begged to differ.

## Chapter Fourteen

LIKE WITH EVERY well laid plan, life—and Murphy—intervenes.

We had control over a lot of the aspects.

One that was out of our influence was when Afan would be around.

As promised, I delivered a list of companies my business allegedly worked for by the end of the next week. I'd hoped to hand it over to Afan, but Musa informed me he was unavailable. My question about when he would be around was met with a non-committal "when he wants".

Not a big help. Even if I secretly felt very relieved, it wasn't in the plan. It shouldn't have been a surprise, not really. I expected the Hashta to stay away from any kind of routine. Anything that would allow enemies to identify him. It was inbred in them.

Besides, I told myself, we needed time to prepare. Our plan was quite elaborate and the devil—no pun intended—was in the details.

I regularly met with Musa after final prayers to discuss

what the companies on the list did and where there was an opportunity to use their data for the cause. He surprised me with his deviousness. I knew he wasn't what he seemed, but the depths of this man's duplicity astounded even me. He was beyond clever. That made it so strange that he wasn't on to us yet. I gave Ebony the credit for that. Her meticulous eye for detail and the enormous clout behind her, supplied me with all the background and data I needed. It was fool proof. Thank goodness she was on our side.

After that first time, I refrained from asking about Afan. I didn't want to bring any unwanted attention to myself, but by the second week I was getting a bit anxious. Afan was the spill of our plan. If he wasn't here, we had nothing.

The helplessness I felt was irritating. We had a lot in place but were on-hold. And if I was irritated, I could imagine how difficult Jonah would be to live with now. For once I was happy I wasn't with my friends.

Keeping up the scam was getting more and more difficult. We were at the stage where the information we had to share with Musa might actually damage the real-life companies we were allegedly working for. Besides being an ethical thing, it would also mean that the company's security department would be alerted and potentially on our tail. Not what we wanted. We needed eyes in the back of our head as it was.

There were heated discussions on which companies we could or could not bring into the firing zone without causing extensive unwanted damage.

EVENTUALLY, Afan returned to the mosque.

Just on time too.

I was about to call the whole thing off. We'd started our crusade to battle a conspiracy, not perpetrate one. The cure was in danger of becoming worse than the affliction. I'd put a deadline on the whole thing, much to Jonah's chagrin, and we were nearing it rapidly.

Afan showed up unannounced in a meeting I had with Musa. My hearts jumped several beats. The Hashta still had that effect on me, no matter my resolve. I recovered quickly, just as well, Musa was observing me closely. We exchanged formal greetings and got down to business.

'Your information is proving helpful,' Afan told me. I nodded but refrained from comment.

'We are doing a first analysis and then will carry out some probes to test the access.'

'If you involve me in the probes, I can help navigate around the safety measures. I can also do a pre-check if you like. Make it look like an annual test.'

'Thank you. If needed, we will contact you.'

Shit. I'd hoped he would let me know in advance which company they would target. That way Ebony could try to intervene and steer whatever they tested without the company knowing or losing any real information. She would just have to monitor all of them if I didn't get prior notice.

'Walk with me,' Afan suddenly suggested.

I looked up, the surprise visible on my face. Musa just smiled.

Afan stood to leave, and I followed. There wasn't anything else I could do. My anxiety returned with a vengeance. Why did the Hashta want me to follow him, and where to? The voice in the back of my head screamed at me that he was on to me. That he knew I was the enemy. But what could I do? Escape was out of the question; I had no other choice than to see it through. No matter what happened.

We left the mosque and walked out into the gravel garden at the side. It was dark, the only lights the solar lamps that lit the winding pathway. I couldn't see all the details in Afan's face, that scared me even more than the man himself. Then I realised he wouldn't be able to see mine either. I took a deep silent breath and slowly let it out, calming my nerves. Images of past atrocities perpetrated by Afan's brethren flashed past my eyes. It took a massive effort to push them away and continue.

I was so concentrated that I almost walked into the Hashta when he stopped suddenly and turned around.

I muttered an apology and quickly took a step back.

'Karief,' his deep voice sounded even more intimidating in the darkness. 'I have a question for you. Think carefully about your answer. It will determine your future.'

My hearts faltered for a beat. I felt the burn of bile as it rose in my throat. Swallowing hard, I nodded.

'Is this a test?' I asked, allowing a little irritation to shine through in the tone.

'Does that offend you?' He seemed genuinely surprised.

'It does,' I replied, deciding that strength—in modera-tion—would be appreciated by this man more than weak-ness. 'Doesn't what I have done show my value. And my loyalty.'

'I do not question your loyalty, my friend,' he stated, amusement in his voice. The kind a cat has when playing with a mouse. 'What I want to know is where it lies.'

I hesitated, genuinely confused. 'What do you mean?' I asked.

'You are a devout Muslim. Karief. We know that. What we also know is that you are a businessman. A successful entrepreneur. A man who singlehandedly built a lucrative and auspicious company from scratch. You have garnered the trust of multinationals, even of the U.S Government. This you have done yourself and you are proud of your achievements.'

'I am. There is nothing wrong with that,' I acted irked by his comments, hoping it was what he expected from a successful businessman. I was very aware I was balancing on a tightrope here. 'Our faith does not prohibit success as long as it is not ill-gained. I am proud of my accomplishments; I worked hard for them.'

Afan laughed. 'And so you should be,' He answered to my surprise, flustering me even more. Where the hell was this going to?

'You deserve the success you have, Karief. There is no contest there.'

'Then what is this about?' My answers were deliberately short.

My irritation continued to amuse him. Then just as suddenly, he became deadly serious again.

'Where is your loyalty?' He let that hang in the air. I stayed silent, waiting for more information.

'Are you a Muslim first?' He continued, closely watching me in the half light. 'Or a businessman?'

Okay. What was the right answer to that. Shit. He'd pushed me into a corner here. My choice would determine how our relationship would progress, and with that, whether I would be able to lure him into our ambush.

Panic threatened to engulf me. I berated myself. This

wasn't helping, I had to decide. Then it struck me. This man was the vanguard of the Establishment. He represented Arand in this dimension, Arand's company. His task was to guarantee a successful business. His goal was not religious. That was a means to an end.

I deduced he would value a like-minded associate. Not a religious fanatic.

'I am a businessman,' I answered resolutely. 'One that is also influenced by Islam.'

He smiled. I hoped that was because my answer was what he wanted, and not because he was already contemplating my untimely and most likely very violent death at his hands.

'But first and foremost a businessman?'

I swallowed hard. 'Yes.'

My inclination was to look away. His intensity sent goosebumps up and down my arms. I forced myself to hold his eye contact and breath steadily, little or no nerves showing.

Finally, he slapped my arm and smiled deeper. 'As I expected.'

'And as you wanted?' I dared to ask.

'Yes. Exactly what I wanted.' His hand pointed to where we had come from, and we turned back to the mosque.

My nerves screamed at me not to turn my back on this man, but I had no choice. He gestured I lead us back, so I turned and walked as confidently as I could, expecting a knife in my back, or a garrotte to slip over my head and jerk me back.

We reached the door to the mosque without incident, and I opened the door to let him in. He passed me and we joined Musa back in the small room. Fresh mint tea awaited us, and I accepted it gratefully, wishing I could slip a shot of whisky in there to quell my nerves. The short walk back here had been nerve-racking. I could barely keep my hands from shaking.

Afan nodded to Musa, which elicited another smile from the imam.

I'd passed the test.

## Chapter Fifteen

'HOW FAR?' Musa asked, looking out of the car window into the dark night.

I turned my head and assured him we were just a few minutes out.

In my rear mirror I saw the other cars were keeping up with us. The big black SUV stayed two car lengths behind, filling my mirror and emphasising the flaws in our plan. A further two lengths behind that one, I could just make out the white four-wheeler.

We'd left San Francisco for the back lands and small towns east of Oakland.

Our departure in the late evening had been eventful to say the least. I'd agreed to pick up Musa, Afan and Mohammed from the mosque and was surprised to see the extended welcoming committee waiting at the white building. Not only my designated passengers, but another six assorted bodyguards. I should have known they wouldn't leave without protection.

One positive: Afan was the only one I identified as non-human. Though he was a big enough threat as it were.

We went through the compulsory greetings, and I tried to suppress my anxiety. Jonah and Sly weren't expecting these many adversaries. I was at a loss on how to get the information to them. My burner phone was secreted under the driver seat. It was out of reach. We'd just have to wing it. Again.

'Shall we leave?' I asked, my nerves under control.

'Just one more person we're waiting on,' Musa assured me.

Was that a smirk I heard from Afan? Whoever our mystery guest was, the Hashta didn't approve.

We exchanged small talk about our destination; my warehouse outside Lafayette. There, I had promised Afan and Musa full disclosure on the security of one of the major Silicon Valley companies. This company was heavily involved in government contracts which offered them yet another way to sabotage US security. It was—understand-ably—a carrot I'd dangled in front of their noses they could not refuse. It was supposed to be my ticket into the Estab-lishment. That was the deal. My initiation and my "ticket-to-heaven". A place I definitely wanted to avoid. We had different plans, and this was our shot at exposing the bastards.

Ebony's team had produced a miracle with the back-ground information and some real juicy titbits to wet Afan's appetite. They were dangerously close to the truth, so we'd agreed that none of the bad guys would be allowed to leave alive and use the information. We had enough issues without the secret service on our backs.

The door to the mosque opened and my blood ran cold when I spied who our last passenger was. It took all of my discipline to stop myself from staring at Aaliyah who casually walked down the stairs and joined our group.

I glanced at Musa, unable to keep all the surprise off my face.

'This is a special woman,' Musa explained, incorrectly deducing that my surprise stemmed from her gender. Up to now the conspiracy had been solely male-oriented, women were not included in important choices within this mosque. I expect it was more a macho, myogenic decision by Musa than dogma.

I managed to nod and tried desperately to curb my raging nerves. This was an unexpected curve ball.

Aaliyah calmly walked up to us, nodded to Musa, shot a dirty look at Afan and barely glanced at me.

I observed Afan. His eye blazed with rage at the sight of Aaliyah. There was no love lost there. Good to know. Maybe the odds had just become a little more even. Aaliyah on our side would be a benefit. Things were looking up, if she took our side.

She continued onwards to the second car and took the passenger seat, completely immune to the sneers of the men who were forced to sit in the back.

Afan took the passenger seat of my car with Musa and one of the bodyguards in the back. The rest climbed into the white pick-up. Within minutes we were immersed in the heavy early evening traffic.

We crossed the bay and bridged the twenty-two miles quickly. I passed through Lafayette and continued on to the industrial compounds on the east side of the city. The late hour assured empty roads as we passed out into the less populated areas.

IT WAS pitch black when we stopped in front of a giant warehouse. There was no name on the front, just a number on the fence. If this surprised Afan, he didn't mention it.

I waited at the gate until it opened, then proceeded on into the parking lot and around the building to the loading docks on the far side of the compound. We disembarked under the flood lights, and they all followed me in through the open dock to the flood-lit warehouse floor.

The building was half full of merchandise. Electronic equipment in closed wooden boxes, others locked away in metal cages on three-story shelving, filled most of the floor to the sides. Harsh lights lit up the corridor between the central aisles where we walked, blanketing the rest in shadow. The sound of our footsteps echoed loud in the otherwise deserted building.

'No one is here?' Afan commented.

'No,' I answered without adjusting my strides. 'I deemed it prudent to have utter secrecy.'

Up ahead was a bank of computers, very similar to the set-up I was used to at Ebony's headquarters. Sly manned the left keyboard, and one of her computer team—the Asian girl—the right one.

When I questioned Ebony earlier on whether that was a good idea—it would after all, be dangerous and bloody— she assured me the girl would be an asset, not a liability.

Jonah and the team hid somewhere in the maze of boxes and equipment. I knew they were there, just not where.

I quickly calculated the odds. There were ten of them. Musa, Afan, Mohammed and the bodyguards. Sly, the girl, Jonah, Ebony's men and myself made seven, but I was counting on Aaliyah to even up the score. That made us just two short. Odds I liked a lot better.

I was starting to feel a lot better about the situation. Until that was, I remembered one of the bad guys was a Hashta.

I stopped in front of the screens and our visitors fanned out to the side of me, the bodyguards stayed three steps back, their eyes on the surroundings. Musa immediately scanned the contents of the monitors, his enthusiastic nods reassuring. This what he wanted to see.

Afan observed the surroundings. He slowly turned full circle, taking in everything on show. His gaze pushed deeper into the warehouse than I found comfortable.

'Afan,' Musa called out to him, pulling his attention back to where I wanted it to be.

The Hashta walked over to Musa and studied the information. He cocked his head in query at some of the data and asked questions. Sly answered in what seemed to be sufficient detail. There were nods all around and the atmosphere relaxed slightly.

It wouldn't stay that way for long.

Afan quickly tired of the explanations and once again roamed the area. He stopped at the second set-up.

A seat was placed in the centre of a black-clad, three-sided photo box. The lighting with reflection umbrellas looked professional. The point microphone next to the seat and the camera on a tripod aimed at the seat completed the image. This was a recording studio.

He wandered through the set-up, then moved over to where we all stood, his body tense and aggressive.

'What's that?' He pointed to the make-shift studio.

I followed his gaze, shrugged and waved it away. 'It's a recording studio.'

'I can see that.' His tone was dangerous. Short and hard. 'What's it for?'

I was tempted to say something stupid like "to make a video" but that would be pushing buttons that were already at maximum stretch.

I glanced up and shrugged. 'We're doing promotional reviews.'

He wasn't mollified.

I turned back to the screens and took a few steps closer. From under my eyelashes, I looked around at the placement of the people in the area. The guards were in a semi-circle about ten metres from us. They were observing the surroundings, none of them looked very anxious, but that could change quickly.

Aaliyah had moved behind the guards and stood slightly sideways between the first and second on the right. The other two were closer to the shelving where I hoped Jonah was hiding.

Musa had taken Sly's seat at the computers, the latter explaining details of the data and pointing to specific screens, his body close to the Imam.

That left Afan, the Asian girl and me. We were placed in a triangle of sorts, with Afan in the middle.

'Why do you have the studio here? Now?' Afan questioned me.

I turned to face him, my hand loosely on the metal frame the computer screens rested on. I smiled at him, not even attempting to conceal my excitement anymore.

'We're going to tape a video,' I explained, my hand gripping the cool metal. 'A confession, if you will.'

'And who are you going to interview?

'We were counting on you and Musa to help us with that.'

Musa looked up at his name. His brow creased in confusion as he felt the tension between Afan and me. The smirk on my face must have alerted him to the change in atmosphere and he tried to push himself up out of the chair. Sly pushed him back. His hand hard on Masa's shoulder.

I couldn't stop myself. 'It's time the world learned exactly what the Establishment really is. And you two are going to tell them that real-time.'

Musa and Afan both looked at the studio and then back to me. Time seemed to stand still. Of course, it didn't and just as Afan turned to grab something from under his cloak a loud crash and a cry grabbed his attention. He watched in anger as two of the guards were felled in one big sweep of Jonah's axe. They were dead before they hit the floor.

Aaliyah took out one of the others with her curved knives, slitting his throat and moving back to avoid the jugular spray. Another guard was felled by the big man's kick and finished off with the axe between his ribs. Mohammed and the others were in life-or-death fights with Ebony's people.

'You!' Afan obviously recognised my big friend. His visage contorted into a hard mask, the lips pulled back, and his brow creased over his blazing eye. He looked from Jonah to me and connected the dots. His final glare was directed at Aaliyah who now stood next to the big man, clearly stating where her loyalty lay.

The Hashta glared at me. Fire blazing in his one eye. His right hand pushed his cloak away from his side and he attempted to free the curved sword from its scabbard.

With a blood curling cry, Afan turned to attack me but was blown off his feet by the chair the Asian girl propelled his way into the small of his back. He staggered and fell to one knee but recovered quickly.

I aimed the iron rod I'd pulled from the frame at his

head, barely missing, and followed up with a kick. He avoided me but was unable to miss the high kick from our resident computer expert. Her foot contacted squarely with Afan's head, and he went down again.

Seconds later he was back up on his feet and had pulled the wicked blade from the folds of his cape. The man was a mountain goat, so resilient, so difficult to keep down. He feinted to the side, then swiped the sword up aiming for a spot between the girl's ribs. She turned away from him, enlarging the distance between them, but saving herself.

Ebony's men joined in the fight, rushing Afan from multiple sides. The diabolical sword held them at bay, wounding anyone who came within striking distance.

Afan took advantage of the space and rushed Sly. I expected him to try and impale our friend but instead he slashed his blade over Musa's throat, almost decapitating him. The shock on the Imam's face was total. This was his ally, but he was also a liability in the current circumstances, and thus expendable. Musa opened his mouth to speak, but only blood came from his lips. His hands grabbed his neck, attempting to stem the flow, without success.

The Hashta's action shocked us. We hadn't seen that coming. Afan took advantage of our surprise and knocked Sly to the side with a well-placed kick to the sternum. The Navy Seal went down, gasping for breath as pandemonium reigned. I heard screams, shouts and shots.

Our computer expert aimed another high kick, but Afan anticipated it and ducked under her blow, bringing the sword up and slashing over her thigh, barely missing the femoral artery and bringing her down. She crawled away from Afan as quickly as possible, a bloody streak following her on the floor.

I threw my strength into a massive swipe with the metal

bar, missing when Afan side-stepped. I continued my turn and followed up with a quick slashing motion from left to right. It missed, but at least it pushed him back from the Asian girl.

I pushed on; sure I could get an advantage as long as I didn't give him room to breathe. I heard a roar from behind me and Jonah joined in the fight, aiming his axe at the Hasha's neck.

'Don't kill him,' I shouted, regretting it instantly. It gave Afan the advantage. He knew we would hold our punches. We needed him alive to record the confession, especially now that Musa was dead. A vicious smile pulled Afan's dark features into a grimace. My hearts skipped a beat from the eerie cry he emitted when he doubled his attack, identifying me as the weakest of Jonah and myself.

Afan countered another swipe from Jonah's axe with his sword. The blade shattered on the axe. It didn't stop him, he pushed through under Jonah's arm and hit him squarely in the crotch with his outstretched foot on the rebound, knocking the big man backwards. Jonah staggered backwards, still holding on to his axe, but no longer able to fight.

Shit. I didn't like the odds now. Sly and Jonah were both down. The Asian girl had crawled away and was stopping the blood gushing from her thigh. From the corner of my eye, I saw Ebony's men down in pools of blood. Aaliyah was more than ten metres away, keeping her distance for some reason.

That left me. Me against the Hashta.

Jonah lay the axe on the floor and slid it my way. I ducked under the remnants of Afan's sword when he rushed me and grabbed Jonah's axe. The weapon was heavy and unwieldy. How the hell did he fight with this thing anyway? But it was all I had. The iron bar was discarded in favour of the cutting edge of the axe, and I swung it amateurishly, aiming for anything I could hit. Naturally, I missed, and shot through, my legs careening as I lost my balance. I fell flat on my face on the floor. From the corner of my eye, I saw Jonah stand up and struggle to move forward, his body still folded double from the vicious kick. His red features showed the enormous strain he was under. His arm reached for the axe, and he hefted the big weapon.

I felt an arm snake around my throat and my head was pulled back violently as I was dragged up on my feet.

'One step and I will break his neck,' Afan growled. Jonah stopped his advance. We locked eyes and I saw how desperate my situation was in his features. Not that I needed the confirmation. I felt utterly helpless.

'Step back,' my captor ordered. Jonah complied.

I was spun to the side, the vice still on my neck. 'You too.' Afan shouted to Sly.

'Do you even know who you are facing?' he screamed in defiance.

There was nothing to lose, I had to distract his attention in some way. Give the guys a chance to jump him, even if it meant more risks for me. I had to push his buttons. Make him careless.

'You're a Hashta,' I answered him. 'A faceless, cowardly assassin from the home dimension. A baby killer. A psychopath. Like all Hashta, you are without value. A parasite. Vermin.'

I felt his surprise in the grip on my neck, then anger as my words hit home. He pushed my body forward in his rage, straining my spine, all attention on me. He growled. The sound freezing the blood in my veins. I'd done it now. Pushed him over the edge. But at least I got his attention.

My body tensed and I waited for the inevitable, he

would snap my neck. I just hoped it would give Jonah or Sly the opportunity to restrain him and continue our quest.

I felt a flood of sticky fluid hit the back of my head and Afan released his grip on my neck.

As I jumped forward in surprise, I turned to look what had happened.

Afan gripped his throat with both hands, striving in vain to stop the pulsing blood that flowed freely from his severed jugulars. The purple liquid gushed out of his body and his life quickly faded. He let go of his neck and his hands searched frantically in the folds of his robes. I realised he was hunting for his amulet. He desperately wanted to transport out of here to where they might be able to save him. I grabbed his wrists and held him away from the transporter, his stare now pleading and fearful.

His hands lost their frantic movements as the life pulsed out of the man. I let go of his wrists. He looked at me one last time and attempted to say something, but no sounds came from his lips. Slowly he sank to his knees, then fell over flat on his face.

Behind him stood Aaliyah, her bloodied crescent knife still in her right hand, the amulet in her left. Her face was a mask of hatred. Jonah stood to the side. He glanced at Aaliyah, then quickly turned his head. The fierceness in her eyes shot sparks at me and dared any of us to say something.

I did.

'Great. Now he's dead.' I shouted angrily. Realisation hit me like a brick wall. Tonight had not been the great revelation we'd hoped it would be. It was a massive cock-up. Instead of exposing the Establishment, these two dead bodies represented the complete failure of our one chance to effectively show the world they were being scammed. We wanted a confession, proof beyond a shadow of a doubt. Now it was gone. Once again, it was our word against the Establishment's. Sure, the authorities could take away Afan's body. They could do all kinds of tests on him. They would have an alien, but the context was gone. We could show the data. We could swear on our honour that there was a conspiracy, but who would believe us? Us: a wanted murderer and other aliens. We were right back where we started months ago. We knew, but there was still no way we could prove anything to humankind.

'We agreed to stick to the plan.'

Aaliyah looked at me in disbelief. 'The plan? And how was that working for you?'

'Isn't that ultimately what you wanted?' Jonah intervened; his tone dangerous. 'Your boogy man exterminated. Besides, we saved your life. You could be a bit more grateful,'

Could he be that short-sighted?

Yes. He could.

I took a deep breath to compose myself before I answered as calmly as possible, 'I am grateful I'm still alive, but our proof is gone. All we did this for is down the drain.' I was seething. It was the relief that the Hashta was no longer a threat, combined with the desolation I felt that all our work, all our sacrifices and stress, had been for nothing. There was no way in Hell I could go back to my undercover persona now and get someone else to confess. That was truly dead-end.

'We can still show the body, and the blood. I can open his chest and show the two hearts,' Jonah continued. 'It's not all lost.'

'Besides, it's not like we really had a choice,' Aaliyah joined in.

I looked at the scene surrounding us. Afan and Musa weren't the only casualties. Mohammed lay to my right, a bullet through the brain. Two of Ebony's men were also among the casualties. One decapitated by Afan's sword, the other mortally wounded by the same weapon and bleeding out from a deep slash to his gut, his intestines spilling out onto the floor. Sly's ministrations were useless, he couldn't stop the bleeding. Tyrone was on the phone, most likely to Ebony. Calling in and getting medical help and a mop-up crew. In addition to all that there were two more wounded, not including Jonah or myself.

'You're right,' I conceded reluctantly. 'Sorry.'

Jonah nodded slightly. I noticed he was still high-strung; the fight had clearly gotten to him too.

'And thank you for saving me. Again.' I added to both to him and Aaliyah, enticing a shrug and a slight smile. Others saving my life was starting to become a very embarrassing habit.

'We're partners,' Jonah explained it away. Aaliyah left it at that.

Tyrone gave me the phone.

'What happened?' Ebony asked.

I summarised the past ten minutes, including Aaliyah's role, and waited for her reply.

'Ok. Then we'll have to find another avenue.' She was so practical. It made me feel a little better. 'Glad you are okay.'

'Yes, but two of the team didn't make it. I'm sorry,' I added.

'I know. Tyrone told me. I'll take care of them and their families. They knew the risks, but still. It's tragic.' Despite the harsh words, I heard emotion in her voice.

'The ambulance is on the way for the wounded, and we will take care of all the deceased.'

'Thanks.'

'I assume you've taken care of Afan's transporter?' I glanced at the amulet hanging from Aaliyah's belt.

'Yes, he's not going anywhere.'

We couldn't let his body be transported back to our dimension. They might be able to resurrect him. That would uncover our operation, not to mention Aaliyah's involvement. Which would be an even more disastrous result to a terrible night.

What should have been the summit of our quest had come crashing down around us.

We were back to square one.

## Chapter Sixteen

WE RETURNED TO SAN DIEGO.

The relief I felt at the end of the undercover operation was tempered by the realisation that we were going nowhere. Our quest had taken us on a fourteen-month adventure, but we had little to show for all our trouble.

It was depressing.

The atmosphere in the room was heavy. Disappointment was rampant in all of us, in the slack shoulders and the way we avoided eye contact and studied the floor.

As expected, Ebony's team had taken care of the clean-up, and nothing made the news. There was a small article in the local newspaper about the missing imam, presumed dead, and mention of a background check that was taking place by the authorities. Ebony had anonymously leaked some of the information we had to the anti-terrorist squad covering the mosque, who subsequently launched a big investigation after a midnight raid on the place. The computers in the basement had been impounded and were in the hands of the Bureau of Counterterrorism, along with a "how-to" manual depicting the security measures taken on the systems.

We hoped the federal geeks would take notice and safeguard the information. Some of it would be useless to them, but the terrorist recruitment would definitely be of interest.

It was a small win. Negligible in relation to the effort we'd invested in the undercover operation, but beggars can't be choosers.

'Now what?' Jonah voiced what we were all thinking.

I shrugged. I had nothing to say. Ebony also drew a blank.

'Was this your only lead?' Aaliyah asked patronisingly.

'No. It wasn't.' I answered irritated.

No one spoke.

'So, what are the others?'

'Don't go there,' Jonah interceded before I had a chance to say anything.

Shit. Another avenue closed. Benedict had been our only other option.

Aaliyah's questioning look was aimed at the big man. She cocked her head when he stayed mute.

'There is one more lead, but he's deep undercover and we can't run the risk of exposing him,' he finally answered with an exaggerated sigh.

'No way you can get a message to him without endangering the mission?'

'No.'

I was getting quite tired of the patronising looks Aaliyah threw our way. She was the reason we were in this predicament now. If she hadn't killed Afan, we could have preceded with our plan and exposed the Establishment.

Okay, not exactly fair. She did save me. But she didn't have to go and slaughter the guy.

'What about you?' I asked her, turning the tables.

She looked surprised. 'What about me?'

'What can you do to help?'

'Haven't I done enough? I've saved your life more than once.'

'Yes, and I'm grateful. But what we need now is a new way into the Establishment. A new lead.'

'Well, don't look at me for that. Bashir has all but convinced my father that women are not supposed to be involved in the business. He's pushing me further and further away from important meetings and decisions.'

'You have no information on the partnership between your father and Gabriel's?' Jonah joined in.

'No. I told you. Father doesn't confide in me anymore. Besides, I still don't believe my father would do such a thing. He hates your dad's guts.'

'It makes good business sense.'

'That wouldn't be enough.' Aaliyah's face was flushed with anger, her lips pulled taunt. Her right hand moved towards the knife strapped to her thigh. 'You are clutching at straws here because you have nothing else. Leave my family out of it.'

'Calm down everyone,' Ebony took over. 'This is getting us nowhere. We have enough enemies out there; we don't need the aggravation to spill over to our team.'

'I'm not part of your crappy team,' Aaliyah spat.

'Really?'

If looks could kill, both ladies would be lying on the floor in their death throes right now.

'Why don't we all sit down,' Jonah tried. 'And have a drink or two.'

'Or ten,' I whispered. Two wouldn't do it. Not with the

unspoken rivalry in the air here. I decided silence was the best option.

'Never mind,' Aaliyah declared. 'I'm leaving.' She turned to Jonah, resolved to have the last stab. 'See you around, big man. I enjoy our little trysts.' With a last mean smile to Ebony, Aaliyah turned her amulet and transported out of the room.

Jonah's contrite look had no effect on Ebony. 'Save it, Jonah. No strings attached, remember?' Ebony strode out of the room followed by the ever-present Sly, leaving just Jonah and me to muse over our next steps.

'Fuck,' he remarked as he grabbed another bottle of beer. Jonah sat down heavily in the sofa and cracked the seal of the bottle. His comment about summed up where we were now.

I joined him on the opposite chair, nursing my own bottle.

The silence was heavy. Neither of us wanted to voice how we were up a creek without a paddle, or more accurately, without a boat.

Ten minutes passed without a word.

'We could always go back to killing them one by one,' Jonah suggested.

I huffed. Sure, that was an option. One we'd discussed many times before. And put to the side, for more than one reason.

'Are you sure we couldn't get a message to Benedict one way or the other?' I tried.

'I wouldn't know how.'

'Maybe Ebony could help?'

'I don't want her to be involved. Not that close to the fire. If he's gone over to the Establishment, then I don't want to put her in any danger. No one knows about her involvement, and I'd like to keep it that way.'

'Do you think he's double-crossed us?'

'No. If he had, they would have found us by now. But I can't run the risk. Not with Ebs.'

'You're right. But there must be some way. Something we could do.'

'What about all the data on the server that we downloaded?' Jonah asked. 'Isn't there anything we could use from there?'

'Most of it refers to the Islamic side of the Establishment.'

'That figures, but are all those avenues closed now? I mean, both Afan and Musa are dead. They can't implicate you in their disappearance. Could you in any way infiltrate a different part of the conspiracy, maybe in another mosque.'

My hearts skipped a beat. Back to undercover work in Islam? Just the thought pushed bile up into my throat.

'I don't think so. I'm not sure what they've shared with anyone else, anyone outside of the mosque. They could have passed around a picture or the basics of my profile. I mean, they were recruiting me for the Establishment. Afan even divulged the conspiracy.'

Jonah shrugged, his eyebrow raising. 'Possible. But maybe they didn't. Maybe you could still infiltrate in another town.'

'A very big maybe,' I answered. Visions of the close encounters I'd had in the undercover mission flashed before my eyes. I felt sick. With all my bravura, two near-death experiences within as many months pushed at my resolve. To say that I was scared was an understatement. Ibrahim and Afan haunted my dreams, the lack of sleep apparent in the bags under my eyes.

'We could ask Ebony if she's seen any communications.' Jonah wouldn't let it go. 'Or any hints.'

I sat forward in the chair to counter the nausea that came in waves over me. Bile exploded into my mouth, and I could only just swallow it on time. Sweat clocked my brow, and my hands began to shake. I couldn't stop them from trembling.

Jonah observed me without a sound. I felt his eyes bore into my head as I leant even further towards the floor with my head between my knees. My hands were clasped behind my head, but it didn't help. They still had a mind of their own and advertised my fear.

I heard Jonah move away and a minute later he came back with a wet cloth that he placed on the back of my neck.

'Don't know if this works with your kind, but it's worth a try.'

I nodded my thanks, not trusting myself to answer him without breaking down or throwing up.

It did help. The cool cloth sent tingles up into my head and countered the sharp stabs of pain. Slowly the trembling receded as I concentrated on the dampness and relief. I swallowed loudly, banishing my stomach contents back to where they came from. That felt better, though the sour and bitter taste remained.

A new bottle of beer appeared on the floor next to me. I gratefully took it and swallowed a good slug. I forced it to stay down. The taste masking the bile of a minute ago.

I held the bottle in both hands and slowly sat back in the chair until I felt the comforting support of the seat.

'You look like hell,' Jonah finally remarked.

'Then it's a good projection of how I feel,' I answered.

I tried half-heartedly to return his smile but failed miserably.

'What got to you?' Jonah broke the silence. 'You must have been in hairy situations before?'

I nodded, took another swig of the beer and looked up at my partner.

'I mean,' he continued. 'You're what? A couple of hundred years old? No one gets that old without some excitement.'

'More than a thousand,' I corrected him. 'In your years. And yes. I have been in tricky situations before. But there was always a safety net. A fall-back scenario. Worst case, I would be reincarnated. Not that I ever got that far.' I swallowed another mouthful of beer.

'In all my years, I've never felt so utterly helpless as the two times I faced death here. So completely out-of-control. There was nothing I could do. My life—my long life—was in the hands of others. Humans—or in the last case; Afan—who wanted me dead. The feeling of impounding doom was so unbelievable, so profound, that it scared me to the core. I was confronted with my mortality. Not once, but twice, during the sting.'

'I was immortal. Maybe not untouchable, but nothing could really kill me. Not for good. I had my family to fall back on, they would pull me out of any ridiculously dangerous situation I got myself in, albeit reluctantly. But they would. Real, permanent death was never a scenario for me. No matter what kind of a pickle I got myself into. It would not kill me.'

'Now. Now. I know what it feels like to be mortal. To lose that guarantee. To feel like you have lost everything, including life. It scares me.'

'I can imagine.'

'Immortality gave me a false sense of security. It made me complacent. I wouldn't die anyway. But that has all changed. The net is gone. No one will bring me back from the brink. That support to fall back on was my lifeline. It's now a big hole. One that keeps me awake at night. I'm not equipped to keep myself alive. I was used to that being someone else's responsibility. And now I can only count on me.'

'And us.'

My lips pulled into a smile. 'And you. You, Ebs and her team. Even Aaliyah.'

'We're your net now.'

'I guess you are.' That made me feel better. The isolation, the loneliness, dissipated and was replaced by a hesitant warmth that flowed through my body.

'You need to get a hold on this, Gabe.'

'I do.'

'Why are you so scared of death?'

'Aren't you?' I looked up, my eyes opened wide in surprise.

His smile was calm as he shrugged. 'No. It's part of life. I've lived with my impending death for a long time. Ever since I was a teenager. Violence does that. It makes you aware of your mortality and you have to find a place for that. I found mine early, when my mother was killed. I resolved to live my life as I wanted to, so that I wouldn't have any regrets. That way, death isn't an interruption of goals or the fulfilment of my life. I live day to day. No apologies. No long-term plans. Nothing that will be catastrophic if it ends prematurely. And what comes after that? I thought I knew. Now I don't. It makes no sense to me to worry about something I have absolutely no control of. If there is an afterlife, I will find out when my time comes. And if there isn't, then there's no use in spoiling my life worrying about it.'

He had a point. More than one.

'You've never been confronted with your mortality,' he continued. 'So I get that it's scary. Especially as you do know where some of the humans go to. That in itself is a nightmare no one wants to go through. But like you said. That's not in the cards for you. Those bridges are burned.'

'You make it sound so easy. Just accept that it's part of you. It never was for me.'

'It is now. You can choose to live your life in fear of what may come, or just live and see when the time comes. The latter will greatly improve your existence.'

He raised his bottle in a toast. 'Besides, we're not about to let you die. You've got things to do.'

I answered his toast in kind and nodded.

'Thanks Jonah.'

'You're welcome.'

The big man never failed to surprise me.

## Chapter Seventeen

WE DIDN'T REALLY HAVE a choice. We had to contact Benedict.

We had nothing else.

The big question was how. How could we contact him without the risk of exposing the archbishop or running into a trap if the Establishment had turned him?

'I can't believe he would fall for their scam. Benedict is a devout man. He believes in a better world. But he's not naive. He knows how the world works,' Jonah explained to Ebony and me. 'Before he joined the church, he was a Navy Seal. He saw the good and the bad in the world. Benedict was in the middle of things no one should have to experience. Instead of numbing to the violence, he decided to counter it. Not by more, but by reaching out as an equal, a brother. He joined the Church to further his goals. There he found hope.'

'Like you?'

'Like me.' His brow creased and hooded his eyes. 'But

unlike me, he knows how to work the system and get the right people on his side so he can make a difference.'

'Why does that make him less likely to fall for the scam?' Ebony asked.

'He's less gullible. He knows what's out there and how people rip-off others. It's part of human nature. Benedict can identify when others try to manipulate him. Unlike me, he will work with that and turn it to his and his goal's benefit. Me, I just start hitting someone.'

We smiled at that.

'He's dedicated to helping others. His own wealth and status are not his priority.'

'He's done quite well for himself.' I pointed out.

'He has. And that has a purpose. He can do more from a position of power in the Church.' He glared at me, daring me to contradict him. 'The two are not mutually incompatible.'

I refrained from pointing out that neither was his background and susceptibility to the lure of the scam.

'We will not know until we talk to him,' Ebony pointed out.

But how?'

'We could send an anonymous message,' I suggested.

'Yeah, and then what? How would he contact us without blowing his cover?'

'Maybe we could get a message handed to him in person,' Ebony offered. 'Possibly during mass, or better, during confession. That's a one-on-one and he can't see clearly who he's talking to.'

'That's true, but I'm not sure whether he still takes the congregation's confessions,' Jonah responded.

'Wouldn't that be announced somewhere?' I picked up the idea.

'Most likely. I'll get the guys to see if any mention is made of his duties,' Ebony acknowledged. 'It's worth a try.'

'Who would pass the message to him?' I asked. 'We can't get close. The Establishment will no doubt be watching out for him.'

'And not you, Ebs.' Jonah stated resolutely.

He was rewarded with a chuckle and smile. 'Don't worry, big man. I wasn't planning on doing the field work.'

'Good.'

'I'll get someone to pass on a message,' she continued. 'You get it to me, and I'll make sure he gets it. Do you want him to give you an immediate answer?'

'Preferably, yes. I don't want to have to repeat the process, because if he has been turned, they could use that to trap the messenger.'

'Okay, you two decide what, and I'll contact someone in Miami.' Ebony stood up and with a last brush of her hand on Jonah's shoulder, left the room.

Now the really difficult part came down to us. What would we ask Benedict that would irrevocably prove his loyalty?

'That should do it,' I remarked, happy with our progress.

'Yeah, if he still takes confessions.'

'If not, then we'll have to find another way to pass the message on.'

Confessions would be ideal. There was no one else around. Just Benedict and the messenger on opposite sides of a semi-transparent screen. If done properly, Benedict would not be able to see who had taken the confession. The messenger would be in the pews before Benedict came and could identify him without it being obvious. There would be a safety zone. No direct face-to-face contact. I didn't want to endanger anyone else.

Jonah was adamant on the archbishop's loyalty. But I had my doubts. I wanted to believe he was still on our side, but it seemed very unlikely. We'd only spoken to him briefly. Okay, Jonah a little longer. The archbishop seemed convinced then, but now he'd had ample time to ponder the strange tale we'd made him party to. Why would he believe the ridiculous accusations we'd spun? They sounded weak— even to me—and I knew they were real. Aliens, slavery and the complete demolition of his faith. Sounded like bullshit.

We would find out soon enough.

Ebony's nerds confirmed Benedict took confession once a week. Tuesday evening, after mass, he would be available for two hours. It was on a first-come first-served basis. No appointments. You just took your place in the pew and waited your turn. That was a bonus. We didn't want to leave more traces than necessary.

Ebony supplied the messenger. A middle-aged Hispanic woman who would effectively fade into the background of the church and the normal congregation. Non-descript in her slightly baggy clothes and head scarf, she would avoid contact with anyone besides the archbishop. She would enter the church ten minutes after the mass ended and kneel in one of the pews. When it was her turn, she would deliver the message, wait only a minute for an answer, then leave. There would be enough people in the church for her to disappear in the congregation. Once outside the building she would make her way around the corner to a waiting car.

It sounded fool-proof, if Benedict was still trustworthy. If not, then the two men at the back of the church would come into play and cause a distraction, allowing the messenger to slip through the doors and out to the street.

'She's not from Miami,' Ebony explained. 'So there's no chance anyone will recognise or identify her. They'll pull a blank if they try to find her afterwards, we'll make sure she's hundreds of miles away.'

That made me feel marginally better. I refrained from asking Ebony if the woman was trustworthy. Of course she was, otherwise Ebony wouldn't have chosen her.

'Besides,' she added. 'We'll be able to hear and see everything from here.'

'How's that possible?' Jonah asked before I could.

'She will be wearing hidden cameras and microphones. We will be able to follow every move she and Benedict make.'

'Isn't that dangerous for her?'

'Only if someone becomes suspicious of her. She's prepared. So, that won't happen. And as I said, she won't be alone. If the shit hits the fan, we'll get her out.'

Ebony smiled at us. 'Come on guys, you've seen all the movies. The equipment we use now-a-days is much better than what you could ever see in a film. The microphone looks like a regular hearing aide, even works as one just in case it is scrutinised. The camera is state-of-the art. It's embedded in a contact lens. No way anyone will find it on her. The equipment emits the data hidden in a used frequency. It's basically invisible.'

That made me feel slightly better. Not good, but it was a start.

'Besides,' she added. 'She's a pro.'

I know Ebony was trying to make us feel better, but with every additional person involved in my—our—quest, I felt an extra burden on my shoulders. I was responsible for them. For pulling them into life-threatening situations. Yeah, sure. I knew in the end; this would benefit humanity. And I almost convinced myself that was why I was doing all of this.

It wasn't.

Ultimately, it was for me. I knew that. It was a selfish goal. One that hopefully would benefit them, but it was about my mental well-being. I couldn't live with what my family—and me by extension—had done for centuries. I felt personally responsible for the scam. It wasn't my idea. But I'd gone along with the whole shakedown. I'd reaped the rewards. I'd enjoyed the fruits of the slavery, of the torment of human beings. People I saw as products. Cattle, if you will. I'd intentionally distanced myself from any kind of emotional contact with humans. We all did. It was a coping tactic. A way of living with what—in our core—we knew was wrong. At least, that was what I felt.

That was why this was for me. It's egotistical. I recognise that, and I hate myself for it. But I don't know how else to cope. My people, my family, are responsible for the biggest scam in human history. They intentionally used the human susceptibility to a higher power as leverage to achieve their own goals. Money. Status. Power. Humans were no more than a means to an end. Inconsequential.

It made me sick.

…I made me sick.

I hated myself.

This was my redemption.

I hoped.


TWO DAYS later we were gathered around the computers in Ebony's command centre. The regular set-up I was used to—and in awe of—was dwarfed by the array of large screens and equipment on show in the cavernous building we found ourselves in.

The three people manning the computers were the team we met in Vegas. The Asian girl with the braids, the geeky guy and the pretty African American girl who looked way too young to be involved in this shit.

I nodded to them as I moved up to the console. From that advantage point I could view each of the countless screens. Not that the content meant anything to me. There were shots of meetings, others of encounters in dark, filthy alleyways, high-level overviews of towns and interiors of multiple buildings.

I glanced at Ebony. She looked completely at home in these surroundings. This was her team. Her command centre. I realised this was the centre of her business, whatever that was. For the umpteenth time I realised how little I actually knew about our computer wizard.

I looked at Jonah. He was just as surprised as I was, in complete awe at the surroundings. It confirmed my assumption that he had not been party to these details of his love interest's life.

'You are not here,' Ebony stated resolutely. 'You are not seeing any of this.'

I shook my head. 'Blind and dumb.'

'Especially dumb,' Jonah jabbed.

Trust him to spoil the moment. Even in jest.

'I'm impressed,' I confessed.

Ebony smiled, then turned to her geeks. 'How is the link?'

'Perfect,' the girl with the braids said without taking her eyes from the second terminal in the centre of the wall of screens.

Jonah joined us and we concentrated on that screen.

The image showed the inside of the basilisk in Miami. A high vaulted cavernous building with its countless marble and stone columns. The beautiful stain-glass windows depicted the saints and meaningful events from the scriptures. Opulence was present in the gilding of the statues and the artefacts on the altar.

The atmosphere was subdued, despite the immensity of the building.

The image moved from left to right as the messenger scanned the church interior. The pews were arranged in four blocks of twenty or so rows. The dark wood and subdued lighting exactly what you would expect from a centuries old church. Statues of saints stood on stone pillars, lined the chamber, peering down on the few people seated or kneeling in the pews. Most of the congregation were middle-aged women, dressed in dull earth colours and all sporting scarfs over their hair. It looked like a scene from a nineteen-seventies Italian film.

Our messenger approached a pew on the far-left block, parallel to the ornately crafted confession boxes that stood against the wall. Another woman was waiting, so our girl took a seat behind her. She knelt down and put her hands together in prayer. From under her scarf, she scanned the immediate vicinity. A priest stood behind the altar, scouring the believers. He had more of a bodyguard aura than a man of the cloth and looked out of place. I had to remind myself how Jonah must have seemed foreign in his day as a priest and smiled at the thought. You could not judge a man by his appearance alone. Maybe he was a priest.

The messenger turned her head to the left and we saw Archbishop Benedict approach the confessionals. His white robe was enhanced by the deep purple stole draped around his neck that hung down almost to the floor. The man's steps were powerful and the impression he portrayed was of a strong authoritative man. When I saw him months ago, he'd been seated behind his desk. Now I understood why Jonah described him as impressive and compelling. He made an entrance. That was for sure.

Benedict smiled and nodded to the woman in front of our messenger, turned and opened the left door of the confessional. The woman entered the door on the right and silence once more reined in the church.

Ten minutes dragged on before the door was reopened and the woman left the dark confines of the confession box. This was the sign to our girl that she could take the vacated place.

The inside of the confessional was dark, the only light a small, subdued lamp overhead. The curtains over the ornately carved shutters on three sides let in little light, effectively screening the sinner from the outside and the man-of-the-cloth on the other side of the screen.

'Forgive me father, for I have sinned.' She started the ritual. 'This is the first time I have been in a confessional.'

'For which sins would you ask the lord for forgiveness?'

'Well, actually,' she continued. 'I'm not here to talk about my sins.'

Benedict's profile turned in the window as he swivelled his head to face her. 'What sins are you here for, my child?' The surprise was clear in his voice.

'I'm here because of the sins of the Church.'

Benedict remained silent for almost two minutes.

'Could you elaborate?' he asked.

'I'm talking about the lies. About the Heaven that is promised.'

'Why do you think Heaven is a lie?'

'It may not be for all of us, but for young men, it is. And you know.'

'Who sent you?'

'An old acquaintance and the fallen son of God.' She spat out the last word, emphasising the reference to my father and not any other perceived deity.

'And why did they ask you to come here?'

'They have not heard from you, Father.'

'No. They have not. It has not been opportune. I am watched.'

'That is why we chose this approach,'

'They sent you here to do what?'

'To make contact and ask if there has been any progress.'

'I have been approached by the organisation,' Benedict reported. 'They have asked me to join their ranks.'

'At which level?'

'They hinted at the highest level. No definite offers have been made, but I have been initiated into the fold. They include me in some low-level strategy brainstorming. I expect them to test me and monitor my loyalty.'

'And where does your loyalty lie?' She was blunt.

'My loyalty lies with the Church, the Almighty God and his true followers. The real god. Not the imposter.'

'Thank you, Father. That is what I came for.'

'They doubt me?' He sounded irritated. 'I suppose it is to be expected. There has been no contact, and the offers are extensive. They might convince any man.' He paused.

'In this case, they have not,' he added.

'Do you have any leads they can work on?' She asked, running through the script we gave her.

'None that would be opportune at the moment. I have to be careful I do not arouse any suspicion. They are watching me carefully. It seems everyone doubts my allegiance.'

WE SAW our messenger reach for the door.

'Take a message back for me, please.' Benedict stopped her. She sat back in the seat again.

'Tell my big friend that he and his partner are top of the wanted list. There is a massive operation underway to find them and eradicate the threat they pose. This was shared with me because of the last visit where they killed my assistant. I said I wanted to know what was being done about avenging the death of one of the brethren. I insisted,' he added. 'The organisation has been able to trace the friends to the west coast. They are close. Tell them to be careful and watch their back.'

'Thank you, Father.' With that she opened the door and exited the confessional. She took a spot in one of the pews and pretended to go through the absolutions common after a confession. After five minutes she left the church and walked around the corner.

No one followed her. She continued for three blocks then ducked into a coffee shop where she made her way to the back exit where a van waited. The sliding door closed behind her, and the vehicle sped off through the alleys and was soon on the highway out of the city.

Ebony took hold of the microphone. 'Thank you, Mercedes.'

The image moved up and down as our messenger nodded, then faded as the technician broke the link.

'Do you believe him?' Ebony asked Jonah.'

'I do.'

She turned to me and cocked her head, silently asking me the same question.'

'Jonah knows him best. I refer to his opinion.' I answered. 'He sounded sincere. And surprised.'

'Okay, then we will proceed with that assumption.'

'Too bad he couldn't give us anything to go on yet, but that was to be expected.' Jonah sounded relieved. Understandable.

I nodded.

# Chapter Eighteen

THE PHONE in my pocket vibrated indicating a text.

With my hands on the steering wheel of my new car I decided it could wait. The big Audi purred along the Pacific Coast highway, and I was enjoying the ride immensely.

This was definitely one of the perks of this world. And of having money. I'd picked up the car earlier that day and was putting it through its paces. First, speed on the Interstate, then the versatility and sublime steering on the Pacific Coast highway. The top was down, and the sun burned the back of my neck as I made my way south. I was coming up on the exit I needed for the ranch and slowed to let the other traffic pass when the text came in.

I filed it away in my head for later and continued on my way. If it was important, then whoever it was would call me.

Leaving the highway, I cruised through small towns and villages up into the mountains.

Something nagged at the back of my brain. A thought I just couldn't get hold of, that wouldn't manifest itself. I tried to push it away and enjoy the ride, but familiar goosebumps ran up and down my arms.

I'm not psychic, I don't have premonitions, but I do listen to my instincts. There was something off here.

A thought occurred to me.

The mobile that received the text message was the burner phone. Not many people had that number, so whoever texted me—unless it was a random wrong number —was part of a very select group of people. People I should answer.

I pulled the car over to a leeway on the side of the road and pulled out the phone.

Dread sent shivers up my body as I keyed in the six-digit code and opened the text app.

My blood ran cold.

The text was short. "They know where he is. Ranch. Action imminent."

The words were bad enough, but what chilled me to the bone was the sender. The text was from Benedict's burner phone. The one we had given him months ago.

This could only mean the Establishment had found us again, and specifically Jonah. I forwarded the text to Jonah's mobile and pushed the speed dial to warm him. No answer.

Pulling the car back into the sporadic traffic I sped down the road to the ranch, I was about ten minutes out. Too long. I accelerated and swerved around a coupe to an empty highway. Revving up the big car, I made short work of the distance.

Jonah wasn't answering his phone.

Surely, I wasn't too late?

Please.

I called Ebony, no answer. I tried again. What was it with these people? Didn't anyone answer their phone anymore. Come on. I was panicking. I had to get rein-forcements.

On the third try, Sly answered.

'Tell her the Establishment is on its way to the ranch,' I shouted into the phone. 'I'll be there in three. Just make sure you get men there. I don't know how many there will be, but they're out for blood.'

'Done,' was the only answer, after which Sly hung up. Never a man of many words, he was already onto the case. That made me feel marginally better. But they were twenty miles away, at least. I had to get to the ranch quickly.

I tried Jonah's phone again. No answer.

My anxiety increased exponentially with every ring tone. Nothing.

'Pick up the damn phone, Jonah!' I shouted to no one in particular.

# Chapter Nineteen

JONAH WASN'T ANSWERING my calls, in this situation, that wasn't a good sign.

My drive to the ranch strongly resembled a street race, overtaking other traffic left and right, honking my horn if they didn't get out of the way quick enough for me.

I parked the car, ran up to the locked wrought iron gate and punched the intercom button. I heard the bel ringing but no one answered. More bad signs. My incessant pushing of the button didn't help. No answer.

In near panic, I looked left and right for a way to get inside. I had to get to Jonah. Checking no one was near, I scaled the wall and jumped over into the park-like grounds, racking my brain whether Ebony kept dogs here. I sure as hell hoped she didn't.

Jonah's bike was in the drive. That meant he was here somewhere. He wouldn't leave it unattended. Not outside. It was his baby. I ran towards the house. The doors were closed, the windows too. I pushed the bell, holding my finger on the button continuously. Someone had to be here. Surely, I wasn't too late.

I banged on the door, tried to look in the windows, contemplated to break through the triple paned glass, but decided against it, and returned to my attack on the door.

Finally, I heard a voice from inside the building.

'Okay. Okay. I'm coming.'

The anxiety dropped off my shoulders like a coat. It was Jonah. He was here. He was all right. Thank goodness for that. On the way here I'd gone through every scenario, most of which ended badly. Yet here he was.

He opened the door in a pair of boxer shorts and nothing more. His bare feet slapped on the floor as he moved back around the door.

'What the hell, Gabriel? Where's the fire, for fuck's sake.' He was angry at my interruption.

'Open the door and let me in, Jonah,' I ignored his questions. 'Why the hell didn't you answer my calls? I've been calling.'

'What the hell for?'

'They're on to you,' I shouted. 'The Establishment knows you're here.' They're planning an attack.'

'Why the hell didn't you say so?' Yeah sure, now it was my fault. I pushed my way into the house and Jonah closed the door behind me.

He led the way into the living room. Garments littered the floor, that explained where his clothes were, though some were clearly a woman's.

'Ebony's here?' I asked, suddenly concerned for her too.

He turned and stared at me but refrained from answering. I scrunched my brow, not sure what to make of it.

'Hi, Gabe.' A woman's voice came from the kitchen.

It wasn't Ebony.

Aaliyah stood behind the counter constructing a sandwich. She was hastily dressed in Jonah's t-shirt, the neck opening so wide it slid off her right shoulder. Her full, black hair was loose and fell down beyond her waist.

She looked fantastic.

I understood the attraction. No doubt about that. But this was Ebony's house. Jonah was her man.

'What the fuck, Jonah?'

'None of your business,' he countered angrily. Aaliyah watched our interaction with a smile on her face.

'This is Eb's house.' I pointed out.

'So what? She lets me stay here.'

'And play here?'

'If I want to. What do you care?' His face was quickly flushing with rage. Or was it guilt. He knew what I meant. I saw how uncomfortable he was.

'I care for Ebony. You should too.' I continued my rebuke.

He stayed silent.

Jonah glanced at Aaliyah. She took another bite of her sandwich and shrugged her indifference.

'We're not exclusive,' Jonah stated with less certainty than he wanted.

'She loves you; you know?'

He flinched. 'She shouldn't. I'm not worth it.'

'She thinks you are.'

'Well, I'm not.'

'So, this is all to prove your point, is it?' I pushed. 'This is how you repay her for everything she has done for you?'

'Lay off me, Gabe, back off.' His rage was nearing boiling point. He walked up to me and invaded my space, his deep breathing a clear indication of his struggle to keep control. I stared up at him, just as stubborn.

'What brings you here, anyway?' Aaliyah changed the subject.

I stared at her. What…?

Her question brought me back to our immediate threat. The Establishment. I turned and walked to the counter, alleviating the tension.

'The Establishment,' I declared. 'They're on to Jonah and planning an attack. They want him desperately.'

'And you,'

'And me,' I conceded. 'And they would be very surprised to find you here.'

'Fuck.' She instantly recognised the implications, dropped the food and gathered her clothes, leaving the room to get dressed.

The soft whirring sound behind me was barely audible over the loud crash of the front door that was blown off its hinges. I turned just in time to see two figures materialise. Rafael's surprise surpassed my own and I rushed him before he registered I was here too. I barrelled him off his feet and knocked the sword out of his hand. Momentarily flustered, he failed to have his defences up and I landed him a hard fist to the chin. He went out like a light. I swivelled off my brother and side-stepped to avoid the body of the second man falling on me. He'd encountered Jonah's double fisted blow.

We turned towards the door where five black-clad figures sporting a variety of bladed weapons fanned out into the room.

It was up to Jonah and me. Aaliyah was nowhere to be seen. We could only count on ourselves.

We stood back-to-back as the enemy circled us. Jonah wielding his ever-present axe and me with my long knives— my weapons of choice.

'Get them alive,' the one we identified as the leader called to his men. Good to know. At least they wouldn't kill us.

'If possible.'

I didn't like the addition.

The one to my right nodded almost imperceptibly and feinted to his left, attempting to pull my attention away from my other side. I turned left and slashed my right knife into the gut of the man opposite the nodder. Then turned immediately and my right blade made contact with the initial would-be ninja. He screamed and grabbed at the stump of his arm where his hand had been.

Two down.

I glanced back and saw that Jonah had made short work of two more of the bad guys, that left one still upright. He backpaddled and called out.

Another group came in through the door. Six more heavily built men in black. Again, no guns, just knives, machetes and one samurai sword.

Strange, but better than fire power. This lot had to get close. Guns allowed distance. Someone made a stupid choice; one we were happy with.

That's when it all went to hell. The fight began with a vengeance, Seven of them against two of us.

Knives and Jonah's axe flashed by on all sides. Blood— mainly red—splattered everything including Jonah and me.

It got slippery underfoot.

Bad guys fell left and right. None of them as adept as us with their weapons. I was elated. Out of the corner of my eye I saw Aaliyah had joined the fight, immensely improving our odds. There were only a few left. One Jonah had on the floor, another locked in combat with Aaliyah and the one I'd almost decapitated.

This was going well. I congratulated myself. Allowed a smile on my lips as I dispatched yet another of the attackers.

I felt elated... Just before I felt a massive blow to my back between my shoulder blades. I recognised my own blood dripping down my back as I smashed into a chair on the way to the floor. I rolled over, the machete narrowly missing me and sending foam and fibre from the sofa I ducked under two metres up in the air. I continued rolling and crashed into the heavy wood and metal coffee table, driving the air out of my lungs.

I lay on the floor catching my breath, the edges of the cut on my back already healing. The attacker had hit me with the pommel of the machete, not the blade, intent on incapacitating me. Then he would finish me off once I was on the floor or take me alive.

It looked bad.

Until Jonah swiped his axe and the attacker's head rolled off his dead body.

Jonah pulled the man off me and held out his hand to help me to get up off the floor.

He'd saved me yet again. The smile on his face informed me he would rub that particular detail in. I smiled back. We made a great team. Most of the time.

Suddenly his body jerked upright.

To my shock, I saw Rafael's sword exit Jonah's torso just under the sternum. The wicked weapon ran him through, up from his gut to his chest, the sharp edge destroying the organs it encountered on the way. Jonah tried to grab the blade and push it back but only succeeded in cutting his hands. The shock on his face mirrored mine.

'Noooooo.' I heard my own voice as though it were someone else's. Jumping to my feet I caught the big man as he fell forward, the sword pulled out of his body by my brother.

Raphael stood there in disbelief. He stared at the sword, then at Jonah and finally at me.

I screamed something unintelligible, grabbed my knife off the floor and pushed it hard into my brother's neck. He dropped his weapon and clawed at my hands, but I wouldn't let go, my anger focussed on this, my enemy.

Purple blood sprayed over me where the jugular was slashed, he was rapidly bleeding out. Still, I didn't let go of the knife. I pushed even harder, almost severing his head. With my left hand, I pulled the amulet from his chest. He wouldn't survive this; I wouldn't let him. Not after what he'd done.

The amulet fell to the floor, and I stamped on it hard, smashing the delicate mechanism.

'Gabriel!' Aaliyah's shouts brought me back to the present and I dropped Raphael. He sank to the floor, dead before he touched the blood-soaked ground.

She was kneeling on the floor next to the big man. His normal coffee colour had faded to a sickly pale flat tint, the blood gushing out of the massive wounds in his chest and back. My feet were glued to the floor. The weight of what had happened immobilising me.

'Help me!' she shouted. 'We need to stop the bleeding.'

I took one more look at the scene and grabbed my phone from the floor where it had fallen to in the heat of the battle. I speed dialled Ebony, willing her to pick up.

Her anxious voice came through the speaker. 'What, Gabe?' I heard car sounds in the background.

'Ebony' I screamed into the mobile. 'Ebony, there's been an attack at the ranch. We need the doctor. Now!'

'Jonah?'

'Yes.'

'How bad?'

'Bad.' I answered. 'Very bad.'

'Will he make it?'

'I don't know. I really don't.'

'We'll be there in under five.'

'Hurry, please.'

'They're on their way,' I turned to Aaliyah and the terrible scene in front of me.

Jonah lay on his back, the pool of blood rapidly expanding beneath him. I grabbed a throw from the sofa and ripped it to pieces.

'Turn him onto his side,' I ordered. 'Then press this into the wound. Hard!' I handed her the material, grabbed hold of Jonah's shoulder and pulled him onto his left side. Aaliyah pushed the material solidly into the seeping wound on his back and I did the same on the front.

It was a downhill battle.

The blood pulsed from the massive wounds around our make-shift bandage.

The big man groaned loudly at the extra tension on the wounds.

'Sorry, Jonah,' I stammered. 'We have to stop the bleeding. Doctor Patel is on the way. Stay with us.'

He looked at me, his eyes searching for what? The truth? That he was dying?

I couldn't look him in the eye. He knew. He could see it in our desperation.

'Get them, Gabe.' His voice was still strong. 'Make them pay. Bring the fuckers down.'

'We'll do it together,' I stated. Not even believing it myself.

He chuckled, the laughter slipped into raw coughs as his

body convulsed. Blood collected in his mouth, and he spat it out in dark crimson drool. The colour was stark against his rapidly paling skin, emphasising how quickly the life was flowing out of him.

I looked up at the kitchen clock, willing it to go quicker to get the doctor here.

'Stay with us, Jonah,' I shouted. 'Fight it. Don't let them win.'

'I'm losing this one,' he stammered.

'No, fight it. We can't lose you,' I shouted to him. 'Eb is on the way. keep breathing.'

'Tiny.' He attempted a smile. The blood dripped from the edge of his mouth and spoiled the effect. 'Tell her I love her.'

'You tell her.'

He shook his head, then coughed blood. 'Tell her.'

'She knows.'

I kept the pressure on his chest but couldn't stop the blood from seeping through my fingers, the material beneath was already saturated. I glanced at Aaliyah; she wasn't doing any better. She shook her head. We were losing the battle.

Suddenly, she lay him back down on the floor and grabbed for something on the floor behind her. I wanted to shout at her, scold her for not helping to keep him alive. Scream that she had to assist me.

Her countenance stopped me. She held up the vial with bright green liquid. It was the last resort. One I didn't want to contemplate yet. It felt like giving up, and I wasn't ready for that.

'The doctor is on the way. He'll be here in a few minutes.' I said desperately, glancing at the clock again.

'We don't have minutes,' she answered.

I wanted to scream at her. Tell her that wasn't true. But I knew it was. There was no escaping Jonah's grey parlour and the still expanding pool of blood. He was bleeding out. I knew it. Aaliyah knew it. So did my friend.

Jonah was dying.

There was nothing we could do to stop that.

Nothing we could do to save him now.

Only afterwards.

Our only option was to make sure he would be reincarnated, and we could get him back. That meant Aaliyah's family.

Mine would have a field day on him. We couldn't let them get their hands on him. There were probably only a few Christian nanos left in his body—if any—after more than a year out of the Church. He probably wouldn't end up there, but we couldn't take the chance. He had to be harvested by Aaliyah's clan. Their nanotech had to be prevalent in the body. That would alert them to his soul.

We wanted him back.

Reincarnation was the only way.

# Chapter Twenty

'DRINK THIS,' Aaliyah dripped the contents of the small flask between Jonah's lips. The bright green liquid was stark against the pale grey of my partner's skin. 'Please, Jonah,' she cried out to him. 'Open your mouth. Drink this.'

'Swallow the nanos, Jonah,' I added my voice to Aaliyah. 'Please. Just swallow.'

He opened his lips slightly and Aaliyah emptied the small vial into his mouth. Some of it dripped out of the corners of his mouth, but I hoped enough went down his throat. He coughed at the liquid as it made its way into his body.

'Will that be enough?' I asked Aaliyah. 'He might not be able to swallow them. And, in the best case, they will only be in his stomach.'

She looked around in panic. I followed her gaze.

'Please, get it,' she pointed to her coat. 'There are more vials in there. We need more.'

I grabbed the garment and brought it back to her. Glancing down at my partner I saw the green liquid seep out of his mouth. He wasn't able to swallow. His eyes were glazing over, the life ebbed out of him with every second we wasted.

I rummaged in the coat pockets and found another vial. I looked at Aaliyah, mirroring her anguish and panic. How the hell would we get it into Jonah if he couldn't swallow?

Another way came to mind, but my emotions didn't want to go down that road. I frantically tried to think of a more acceptable option. There wasn't one, and we only had a matter of seconds.

I grabbed the vial, opened it and poured the contents into Jonah's deep chest wound. The viscous liquid entered his body directly through the damaged tissue and a silent cry left his lips as his body tensed and bucked at the invasive nanotech. Harsh spasms racked his frame for what seemed like forever but was no more than a few seconds. My blood ran cold as I watched my friend battle for his life and lose.

'I'll find you,' Aaliyah said between tears. 'Make sure you're there. Fight for the new life.'

'Fight for your reincarnation, Jonah,' I added, shouting at him. 'Fight! Fight! Come back to us!'

Jonah's frame convulsed violently, then slowed until he lay still in the ever-expanding pool of his bright red blood.

The silence was even more startling than the spasms.

'Jonah,' Aaliyah called out. 'Jonah!'

She screamed at him.

He was gone.

I couldn't believe it.

Jonah was dead.

I turned to the other bodies.

Rafael lay on his side, my knife still embedded in his neck and the shattered amulet beside him. His eyes were open in death. I should close them, but I didn't want to touch him. There was a very real chance I would vent my anger on his corpse.

He was my sibling, and I'd killed him. But my feelings of intense loss were not for him, they were for Jonah.

It was a cliché; my brother from another mother. But that was how it felt. In the time I'd known him, he had become more important to me than the younger sibling I had known his whole life.

TWO OF EBONY'S armed guards came in the door cautiously.

They were professional, canvassing every corner and covering each other. I stood where I was, letting them do their work. They glanced over Jonah's body but continued to case the room.

One spoke into what I expect was a microphone. 'All clear.'

Two more burly men came into the house, followed by Ebony. Dr Patil pushed past her and moved quickly to Jonah's side. He placed his fingers on Jonah's neck and waited with bated breath, then looked up at Ebony standing in the doorway and shook his head slowly.

She flinched but kept her face in check. Behind the hard exterior I saw the immense pain in her eyes. She glanced at me, and my hearts went out to her. I had trouble suppressing my own tears.

Ebony knelt down beside Jonah and softly pushed strands of his hair from his forehead. She swallowed hard, touched him on the shoulder, then stood up.

'How long ago?' Dr Patil asked.

I shook my head, thinking. 'About a minute, two maybe, before you came in.'

He looked up at Ebony and I imagined I saw a slight nod. I found it strange, but left it at that, all of my attention on the unbelievable loss we just experienced.

Dr Patil placed Jonah's hands on his chest and beckoned to his assistant who came in pushing a gurney. A block of concrete landed hard in my gut at the sight of the black body bag on top of the gurney. He was dead. My friend and partner was gone.

I walked over to Ebony and took her hand. She let me steer her out of the room. We didn't need to see this.

# Chapter Twenty-One

LIFE CHANGED after we lost Jonah.

Dramatically.

Aaliyah transported back home immediately after Jonah's last breath. She vowed to find the reincarnated version and somehow bring him back.

I wasn't sure that was even an option.

The recruits' bodies were artificially grown in record time in our dimension. They weren't created to survive a transportation. They were vessels so the humans could work. Created specifically for that purpose and—though never said out loud—not for durability. We wanted maximum usage for at most ten years. Then the body would deteriorate rapidly, necessitating a new purchase. It was the basics of commerce; secure the demand.

We weren't the only ones to build that into the reincarnated bodies. All the families did. Maybe some were less greedy than others, but it was a fact of life. Grunts were temporary.

We didn't move the souls to a new body once the temporary one was worn out. There was no use, not unless an accident happened within the first six months. After that, it was redundant. For most of the grunts, the soul died long before the new body. Besides, why invest more money on a spent product.

I shivered at the callousness of my kind. The same complete disregard of human life that characterised my life and my beliefs before I met Jonah. Sure, I had doubts then. But he gave them a name. And me a goal.


WE HAD to continue without him. We owed him that.

I owed him that.

The large van and a private ambulance stood in front of the ranch. Seven burly guys dismounted from the vehicles and pushed past me into the house. I recognised one or two of them from my father's visit. They had bailed us out then. They were too late now.

They reverently packed Jonah's body in the black body bag, placed him on the gurney and brought him out to the ambulance. Ebony followed him.

'This isn't over,' she said to me before the EMT closed the door and sped off.

I nodded. What else could I do?

I turned back to the carnage in the house.

'We have orders to bring all the bodies,' the man I identified as Clyde stated. I nodded. We couldn't leave them here to be found by random humans.

'What will happen to them?' I asked. After all, one of the corpses was my brother.

'You'll have to ask Lady E for that,' he answered as expected. 'You have a vehicle anywhere near?'

'The Audi, outside the gate.'

'Give me the keys, one of the guys will get it and follow us back.'

I handed over the keys and was about to ask what I was supposed to do without transport when he added, 'you come with me.'

I glanced back at the bodies just in time to see the body bag zipped up on my brother. A sharp pain shot through me. Not for him, for my mother. One of her sons just killed another. That was how fucked-up our family was. It would break her heart. She always wanted us to get along, like any mother. She was the counterweight to my father's coldness.

My dad.

He would go ballistic. Defeat was not in his vocabulary. Losing a son was probably not even that big a thing for him, it was more the lack of control and the fact that I had done it. And maybe because he didn't have the essence. He couldn't reincarnate Rafe, that was a failure, and dad didn't suffer those well. He would never know for certain what happened to Rafe, but he could no doubt join the dots.

Clyde and I open the doors to one of three SUV's that had materialised outside the house.

'Lady E can't stay here anymore. This place has been compromised. It's on the enemy's radar now. She told me to bring you to her new headquarters.'

I wasn't surprised. If this place was no longer safe, she would have multiple other locations. Ebony was ten steps ahead of anyone else. Always.

Clyde pulled out after the two vans. I looked in the mirror and felt the guilt weigh heavily on my shoulders as the sight of the pretty ranch retreated into the black sky.

I stared out into the pitch black of the night. There wasn't even a moon. Just a faint glow from the stars, and even those were tempered by the clouds that quickly rolled in, heralding the predicted storm.

Within minutes, thick drops of rain battered the windshield, and the wind blew them almost horizontally against the SUV. Clyde seemed oblivious of the bad weather. He expertly handled the big heavy SUV. The sheer weight of the bullet-proofing offered a steady drive no matter how hard the wind blew. This storm was going to be historic, according to the weatherman, but it had nothing on the battle that was raging inside me.

The anger at my family for my best friend's murder warred with the terrible guilt I felt that it was all my fault. Jonah died protecting me. It should have been me. Not him. I should be lying in the body bag in the back of the truck, not the big man.

If I had just stepped to the side. If I'd killed Rafe earlier. If I had never met Jonah.

If…If…if.

Yeah right. Who was I kidding?

I alternated between blaming Jonah and myself.

Mainly myself.

And what about our quest? How on earth were we going to proceed without Jonah? And should we even try? It was his goal originally. His life's work.

How could we not continue? It would be a disrespect to his memory if we didn't. Not to mention I had nowhere to go and would be hunted down like a dog by my family for eternity anyway.

Now we just had to find out how.

Something inside me said Lady E would have a plan.

I hoped to hell she did, because I didn't.

The plan turned out to be deceivingly simple.

Keep going.

Besides, he might come back.

We were leaning heavily on Aaliyah for that, but we had to have hope.

I hadn't heard from her since she evaporated into thin air after Jonah died. I assumed she was back in our dimension finding our big friend.

It struck me how little I knew of the whole procedure. How long would it take for his soul to reach our dimension? What happened after that? And when would it be paired with a body? Besides, how did they actually grow the vessels to resemble the original human body of the subject?

I would just have to trust Aaliyah.

The enemy. The friendly face within the enemy? Whatever.

I was driving myself nuts here.

A thought struck me. 'What happened to Jonah's body?' I asked Ebony.

She looked at me and I was sure she was about to say that it wasn't any of my business, when her face softened. She set down the tablet she was using and came over to where I stood.

Ebony took my hands and looked up at me. There was a slight hint of moisture at the edge of her eyes.

'I took him to doctor Patil's Clinique. There he was officially pronounced dead. Patil took care of the autopsy and all the paperwork. Jonah is now officially deceased. That means we can have a ceremony if we want before he is cremated.'

Her words cut deep. They brought home the message that my big friend was officially gone. Ebony read my mind. 'We don't know if he's coming back.'

I looked at her and nodded. 'No, we don't.'

'Has it ever been done?' She asked.

I shook my head. 'No. Not that I know of.'

'But it is possible?'

I shrugged. 'Technically, yes. The bodies are replicas of ours in most aspects. And we can survive here. So, it should be okay.'

'But?' She saw right through me.

'But they are not made for endurance.'

'You live forever. Or nearly anyway.'

'Yes. We're basically immortal, in our timelines and here. But the bodies we grow for the grunts are not the same.'

'An inferior copy?'

'Something like that.'

We were quiet. What was there to say after that revelation.

I decided I couldn't sugar-coat it anymore.

'And that's only if Aaliyah finds him.'

Ebony stared at me, probing my eyes for more.

She sighed, kissed me on the cheek and let go of my hands. 'She'll find him.'

I refrained from reacting.

# Chapter Twenty-Two

THE CREMATION WAS small and very private.

Besides the staff, just Ebony, Sly and me. And of course, the ten guards that patrolled both the crematorium and its grounds. No-one was allowed anywhere near the service. Clyde and his team made sure of that.

The Church was also absent. Ebony had vetoed informing Benedict. He would no doubt have heard on the news, or maybe through the Establishment grapevine. The latter were probably rejoicing now. Paparazzi had been warned to stay away. They had taken the barely veiled threats seriously, no one was here.

The short service—if you could call it that—only lasted twenty minutes. The closed casket was brought into the room on a wheel bier. Ebony and I formed the two-person procession behind it and took our chairs while the pall bearers moved the casket onto the conveyor belt.

There were no speeches. No memories spoken out loud. We just sat there silently, each submerged in our own thoughts.

Ebony nodded to the funeral arranger, and he moved toward the console where he flicked a switch. The dark blue velour curtains parted softly, and the conveyor belt slowly moved the casket backwards into the dark beyond. We stood and watched our friend leave us. When the curtains closed again, Ebony took my hand, and we walked down the aisle out of the now oppressive room. My head hurt and the feeling of guilt lay heavily on my shoulders.

We continued walking out of the building to where Ebony's car waited for her.

'Are you coming back with us?' she asked me. 'The boys can bring your car.'

I shook my head. 'I need some air, sorry.'

'No problem.' She smiled. 'See you tomorrow, Gabe.' She kissed me on the cheek and got into the car.

The sleek car sped away, and I took a deep breath.

I walked to my vehicle, clicked the remote and started up the sporty German machine. The crematorium was left behind in seconds as I sped out of the secluded grounds onto the highway.

I had no idea where I was going to. I just wanted to be alone for a while. At intersections, I randomly picked a direction and kept on driving.

The radio music blasting out of the speakers was set to one of the old rock channels. The dark verse of the Deranged's Sound of Silence echoed in my head. It seemed appropriate. Jonah had not been one to keep silent if he observed what he perceived as injustice. I thought how dangerous silence was, much more than to speak out. The links to our current circumstances were apparent, and maybe just as hopeless.

With all my hearts I hoped Aaliyah would be able to

bring Jonah back to us. Our quest wasn't finished. He wasn't finished. We needed the big man.

Every day that went by without word from Aaliyah was another closer to never seeing him again.

I know, I'm being sombre. Death does that to me. That, and the odds that were rapidly stacked up against us.

I drove for hours and finally stopped at an all-night diner. It was five in the morning when I pushed the door open and stepped into a replica of a fifty's diner straight out of Happy Days. The long counter hugged the right side of the long room. A metallic base with what looked like a bright red Formica top. Black round bar stools with chrome legs stood on the checkered black and white tiled floor. Along the left side booths with the same bright red seating hugged the windows. In the background I heard sixties music from the Wurlitzer Jukebox near the cash register.

There were three other customers. A middle-aged woman whose hospital scrubs poked out under her long cardigan sat near the door. A cop and an old man hugging a cup of coffee, were seated further up the counter.

I took a booth and slid into the seat facing the window. I kept my car in my line of sight as I stared at the darkness. A few minutes later a pretty thirty-ish waitress took my order of coffee and a bagel and left. I turned back to the dark. There was something at the edge of my mind that wouldn't come into focus. It was just out of reach. I was sure it was important but couldn't put my finger on what it was.

The coffee and bagel were placed in front of me. I thanked the waitress and attempted a smile. She returned the sentiment and left when the cop called for another coffee. I lowered my gaze to the sirupy black brew. What I really needed now was a stiff drink, but that was out of the question. What if I was pulled over with a strong alcohol breath? I would pass any breathalyser test, but the blood test would be a very different matter. I couldn't run the risk. Not that the alcohol would help dull any of the dark thoughts I was experiencing. I'd need a lot more than a few bottles of booze for that.

No, the best cure for my guilt was action. I—we—needed to do something, something useful. Brooding wouldn't help anyone.

I took my phone out of my jacket pocket and opened the organiser app. I needed to do a brain dump. I typed everything I could think of into the app. Never mind how irrelevant it seemed; I jotted it down. The contents would be aggregated, and I could let loose a load of algorithms to find any links I'd missed.

Twenty minutes later I closed the app and sat back. Taking action was much better than beating myself up. My newfound energy woke up my stomach as well. The loud rumbles a clear sign my appetite had returned with a vengeance after a few days of minimal food craving. I smiled at the memory of Jonah's insatiable appetite.

I called the waitress over, ordered yet another coffee refill and asked for the menu. It was her turn to smile now, and it lit up the room. She really was very pretty.

I ordered banana-pancakes and even more coffee. It was delivered to my table within minutes accompanied by a bottle of maple syrup.

I dug into the food with gusto, my dark mood at least temporarily lifted.

My belly full, I sat back and observed my surroundings.

The diner was busy, the counter almost full and most of the booths occupied. I glanced at my watch, almost six-thirty. The amount of people in medical scrubs convinced me there was a hospital nearby. Their numbers were further inflated by hard-hat workers, in for a quick breakfast before work started. A building site I guessed. The cop and the nurse had left, the old man was still hunched over his now empty beverage.

The single waitress had been joined by two more who rushed between tables and the counter, continuously taking orders and filling coffee cups. There was light banter and occasional laughter. The place was jamming.

'CAN I GET YOU ANYTHING ELSE?' The pretty waitress smiled down at me.

I shook my head. 'No thanks. The pancakes were great. And if I drink anymore coffee I'll start bouncing.'

Her laugh was warm and inviting.

'I couldn't help noticing you looked so sad when you came in.'

'A good friend was cremated yesterday,' I answered softy.

'I'm sorry.' She sounded very sincere.

We were silent for a moment and my gaze went back to my hands on the table.

'Looks like rush hour has started,' I continued, suddenly not wanting her to leave.

'Yes,' she answered. 'Six to nine is the morning sprint. Then four to seven.'

'Shift changes at the hospital?' I guessed.

She nodded again, her cute brown bob dancing around her face.

'What about you?' I dared to ask.

She looked at me, hesitated a minute then returned my smile. 'I'm off in twenty minutes.'

I nodded, not sure what to say after that. I was no

stranger to human women. I'd had my share of encounters in the many years I roamed this dimension. But there was something about this woman that stopped me from my normal cliche macho behaviour.

'If you like,' she continued. 'We could talk a bit. I'm off soon and you look like you could do with the company.'

I smiled. 'I'd like that. If you're not too tired. After your shift and all.'

'I'm good. See you later then.' I nodded and she left to help her co-workers with the morning rush.

Sure enough, twenty-three minutes later she slid into the booth opposite me.

I tried to smile, by the look of sadness on her face, I failed miserably. 'Thanks,' I mumbled.

'You're welcome.' That smile again.

'I'm Gabriel,' I formally introduced myself.

'Kate,' she answered as we shook hands.

We continued with small talk. The weather, music, that kind of thing. Though the noise in the diner made it very difficult to understand each other, I had to ask her to repeat herself more than once.

'Let's leave, shall we?' She suggested, looking around. 'I live nearby, it's quieter, and more private.'

'Are you sure?' I asked. 'You don't know me.'

'I have a gut feeling you're a safe bet,' she laughed. 'You're too sweet to be dangerous.'

If only she knew.

Her home was a small, detached house on a quiet street about a mile from the diner. The well-kept garden—though tiny—was welcoming, as was the house.

'I guess it's too early for alcohol?' she asked, two cans of beer in her hands.

'We've been up long enough,' I laughed.

She put the cans on the table, one in front of me.

'Your friend,' she asked softly. 'Were you very close?'

I knew I shouldn't tell her, but the need to share my pain with someone was too strong to ignore. 'Close might not be the right way to describe our relationship,' I answered with a smile. 'Sometimes, we were at each other's throats, sometimes even literally. And ours was more a relationship of circumstances. We shared the same goal. At least, that was how it started.'

She nodded to urge me onwards.

'We were both involved in uncovering a massive scam.'

'Are you with law enforcement?'

'No. Not really. We identified the scam and were gathering some proof before we could go public.'

'Private Investigators?'

'Something like that, yes. But it was personal for him because it wrecked his life.'

'And for you?'

'For me,' I hesitated. 'For me it was personal because it was my family.'

'The ones perpetrating the scam are your family?'

I nodded. 'I didn't realise exactly what they were doing until I met the big man. That's what I called him. The big man.' I smiled at the thought. 'He was. Big, I mean. He towered over most people. Definitely over me. Frankly, I was terrified of him to start with, but he grew on me. We became close. Like brothers. My new family.'

I looked up at her face. She smiled and I felt a warmth sting at the back of my eyes. Cry? Are you kidding? I don't do that. Not that there are no tears in my dimension. My kind can cry, just like you. It's just that all my tears were knocked out of me by dear old dad. I can't remember when my last time was. It wasn't done. Not in my family.

My automatic reaction kicked in and I pushed my emotions back.

'You're allowed to grieve, you know?'

I looked up at Kate. There was genuine empathy in her eyes. She took my hand and squeezed it.

'Thanks,' I answered, smiling back.

We sat in silence, her hand still in mine.

Kate leaned forward and kissed me.

I kissed her back and took her into my arms, the warmth of her body soothing my feeling of loss.

One thing led to another and early in the afternoon I woke up in her bed feeling better than I had since Jonah died.

It wasn't just the sex. Sure, that had been mind-blowing. But the warmth of another person, the empathy. The connection. Even if it was just for one night, or day, in this case.

I dressed and made some coffee in her kitchen, brought Kate a cup and kissed her softly on the forehead.

'Hi, sleepy,' I said softly.

She smiled and opened her eyes slowly, hanging on to the peaceful numbness of sleep.

'Thank you,' I said sincerely.

'You're going to be ok,' she said.

I nodded.

'Now go get them, Gabe,'

One last kiss.

Then I left.

# Chapter Twenty-Three

'I CAN'T FIND HIM.' Aaliyah's voice shook, the flush on her face mirroring the anxiety she felt.

My hearts sank. Jonah had to be there. Surely, he'd come through the reincarnation. I knew it was invasive, but he was a fighter. There was no way it could have beaten him.

Unless…

Unless we were too late with the nanos, and he hadn't made it to Arand's reincarnation facility. I didn't want to think about the other options that were left, but my mind kept returning to what might have happened.

Worst case scenario: Jonah still had some Christian nanos in his body when he died and Arand's hadn't worked. That would bring him into my father's compound. I shuddered at the thought.

If they found him—and believe me, if he ended up in that compound there was no way they could miss him—his new life would be hell. Plus, Ebony and I would be in grave danger. My family would pick his mind, drive him crazy. Torture him until he broke. And there was nothing we could do about it.

In my father's compound he would be lost for us. There was no way we could know if he was there and what had become of him. We couldn't help. I contemplated transporting back home to find him. But even though my transporter worked now, I didn't trust it not to show up on the radar if I went home.

Now that would be a family reunion. My father and Michael would have a field day. I would gladly give my life for Jonah, but in this case my sacrifice would be totally futile. It wouldn't help the big man and it would only compound our predicament. I had to think of something else.

Or—a speck of hope—he could be gone, really gone. Not reincarnated. None of the nanos had taken. Jonah was off to wherever humans went without our interference.

I hoped for the last, if Aaliyah couldn't find him.

'Where did you look?' I asked, immediately regretting my question and the somewhat accusatory tone.

Aaliyah looked at me, fire in her eyes and her face a mask of anger.

She slowly answered me, emphasising each word. 'Where do you think?'

When I didn't answer she added sullenly, 'I looked everywhere. In the lab, the growth plants, the grunts holding cells. Everywhere. Nothing.'

'Not even a trace.'

She shook her head.

'It could be too early,' I suggested, grasping at straws.

There was hope in the way she picked up the idea. 'Maybe. It's only been a few days.'

A week actually. But I refrained from pointing that out.

'It's possible he's in limbo somewhere because they can't recognise him,' she contemplated. 'Normally the soul is recognised by the computers because the nanos administered are recorded. His weren't of course.' She looked up at me. Hope reinstated in her dark eyes. 'I might have to wait a few more days. See if he is classified as an "unknown". Then I can find him.'

'What will that mean? An "unknown". What does that entail for how they'll view him? Will they still reincarnate him?'

'Yes, they will, once they've scanned the DNA readings from the nanos. Usually, the DNA sequence is already in the computer, and they have the blueprints for the body. With Jonah they don't have the designs yet, so they will have to make them. That will take time. It's logical that he hasn't shown up yet.'

It sounded legitimate. The bodies of the grunts were built from the blueprints. The data was passed on to the computer that created the design for the body. Upon death, the nanite relayed the status to the computer and the creation of the vessel was started, ready to house the soul when it arrived.

Jonah's DNA was absent. The designs for his body had to be created from scratch. That was the delay.

We silently agreed to hold onto that straw.

'I'll continue looking for him' Aaliyah declared, her tone much stronger now.

I nodded and smiled, fearful of breaking the fragile confidence we had.

Aaliyah transported out of the room and left me alone to my doubts.

God, I hoped we were right. I couldn't face the idea we might have sentenced Jonah to my family.

Shivers ran up my spine and a cold hand gripped my hearts.

## Chapter Twenty-Four

'WILL she be able to find him?'

Ebony and I were in a country house far away from the busy streets of the city. Her current hide-a-way was another massive ranch style mansion in the hills outside San Diego. The place would easily house a family of ten with room to spare. Opposite the main house was a collection of stables, barns and servants' dwellings.

There were presently seven people in the complex. Ebony, her bodyguard Sly—who doubled as the cook—and me in the house, the rest were patrolling the grounds around the buildings. A further contingency of rough looking guys on horseback or riding dirt-bikes kept an eye on the hundreds of acres that encircled the ranch. This was truly a place to disappear.

'She will,' I answered with more conviction than I felt, remembering the last time I spoke to Aaliyah.

Ebony kept up a controlled appearance, but one look in her eyes showed me it was no more than skin-deep. She hurt inside. Jonah had been much more to her than I—or even she—had realised. I felt the loss. Hers and, to be honest, mine too.

The big man had grown on me. We were closer than I had ever been with one of my siblings. Sure, we'd argued. But which brothers didn't?

'How will she know it's him?' My half-hearted attempt hadn't been enough to convince her.

'The nanos will have activated almost immediately because he was slipping fast. They send the information to the computers and the soul is picked up.'

'Yes, I got that part,' Ebony persisted. 'But once the soul is reincarnated, how will Aaliyah know it's him?'

'The information the nanos send included a breakdown of the DNA, that enables the plant to build a body that is almost identical to the one he had here.'

'What will be different?'

'Superficial things. Like the beard and the tattoos. They're not determined by the DNA sequences. They are conscious choices he made. But his general physique, length and skin colour will be the same. His musculature might be less than here, because it is as much a question of training as genetics, but the basis will be there.'

'A Jonah without the tattoos or scars?'

'Yes.'

'That will be strange. I've only known him like he was.'

We were silent for a moment.

The bodyguard brought us coffee. We thanked him and he moved back to a respectful distance to give us space to talk. Despite everything, I think he still didn't trust me.

That was one thing I'd noticed in the past few days. The guards Ebony had surrounded herself with were completely devoted to her. I didn't doubt for a second that each and every one of them would willingly die for our tiny computer wizard. Not for the first time, I found myself wondering what the foundation was of her hold on these people.

'What about his mind?' Ebony brought me out of my reverie.

I shook my head. 'I don't really know. I spoke to some of the recruits on one of my last visits. They seemed to remember a lot of their previous life. But I didn't know them before they died so I don't have a good frame of reference.'

She looked worried.

'The last guy I spoke to was very aware of his situation. And who brought him there. There was a lot of anger. I think the new Jonah will most likely be very much the same in temperament as the one we knew.'

That brought a smile to her lips. 'Heaven help them then.' We both chuckled at the thought of a reincarnated Jonah wreaking havoc on the transportation workers in my dimension.

The lighter atmosphere was short-lived. 'What if your family finds him first?'

'They won't,' I tried to sound convincing. 'There's no way any of my family will be anywhere near Arand's transportation hubs. Arand's is much more sophisticated than my family's and I very much doubt he'd risk them stealing his secrets again.'

I hoped I was right. I shuddered to think of what would happen to my friend if my father or one of my brothers got wind of Jonah's presence. They would no doubt try to extract every last bit of information from his soul's memory. Most likely not in a friendly or remotely pleasant way. If they found out Rafael was indeed dead and we were responsible, they would vent their anger on Jonah. Life in my dimension was not pleasant for a human. For Jonah it would be the true definition of Hell.

I said a silent prayer to Aaliyah to find the big man quickly. Before his bad situation became much, much worse.

# Chapter Twenty-Five

'HE'S IN THE HOLDING CELLS.'

Ebony and I let out a collective sigh of relief.

Ebs, because Aaliyah had found Jonah and he had been reincarnated. Me, mainly because he wasn't at my family's compound. That option had haunted my dreams for the past weeks to the extent that I didn't want to sleep anymore. It didn't help, the nightmares followed me into daytime.

'Thank you.' Ebony took Aaliyah's hands. 'Thank you for finding him.' For a moment there was a connection there. Both women so happy that their reluctantly shared love-interest was alive.

'Has anyone recognised him?' I asked, trepidation causing the words to come out harder than I meant. I tried to soften the blow with an apologetic smile.

Aaliyah shook her head. 'No. Thankfully, they haven't. They have no reason to. I mean, Jonah's known in your family's religion, not generally in Islam. There's no reason they should think he is anything other than just another grunt. His skin colour helped a bit. If he'd been white, he would have stood out more. But his darker skin blended with the Arabian recruits. They think that's his origin. I overheard one of the scientists declare that he had probably been an onlooker at a suicide bombing who'd been administered nanos at the moment of death by an enthusiastic recruiter.'

I cocked my head in agreement. It sounded plausible. We'd done the same.

'What now?' Ebony asked. 'How do we get him back here?'

Aaliyah let go of her hands and stepped back. The lines returned on her brow, and she bit her underlip.

'That's the next hurdle I have to scale.'

Ebony glanced at me. I couldn't lighten her concerns. The question was foremost in my mind as well.

'To be completely honest,' Aaliyah continued. 'I don't know.'

Not what I wanted to hear.

'Is there any way you could buy him or get someone else to do it for you?'

'I'd have to be very careful,' she mused. 'If it comes back to me, I could have Bashir on my back.'

'Do you do any acquisitions for your family?'

'No. I don't. Bashir takes care of that now.'

'A friend then?'

'I don't want to endanger anyone close to me. And it's very difficult to trust anyone else. I don't know who's under Bashir's influence. He's gaining more followers every day. People I thought would never fall for his bullshit, have succumbed to the peer pressure his group exhumes.'

'How far is Jonah in the process?'

She looked at me intently. 'He'll be at the holding

facility for about another week. After that he's up for sale.'
She echoed my concerns.

'Then there's not much time.'

'Thanks Gabe. I really needed you to point that out.'

'Sorry. I didn't mean it that way. It's worrying me and came out wrong.'

She didn't pursue it.

'Have you spoken to him?' Ebony attempted to lighten the conversation.

'No. I couldn't get close without it being obvious I was looking for him. Plus, I don't know how he will react if he sees me. He might recognise me, or not. I couldn't run the risk of him calling my name with others there. I saw him on a screen. When I get back, I'll get close when no one else is around.'

'Is there anything we can do to help?' Ebony asked.

Aaliyah smiled and shook her head. 'No. I don't think so. Just make sure that everything is ready for him when he comes back.'

I noticed the "when", not "if". I wished I was as positive as she tried to be.

'What do you mean?' Ebony asked.

'He'll be disoriented. Maybe even angry. I might have to force him to come. I have no idea whether he will recognise any of us. He might have to be restrained.'

This was not what I had in mind. Shit. An angry Jonah wasn't a positive turn of events.

'And we don't know how his new body will stand up to transportation. He might need medical assistance.'

'We'll have our doctor on standby and the clinic ready, just in case,' Ebony answered. 'Doctor Patil is familiar with Gabriel's physique.'

'That will help.'

We ran out of things to say, the silence heavy on all our shoulders. Anything we tried to voice now would only complicate things or strain our enthusiasm even more.

'I'll go back and give you a heads-up one way or the other before I get him here.'

'Thank you.'

She nodded.

With a push on her amulet she was gone, leaving Ebony and me with a sense of relief tempered by uncertainty of what was to come.

There were a lot of unknowns.

But there was hope. At least we knew where he was. For now.

## Chapter Twenty-Six

THE FAMILIAR WHIRRING sound of a transportation was loud in the silence of anticipation.

Ebony sat perfectly still; her eyes glued to the centre of the room where the air was fluctuating. The forms on the other side were blurring and out of focus as a semi-translucent sheet of light shimmered in the dusky evening.

I forced myself to breath.

Shivers ran up and down my spine and goosebumps covered my arms as a feeling of dread engulfed me. Had it worked? Would Aaliyah be able to bring the big man back. And if so, what state would he be in? It was all out of our hands. What would happen, would happen.

The swirling started to take form. Big form.

'Jonah?' Ebony whispered almost imperceptibly.

The big man's recognisable size was what gave him away.

The whirring stopped and silence reigned in the room. Neither Ebony nor I dared to breathe, let alone move.

Jonah stood in the centre of the room. His eyes were

closed and there were deep lines across his forehead. His frame shook as though a fever ravaged his body. His hands were clenched into fists and the muscles in his arms and shoulders were tense.

'Jonah?' Ebony repeated, now a bit louder.

The figure opened his eyes and slowly looked around the room. He turned to me, and I stared into a familiar face with strange bloodshot lavender eyes. They seemed so out of place, so foreign. His gaze travelled onwards to Ebony who gasped at the change.

There was surprise in Jonah's face. Concentration in the lines on his brow and intensity in his whole stance. Like he was desperately trying to remember who we were.

His head turned to me, then back to Ebony and he took a hesitant first step towards her. His frame crumpled and he sank to the ground. His eyes were closed, and his rigid body went limp.

'Jonah!' Ebony ran forward and knelt down beside the unconscious form.

A second whirring sound started to my right and Aaliyah materialised in the haze. As soon as her form became solid, she rushed over to Jonah and Ebony.

'What's wrong with him?' Ebony asked. 'Is he okay?'

Aaliyah glanced up at me, then proceeded to examine Jonah. She placed two fingers of her hands on either side of his neck and counted.

'His hearts are pumping,' she answered both of us. 'His breathing is regular. The muscles are relaxed.'

I let out a sigh of relief. Ebony closed her eyes and took a deep breath.

She stood up and addressed the ever-present guard. 'Get doctor Patil please, Sly.'

He nodded and left the room.

'Let's put him on the sofa,' she suggested. The three of us picked up the slack form of our friend and softly placed him on the long chaise, his head resting on some of the colourful cushions.

I took a good look at my former partner.

He looked the same, but different. His basic physique was the same, slightly less muscle, but close. The dark hair resembled the colour he had when we met even if it was a lot shorter now. The stubble of a beard made his now relaxed features very familiar. My eyes travelled down to his arms and torso, and I realised what made him so different now.

'It's the tattoos and scars, or lack thereof,' Ebony beat me to it.

The new Jonah's skin was pristine. No tattoos, no scars, nothing.'

'Makes sense,' she answered.

Jonah's breathing was deep and regular. His features were relaxed as though in deep sleep.

The door opened and the doctor came in. He had been waiting in another room in the vast complex, just in case. He moved over to the sofa and opened his familiar black bag. He took out his stethoscope and was about to start his examination when he looked up at me and Aaliyah. He listened to the hearts, observed his breathing and gently pulled one eyelid open to look at Jonah's eyes.

'Is this normal?' he asked Aaliyah.

I moved closer and saw that Jonah's violet-purple irises were surrounded by what you would call bloodshot whites. Only in our case—and now his—there was a decisive soft purple hue to them. Logical, as our blood is purple.

'I think so,' Aaliyah answered. 'Transportation has probably burst some calliparies in the white of his eyes.'

Patil nodded his agreement and continued his examination.

After a few minutes he sat back and looked at the three of us. 'He seems to be in a deep sleep. His breathing is good. One of the hearts has a slight flutter, but otherwise they seem to be strong. I'm not sure what else I can say. I don't really know what I'm looking for, the majority of my dealings with your kind has been after they were deceased or Gabriel who seems very healthy. I can't really give a prognosis other than that sleep and rest will probably be good for him.'

'Thank you, Doctor,' Ebony smiled.

'What do we do now?' I asked.

'Wait for him to wake up.'

'Will he be okay?'

'I have no idea. This is not regular medicine. They don't teach alien physiology in med school. I'm winging it as much as you are. Educated guesses. No more than that.'

We all nodded.

Doctor Patil left us.

'So, we wait?' Ebony asked.

I shrugged. 'I don't think there's much else we can do.'

Ebony looked at me intently, then at Aaliyah. 'Do you have any idea what we can expect?'

'No,' I answered honestly. 'As far as I know, no reincarnated soul has ever come back to earth through our network.' I glanced at Aaliyah.

'Same here. This is a first.'

'Any guesses then?'

We both shrugged.

'Okay, then we'll just play it by ear.' The practical, organised Ebony was back again. I must say, I prefer this one under the current circumstances.

WE WAITED for more than an hour before any movement came from the sofa. I was starting to think the big man's sleep was more than that.

Aaliyah sat next to him constantly monitoring his heartbeats and his breathing. Ebony was back at the bank of computers, searching for something, she didn't say what. I was at the table pretending to work on my laptop.

I couldn't concentrate. My mind kept going back to what we had done.

Initially, when teleportation technology was first discovered, we experienced our own frightening side effects. Splicing, people dying, others going insane. The technology was vastly improved, but I had no idea whether that was good enough for the inferior grunt bodies. The effects I experienced every time I used this travel method, strengthened my doubts.

Different scenarios alternated in my head. What if he didn't wake up? What if he did?

The sounds came first. A soft grunt of pain, followed by heavier breathing.

Aaliyah knelt down next to Jonah's head. Ebony and I dropped what we were doing and moved over, careful not to crowd him. We reasoned Aaliyah was the last person he'd seen in the other dimension and chances were he would remember her.

His eyes opened slowly, and he stared at Aaliyah. She stayed absolutely still, not even breathing. We did the same. Slowly he pushed his upper body off the chaise and swivelled his head around to look at the surroundings.

There was confusion in his eyes. His brow was creased, and his lips pulled into a tight line. When his gaze fell on Ebony his features softened slightly, but the confusion was still there. He lingered a few moments, as though attempting to remember. Then he passed on.

When he finally came to me, his visage hardened. The confusion turned to hatred. His eyes were dark and hooded by his thick eyebrows. He pulled his nose up slightly and his mouth opened as if he wanted to say something.

The tell-tale tingles of fear and excitement moved up my spine and collected at the base of my skull where they became a dull ache. My mind struggled in the fight or flight conundrum, where flight was the preferred outcome. Jonah was terrifying. The anger and resentment that emanated from him was almost overpowering.

I forced myself to hold his stare. Lowering my eyes felt even more dangerous. My breaths were shallow and quick. I felt my hearts beating rapidly in my chest, readying my body for what was to come.

We stayed that way for what felt like an eternity until the link was broken by Aaliyah.

'Jonah,' she caught his attention with her soft voice. 'Jonah. It's okay.'

He glanced at her, then back to me again. The anger now competing with confusion again.

'That's Gabriel, Jonah,' Aaliyah continued. 'He's one of us.' She paused. 'He's one of the good guys.' Jonah didn't look convinced, but the direct threat was gone from his eyes.

'Take a deep breath,' she continued on a soothing voice. 'You're safe here. We're your friends.'

He looked around again. Slightly less anxious.

Aaliyah helped him sit up against the back of the sofa. His skin colour slowly returned to normal.

Ebony took a few steps forward. Jonah turned to face her, and his features softened a bit. 'I know you,' he said.

She smiled at him and was rewarded with a tentative smile back.

'I'm Ebony,' she said, and he nodded.

'Yes, Ebony…Tiny.' He reached out his hand for her. Ebony bridged the gap and took it. The smile was real now, from ear to ear, as he pulled her close.

I decided to stay put. His earlier reaction to me was still foremost in my mind. The pure hatred I'd seen in his eyes was like nothing I'd experienced before, not even the first time we met. I wasn't in a hurry to repeat it.

The moment was broken by a loud rumbling originating from Jonah's stomach.

Jonah raised his eyebrows and looked down in surprise. Ebony's laughter was a welcome lightning of the atmosphere in the room. We all joined in.

Sly returned minutes later with food for our hungry team member. We all moved closer and sat around the sofa while he devoured the meal.

Banter was easy and the mood lightened, even for me. I dared come a bit closer but still kept more distance than the others. No use in pushing the odds. We would get around to discussing his feelings for me at another time.

## Chapter Twenty-Seven

THINGS HAD CHANGED.

Jonah was different.

Fundamentally.

Even his appearance was an unnerving combination of familiar and foreign. I'd never realised how much his exterior determined the man. The tattoos and scars were an integral part of what was Jonah.

His new physique was smaller, less imposing. Maybe because of the missing musculature as much as the absent ink. He was still athletic, just less massive. That was something he could remedy, and he quickly found his way to the private gym Ebony had incorporated in the safe house.

But it wasn't just the exterior.

This was a different man.

The old Jonah had always been very present. Explosive sometimes, but consistently extrovert and the centre of attention. This version was reserved. Standoffish. It felt as though he'd built a wall around himself and no one—not even Ebony—was allowed in. She tried. Man, how she tried.

Initially he tried to re-ignite the passion they had shared, but more often than not, I encountered them at opposite sides of the kitchen the next day, both avoiding each other's eyes.

As days moved into weeks, we found a way to co-exist, because that was what it was. I tried to involve him in what we were doing, but he showed no interest. He would stand there, hear what we had to say, then shrug and leave.

Before he died, you could read his emotions off his face like a neon light. Now he was a closed book. I had no idea what he was thinking. What he felt. It scared me.

His demeanour had an enormous impact on Ebony. She'd wanted him back, now she was not so sure. She sought her release in work, doubling her efforts to find a new way into the Establishment so we could continue our quest.

I tried to help, but she wanted solitude. Or at least not me around.

The atmosphere in the house was volatile. The stress in all its inhabitants reaching boiling point. It was just a question of time. I hoped to hell I wasn't in the centre of it when it erupted.

# Chapter Twenty-Eight

'YOU'RE TO BLAME, YOU KNOW.'

'For what?'

'For my death.'

I stared at Jonah. 'How do you figure that?' I was mortified. How could he believe that?

He looked at me incredulously. 'It's obvious.' He held his hands up in despair.

'My brother killed you. Not me,' I tried.

'He killed me while I was saving you,' the big man said, accusingly putting his finger on what had been eating away at me ever since that fateful night. I tried to push my feelings of guilt away, but he had a point.

'I died saving you.'

Yeah, rub it in, will you? Just what I needed.

I sighed. 'So now you're saying this is all my fault, are you?'

He nodded. Anger started to flush my face.

'You've had a death-wish ever since you found out about the Establishment. The only reason you're alive at the moment is because of me,' I retorted angrily. 'You would have died long ago If I hadn't stopped your senseless rampage. And you know what? You would be in deep shit if you had. You would be slaving away in a mine somewhere in my dimension. Not here. Not alive again. So, stop the blame thing. I'm not falling for it.'

The faint curl of his lips threw me.

What the hell?

He was pushing my buttons again. This truly was Jonah, even if he looked unsettlingly different.

'Good to have you back, big man.' I smiled back at him.

He laughed. 'Gotcha.'

'Yes, you did,' I had to concede.

The smile faltered and I saw something I'd never seen before; uncertainty, and maybe a touch of fear.

'How are you really doing?' I asked him softly.

'I'm not sure.'

I stayed silent to give him space. If he wanted to tell me, he would. The only sound was a faint hum of the wind outside the ranch. A storm was brewing. In more ways than one.

'I feel tired most of the time,' he continued. 'But in some way, very invigorated. It's a contradiction really. I have energy, just in short bursts. When I do, I'm brimming over with stamina, and after a few minutes it's like it all just flows out of me.'

I nodded. It was the same feeling I'd experienced the first few times I came here.

'It will get better,' I answered. 'Give it some time. Your body has to get used to this dimension.'

'My body?' He lifted his right arm and looked at it. Then the left. The puzzlement on his face said it all.

'I feel this body. I know it's what I'm in now. But it

doesn't feel or look like mine. Sometimes it feels as though I'm in a video game. I'm steering this avatar from a console somewhere. It feels disjointed, foreign. Weird.'

I just nodded.

'I stood in front of the mirror this morning for more than an hour. Just staring at my reflection. I watched it move exactly as I ordered it to. I saw my breathing completely in tune with the spectre in the mirror. Everything was in sync. All the time. But still, it doesn't feel like me. I miss my body, my tattoos, my scars even. They were memories of my life. This body isn't. It's new, Unused. Unloved. It's not mine. It's just borrowed.'

We were silent again. What was there to say?

'What was it like?' I finally dared to ask. 'The reincarnation?'

'Like being beaten up, run over by a train, pulled apart by horses and trampled by elephants.'

'That bad, huh?'

He rolled his eyes. 'Hell, yeah.'

He took a deep breath.

'In all the fights I've ever been in, I've never felt that way. The pain was in every fibre of my body. I felt agony in places I never knew existed. My brain felt like it was going to explode.'

His gaze was fixed on a random spot on the floor. There was a nervous twitch in his folded hands, tensing his fingers so much they almost cracked. His face was pale, emphasised by the lack of tattoos in his neck and upper chest.

I stood up and walked to the drinks cupboard where I pulled out a bottle of bourbon and two glasses, sure Ebony wouldn't mind. I gave one to Jonah, poured a generous amount and moved back to my seat where I filled my glass.

My big friend stared at the drink as though he didn't know what it was. Then he slowly brought it up to his lips. He drowned the amber liquid in one go and held the glass out for a refill. I shoved the bottle his way.

The alcohol brought some colour back to his features. A welcome sight.

'There was just pain for a while. It started in the wound, then radiated out. Like it travelled my body through my blood.'

'It could have been the nanos,' I suggested. 'I had to administer them directly into the wound because you were too weak to drink them and there was no time for them to be digested.'

He nodded.

'For a while everything went dark. There was nothing. That was what was most frightening, it was empty. Nothing. No sounds, no sights, no smells. Absolutely nothing. Only the sense of motion. And even that was uncertain.'

'Then panic set in. I wanted to scream, to cry, but nothing worked. I felt hysteria take over, it settled in each cell of my brain and screamed at me to do something. Anything.'

'What brought you out of it?'

'The memory of the last words I heard you say. "Fight!" You screamed it at me. You and Aaliyah. I concentrated on that recollection. That one word. 'Fight." I repeated it again and again. Like a mantra. It pushed the panic back. I gripped onto the conviction that I had to concentrate all my energy into that one action. Fight! Fight to get back. I didn't know how. I just fought.'

He sipped his drink. I waited in silence.

His tale cut me to the bone. This was what all the

kidnapped souls went through. They all suffered the same blinding pain, their only support their unwavering faith. The steadfast belief they would be going to a better place. That they would maybe even see their departed loved ones again.

Their salvation.

And what did it turn out to be? A hoax. A scam. The biggest lie.

And my family was at the base of it all.

'And then I woke up. Kind of.'

Jonah's words startled me out of my contemplations. I felt momentarily disjointed from the here and now.

'The first thing to come back was sound. Far away at first and jumbled. I couldn't ascertain what it was. Just sound. But that one thing gave me hope. It was something to hold on to. I concentrated on it. It came closer. Still unclear. But actual sound.'

'I think the most troubling thing was the sound of my own heart. It thumped with a shadow. A memory. I heard two thuds for every one I expected. It was frightening.'

'After that came light. No forms, but an end to the endless darkness. I became aware of a surface I lay on that touched my body. It was soft, but strong. In my head I alternated between rejoicing and utter panic that I couldn't reach whatever was out there. It was so close, but still so far away.'

'The sounds morphed into voices. I tried to call out, but the words stayed in my head. I couldn't make a sound. I made out individual words but couldn't understand the language. It sounded alien to me.'

'Finally, after what seemed like days in limbo, I was able to open my eyes. Slowly my mind took control of my body. I felt movement when I concentrated enough.'

He swallowed. The paleness returned with the reliving of his death and reincarnation. I sat in silence. Awestruck and at the same time in deep, deep pain that this was partially my doing.

'I raised my arm up to wipe my face and was shocked when an arm came into view that was clearly not my own. No scars, no tattoos. Nothing familiar. I shied away at first, then realised that it moved at my whim. It was my arm. My hand. I raised the other one. The result was the same. It was surreal. Just not in a nice way.'

I nodded. I couldn't imagine how it would be to wake up from death in a body that is not your own.

'The thumping sound was both your hearts,' I explained.

Jonah nodded. 'Yeah, I know that now. But at that time, it was terrifying. I thought there was something wrong with me. A heart shouldn't sound like that.' He looked at me with half a smile. 'You forgot to mention I would have two once I woke.'

'It slipped my mind at the time,' I remarked. We both chuckled at that.

'How do the recruits in your dimension deal with it all?' he asked me.

I shrugged. I'd never asked. Recruits, or grunts, were an invisible workforce. One I'd never thought about, never mind contemplated ever asking what their experiences were. You can compare it with your cattle, or beasts of burden maybe. You don't ask them how they feel. They're there do a job.

'I suspect it's their faith that pulls them through. The promise of a better life after all they have been through.' He cocked his head in agreement.

'Do all the souls make it?' Jonah asked.

'No.' I had to be honest. 'Not all of them.'

'Acceptable collateral damage?' His dark comment cut deep.

'I used to think so. Now I don't. Not now after I've heard what everyone goes through.'

Silence descended again.

'Where do they go to if they don't achieve reincarnation?'

'I have no idea.' I shook my head. 'I hope to wherever they should have gone in the first place.'

Jonah looked up at me. 'You still think there is a real God? A real heaven?' I detected a sliver of hope in his eyes. Again, mixed with uncertainty and a touch of fear.

I sighed. 'I don't know. It's not something I've ever believed in. We don't have deities where I come from. No religion. None other than cold hard cash. We basically live forever, so we have no use for an afterlife.'

'No one dies in your dimension? Not of your kind anyway?'

'Hardly ever.'

'No illness, no fatal diseases or anything like that?'

I shook my head. 'Our scientists have effectively banished any life-threatening diseases or conditions. We live healthy balanced lives, and if anything does go wrong, we can almost always reincarnate someone back into his or her own body.'

'Even if the body is damaged?'

'We repair it first. We hold the essence of the person in limbo until the body has healed enough to function as the vessel again.'

'Limbo?' Jonah remarked with a huff. 'That's what you call it? Makes it sound like a walk in the park. Hate to disappoint you, but it isn't.'

'No. I got that.'

We emptied the bottle into our respective glasses and sat in silence.

# Chapter Twenty-Nine

'BENEDICT CONTACTED US.'

Jonah's voice over the phone over stemmed the sound of the ocean.

I was enjoying a rare day off and had decided to take the car out for a drive along the coast into Mexico. My false passport—courtesy of Ebony's team—worked perfectly at the border and I'd been able to pass without a hitch. We had plans that would need us to move out of the US, so a test was in order. It wasn't really a big risk, not with Ebony's experts, but I wanted to make sure. Besides, it was an excuse to get out and I needed a change of scenery.

I pulled the car up to a leeway and concentrated on what the big man was saying.

'There's a shipment of "Tickets" coming in.'

'How did he contact us?' I interrupted, always the suspicious one.

Jonah stopped his monologue, and I heard an audible sigh. 'Are we going there again? I thought we'd established his credibility?'

Benedict was Jonah's weak spot. He couldn't see past his trust, blind to any criticism or scepticism, especially from me. Well, I was still in two minds about the archbishop. He'd seemed sincere in the confessional. And yes, he'd warned us about the attack. But ultimately it had been too late. It cost Jonah his life. Jonah wouldn't hear of it. He rebutted me constantly about my doubts. I didn't know the man, he did, and all that crap.

Well, Jonah didn't have the experience I had with the Establishment. They could—and regularly did—turn the best of men and women to their cause. Their arguments could be very compelling, especially with ambitious men. Jonah assured us many times that Benedict's ambitions lay with helping people, not in gaining status, but I couldn't get past the fact that—even if that was true—it was bringing him up the ladder in the Church. Better men have been corrupted by power. No one was exempt from the lure of authority and adoration. It wasn't even just a human thing. We were just as susceptible.

So, call me negative. I prefer cautious.

'It was him,' Jonah stated resolutely. 'The message came from a secure source.'

'His phone?'

'Gabriel. When are you finally going to trust him?'

I refrained from answering. He wouldn't listen anyway.

The silence was complete. For a moment there I thought we'd lost the connection. The faint background sounds convinced me otherwise.

'Anyway,' he continued, completely ignoring my doubts. 'This gives us a great opportunity to hit the Establishment where it hurts.'

'How do you figure that?'

'There's a list of the intended recipients along with the equipment. All the contact data and their ratings.'

Now that would be a major win for us. Our leads dried up weeks ago. This limbo we found ourselves in had lasted for almost a month now, we were getting restless and desperate. We had to do something. And I guess—no risk, no glory.

Still, I wasn't convinced.

Maybe I was just too careful.

'That would be a big win,' I replied, throwing my excessive caution to the wind.

'Finally, you approve.' I heard the relief in his tone. That and sarcasm.

'So, when, where and how?' I pushed past my irritation.

'Thursday, so we have time to plan. Location somewhere between Albuquerque and Phoenix.'

'That's a massive area.'

'We're getting the exact route in the coming days.'

'We need to case the route, see where the risks are minimal.' My mind was already working on the parameters. The area between Albuquerque and Phoenix was rugged. Mainly desert, forest and mountains. There were roads, some well maintained, but the majority of the terrain was part of either a nature reserve or Native American country. Both meant few highways and big open spaces without inhabitants.

'So, get your ass back here,' Jonah concluded.

'I'll be back tomorrow.'

With that he broke the connection.

I sat in the car, the midday sun burning down on my head. If we could get that list it would be a major push to our cause. It would invigorate what was quickly becoming a dead end for us. It was so frustrating, knowing so much about the Establishment but not being able to do anything about it. This could be our salvation. It sounded great. It would be. If it was true.

Call me a pessimist. But when things sound too good to be true, they often are.

It still didn't sit well with me.

# Chapter Thirty

I WAS BACK at the house.

My earlier misgivings were tempered by the information Ebony had received through multiple security measures and checks. It was legit. At least as close as we could determine.

I was pulled into the adrenaline of planning. It felt good after such a long period of inactivity. The big man was enjoying it immensely, he almost seemed like the old Jonah. I glanced over at Ebony and noticed the small smile on her lips when Jonah spoke. It was infectious.

The three of us were joined by Sly and four more of Ebony's team. All people we could count on, they'd proved that more than once. Their participation made me feel a lot better. This was some serious fire power here. All seasoned professionals educated either by the army or the streets.

'The route takes them through Socorro and the Seviletta National Wildlife Park.' Tyrone pointed to the spot in the three-D projection on the display table.

'They take highway Sixty through Magdalena and down to Datil. From there they're planning on a more cautious route, off the main highways, through The Apache National Forest down to Stafford. Then back up via the San Carlos reservation where they pick up the Sixty again at Copper Hill Globe. From there it's more or less direct to Phoenix.'

The three-D projection moved with his hand, and we experienced the rise and fall of the environment as we contemplated the route.

'Once in Phoenix, they'll head to a small airfield outside Gold Camp. From there the tickets will be distributed to several small planes destined for locations on the west coast.'

'There are three teams that will run the route today and tomorrow,' Ebony joined in. 'They will take specific parts of the route, two are families, one is an elderly couple. They'll all pose as tourists so no one will bother about them taking photos and filming. The one place that could be an issue is the reservation. We're not allowed to film there, not without a permit. And we don't want to leave a paper trail.'

I studied the terrain on the display. It was rough. High terrain, winding roads. Speed would not be an option here. Not for them, but also not for us.

'We should get the information back by tomorrow end of day.'

I nodded. 'Sounds good.' I turned to Sly. 'What's the basic plan?'

Sly's Navy SEAL background made him the ultimate strategist. We relied on him to come up with the detailed plans. It was best to leave that to the experts. Even Jonah referred to him on that account.

'We know there will be small truck and an SUV following. There are a lot of winding roads along the way. We could ambush the transport at one of the uninhabited spots, somewhere unexpected.'

We settled on a spot in the trail where the steep winding road had several hairpins turns. This would slow down the mini-convoy and put a strain on the vehicles. It would also force them to keep more distance than on the rest of the route. We figured it would be possible to disrupt the progress of the following SUV and create a void between the vehicles. Then we could target them separately.

We agreed on the two teams. The main one for the truck, the other would keep the pursuing guards busy and out of the way.

Jonah and I would be in the first team, together with five of Ebony's people. Sly and three others would keep the SUV down the mountain until we had control over the truck.

We had a selection of our own SUVs and off-terrain motor bikes. The last were powerful on the dirt roads and small enough to slip between the truck and the wall of the cliff if needed.

IN THE EARLY MORNING, we took up our positions. It would be a long wait in the strong punishing Arizona heat, but it was the only way. We had to get there early in case they'd sent out recognisance.

We'd dug holes in the dirt floor and covered ourselves in branches that offered at least some relief. The cars and bikes were invisible under camouflage tarps. Even I couldn't see them from my vantage point. We had a good view of the road as it widened at the top of the windy track. Trees and shrubs lined the mountain side where we were hidden. A sheer cliff bordered the other side of the winding road.

Finally, as the sun started to set over the trees, I felt the vibration of the phone, the signal our quarry was nearby.

There was a revving sound as the truck attacked the first of the seven hairpin bends and ascended the steep mountain side.

We crouched down lower and waited for them to come into view.

The plan was simple. We would use the environment to our best advantage, splitting the two vehicles and their occupants. Sly and his team would stop the SUV as it came around the third hairpin, immobilising them out of reach of the truck. We would then attack the first vehicle and force it to a standstill.

With bated breath, I waited for the rumbling to come closer. Then I heard the tell-tale staccato sound of gunfire from further down the hill. Sly's team had engaged the SUV.

At that precise moment, a small white truck rounded the last bend and chugged up to our position.

We broke cover and opened fire on the front and back tires, shredding the rubber and forcing the truck to a standstill. Jonah shot the driver as he stopped the truck, we'd agreed there would be no survivors.

To our surprise, there was no resistance. No return fire. It took a while for me to register that the truck cabin held only one person: the dead driver. Jonah threw caution to the wind and pulled the tarp open at the rear of the truck.

His brow creased in surprise, and he stared at me. 'There's nothing in here.'

'What?'

'It's empty.'

A second later my phone rang. Sly. I answered.

'There was only one person in the SUV,' he commented.

'Same here.'

'Shit!'

The helicopter rose up over the ridge like an angry wasp. It hovered over the edge while the machine guns hanging from both sides raked the earth around us.

This changed everything.

With a burst of big calibre bullets, it lifted its tail and sped over the scene, annihilating everything in its wake. We dove for any cover we could find.

I lay under the truck with my arms over my head as the missiles hammered into the metal and rocked the vehicle with the impact. I hope the rest of the team had found a better place. This was a trap. I couldn't leave the relative safety of the truck until the helicopter shot over the position. And then, where would I go to? The trees were fifteen metres away up a steep incline. No way I would make it up there before the helicopter came back. The other way was a direct drop down the cliff.

I scanned what I could see of the direct area from behind the wheels. The riddled corpse of the driver lay to the right, his extremities at odd angles from the intensive firepower of the aerial howitzers.

I crawled back further under the truck as the guys in the helicopter mowed over the scene again, shooting everything in sight, indiscriminately.

Gasoline dripped from a hole in the chassis of the truck onto the dirt. I coated my finger and smelled the substance hoping it would be diesel. Petrol could catch fire, and that was a complication I could do without. Luckily it was diesel. Not ideal, but a lot better than the alternative.

I timed the interval between the runs, desperate to calculate the window to move. I was still without a clear idea where to run to, but the spot I was in was a death trap. The truck was the main target for the heli's runs.

Again, high calibre bullets hammered into the chassis. One penetrated the metal and crashed into the dirt next to my leg. I pulled my extremities in and curled up as much as possible, creating a small target. More bullets spat up sand and rocks where my head had just been, convincing me they had some kind of infra-red tracking on board.

They were getting close. Too close.

I waited another ten seconds, then I would chance it once the heli had passed again.

Nothing came.

The only sound I heard was the gently hovering chopper. I lowered my arms from my ears and attempted to figure out what was happening. It was impossible to hear much over the sound of the rotors that echoed under the truck. I had to shuffle forward to see where they were. It was a risk, but what other option did I have?

Crawling forward, I glanced out into the dust. Nothing. I had to move further out. Big risk. But I had to see where they were and what was happening.

My crab crawl brought me up to the light, out from under the relative safety. I pushed my head out and scanned the air to the front and left side. It wasn't there.

Where the hell was the chopper?

I moved further out from under the truck. Maybe they thought I was already dead? But the sound was still there. Just out of sight. I hoped that meant I wasn't visible either.

A shrill whine to the back of the truck proved how wrong I was. The pilot had been waiting for me to move. He swung the helicopter around and faced me full-on, the angry machine guns focussed squarely on the square metre where I crouched.

I was done for.

I could see his features, the vicious grimace of his tight

lips, the upturned nose, the glint in his eyes. He had me, and he knew it. I could see him laugh and say something in his microphone.

This was it. Even my healing capabilities were useless against this fire power. I stood up, my ego not letting me die cowering in the dust.

Again, he laughed, savouring the moment. There was nowhere I could go; he knew I was helpless.

The smile was glued to his face. I watched and anticipated the impact the bullets would make on my body. The damage.

Out of the corner of my eye I saw something careen into the helicopter tail, exploding the rotor and knocking the chopper out of the air. The machine spun around uncontrollably, and I took great pleasure in the glimpse I got of the panicked pilot.

The helicopter plunged down into the cliff wall and detonated as it crashed into the sharp rocks. I dove to the side as debris showered the scene. The sound of the screeching metal and the final explosion numbed my ears, drowning out any sound.

I felt hands grab me and pull me out of the road. I got back on my feet and followed my teammates down the incline to where we had left the other vehicles.

The incessant whine in my ears relented and I shook my head to clear it.

At the vehicles I pushed into the passenger seat of the first SUV and belted myself in. Jonah closed the front door on the driver side and took off at speed. I saw the other car and one of the bikes speed up ahead of us. The second dirt-bike was missing, and I realised that was what had struck the helicopter.

Tyrone's quick thinking saved my life and that of the

rest of the team. He'd revved the bike and sent it off the cliff into the helicopter, aiming it perfectly at the hovering machine.

We'd come out alive, all of us.

But it was a screw-up. No tickets and no list. Instead, we'd been lured onto a trap.

Because that was what it was; an ambush. No doubt about it.

The look on Jonah's face told me he'd come to the exact same conclusion. We'd been set-up. And it had almost killed us.

I grabbed the burner and called Sly for news on the second team. Thankfully he answered.

By some miracle, no one from our teams had been badly wounded. The main casualties were our egos and confidence.

At the junction, we split up and raced away, Jonah and I taking the right-hand dirt track.

He drove as quickly as he dared, trying to minimise the dust cloud that inevitably followed in our wake. There had been one helicopter, who was to say they didn't have another one. One that could follow our trail.

In the waning light we avoided using the lights and sped on under the cover of the trees and the impending night.

# Chapter Thirty-One

'WHAT THE FUCK HAPPENED?'

'We were betrayed,' Jonah answered. His tone still dangerous.

'Betrayed?'

'How else would they have known where to look. We were careful. There were no tails, nothing. We made sure. Ebony scrambled all the communications. It's not possible they found us by accident.'

Silence.

'Who?' I dared to ask.

'I don't know, but we have to find out a.s.a.p.'

We hurried on, anxious to get away from the scene of our failure. It was still potentially dangerous. They would find out soon enough that the helicopter was down and if there was another team close, they would search the scene for us. The bodies were a dead give-away, they were theirs. None of ours.

I wanted to put as much distance between us and our attackers as possible. I also desperately wanted to make sure we didn't inadvertently lead the enemy to Ebony. My partner's sullen and brooding demeanour told me he was thinking the same.

Twenty miles later Jonah dared to turn on the lights as we bumped onto an asphalt highway. He floored the SUV as much as he dared to get even more distance between us and the scene. We would have to contact Ebony soon, but we wanted to make sure we were on safe ground before I did. That meant getting rid of the car, or at least the plates.

At an all-night diner and store, we parked the car in between three eighteen-wheelers, effectively screening it from anyone travelling the highway. Jonah left to use the diner's bathroom and clean up his cuts and bruises. The majority of the blood was in the t-shirt on the floor of the SUV. Purple blood still threw him, and he wanted to get any trace out of view. He wore his jeans jacket over his bare chest, the bottom concealing any blood on his jeans.

I left the car and hunted around for a vehicle I could switch plates with. There were more than twenty four-wheel drives and pickup trucks in the car park, along with seven eighteen-wheelers and a bus. I discounted three possible "donations" due to visibility from the diner and settled on an old Ford F150. It was battered and sported what looked like bullet holes in the side panel.

The pickup was completely out of sight of the diner and the store. I unscrewed the plates and hid them under my jacket. Back at our car I swapped the plates and threw the old ones in the loading bay of one of the trucks that gave me cover. I wasn't sure whether Ebony would be happy about the switch, but something told me the old plates had not been delivered with the car anyway. She valued privacy. That and the nature of some of her businesses necessitated staying under the radar. I wasn't worried they would be able to trace the plates back to Ebony. She would have thought of that before she gave us the SUV. But I didn't want anyone ambushing us if they recognised the registration.

I walked over to the store and saw Jonah dressed in a new t-shirt, black jeans and his trusty jeans jacket. He was filling a cart with supplies, mainly food and drink. I joined him and he pointed to the clothes department.

'You stink,' he pronounced.

My raised eyebrow didn't make an impression, and he nodded again in the direction of the clothes. I conceded and walked over to three racks of t-shirts in mainly blue and black. Most had an image of some sort on them, none that meant anything to me. I pulled out a plain black shirt and rummaged around in a box of jeans until I found a pair that were my size. These were not the clothes I preferred, but there was nothing else. Unless I wanted checked flannel shirts, and that was too much for me. I'm the three-piece-suit kind of guy, silk shirts and all. I added underwear, a polo shirt and two hooded sweaters to the pile of clothes and made my way to the front of the store.

Jonah joined me at the cash register, and we paid cash for the supplies and clothes. He pushed a container of shower gel in my hand and pointed me to the bank of paid shower rooms for the truckers. After ten glorious minutes of piping hot water and dressed in my new unfamiliar clothes I joined him in the diner.

Jonah was already halfway through a burger when I slipped into the booth opposite him. He looked up, cocked his head in appreciation of my new attire, though probably more for the lack of diesel odour, and signalled to the waitress to come over.

'What can I get you, sir?' The pretty blond asked flirting with the big man. Jonah pointed to me.

'He needs something to eat.' She looked disappointed but gave me a hesitant smile anyway. I glanced at my partner who barely hid his amusement. Yes, he still had it.

'A burger and fries please,' I ordered. 'And a cup of coffee.'

She smiled and looked back at Jonah.

'Anything else for you?' she asked, obviously flirting.

Between bites he managed to answer, 'Another one for me too.' He held up his half-empty beer glass. 'And a refill, please.' His cheeky smile and wink made her blush, and she left to place the order.

After she left, the atmosphere changed dramatically. The temperature lowered by at least ten degrees and the scolding sullen Jonah was back again. Shame that hadn't disappeared with the tattoos.

'What's eating you?' I asked.

'The idea of a traitor.'

'You've been thinking about it.'

He nodded between bites.

'Who?'

Silence. Jonah pushed the cleared plate to the side and downed the last of his beer. He held the empty glass with both hands and turned it slowly from one side to another. I was sure he already had a decision but decided to go through the motions anyway.

'Who are the possible culprits?' I asked.

'Aaliyah. Sly. And Benedict.' He almost spat out the last name.

'Can't be Sly.' I answered. 'He's devoted to Ebony. He wouldn't betray her, or us as the extension.'

'Aaliyah?' He looked at me, hoping I would find a reason why it would be her.

I had to disappoint him. 'I can't imagine it could be her. She wouldn't endanger you.'

Silence returned and he studied the glass again.

Our reflections were interrupted by the waitress. She placed our order on the table and smiled again at Jonah. He returned it, though a bit half-heartedly. A call from another table took her to other customers.

'It has to be Benedict,' Jonah stated resolutely as he pulled his second plate of food towards him.

I decided to stay silent. Nothing would be achieved by contradicting or agreeing with him.

We ate in silence, the atmosphere heavy.

'What do you want to do?' I asked Jonah as he finished his last mouthful.

'We confront him and sort this out.'

I nodded.

We would have to go back to Miami.

# Chapter Thirty-Two

HE WAS hell bent on confronting Benedict. Ebony and I couldn't talk him out if it, no matter what we tried.

One advantage the big man had was that Benedict presumed him dead. The archbishop was in for a hell of a surprise.

Jonah was back.

… …Kind of.

Our biggest issue was how to approach the archbishop.

The security in his home had been improved immensely since our last visit. Repeating the confession approach wasn't an option either, we were too obvious. There was no way Jonah would agree to a substitute to ask the questions. He wanted to look his old mentor in the eye.

'What about transporting me?' Jonah suggested. 'Ebony repaired your transporter, didn't she?'

I cocked my head and shrugged my shoulders. It was an option, but not one I was in favour of.

'We're not sure your body would be able to withstand the trauma again,' Ebony warned.

'And it's not one-hundred percent certain my family won't be able to pick up the signal.'

'I thought you'd tested it?' The big man was adamant.

'I did,' I answered, my irritation building. 'And threw up all over the place.'

'We're still working on the details,' Ebony confirmed. 'It should get better, but it needs more tweaking.'

'Yes,' I agreed. 'But with my body. I don't know what will happen to yours.'

'Why should it be any different?'

'Your body wasn't made for transportation,' I explained yet again. 'We've been through this before, Jonah. It's not safe.'

He opened his mouth to protest but thought better of it and sulked. Great. Just what we needed. A sullen and morose Jonah. His mood-swings had always been legendary, but since he'd come back, they were in a whole different ballpark. When he was like that, any discussion was destined for failure. He became cantankerous and pouted like a spoiled child. It got on my nerves.

I know, I shouldn't react, he'd been through a lot. But it was getting more and more difficult to ignore his negative disposition.

His stare was dark and cut through my own frustration. The purple irises held mine. They were still alien, weird. Scary even, on Jonah. They emphasised the change in my old friend. Not for the first time, I questioned our choice to bring him back.

Tingles started at the base of my spine.

'There might be a way to talk to Benedict.' Jonah surprised us at breakfast next day. I looked up from my pancakes and swallowed the last mouthful.

'How?' I asked.

'Twice a year, Benedict goes to pray in the crypt where his mentor has been laid to rest. It's a communal crypt for clergy in Miami in the main cemetery. A big stone construction with a lot of underground corridors and separate rooms cut out of the rock. It's a form of meditation for him as well as a connection to his predecessors.'

This was interesting.

'You've been there?'

'Once. I briefly went inside, then left him alone to his prayers. I stood watch outside.'

Ebony was intrigued as well. 'So we can expect a guard outside?'

'I think so. Especially after Francis.' We nodded our agreement.

'How many entrances were there?'

'Just the one that I could see.'

'There might be options,' Ebony suggested. 'In a lot of cemeteries, thieves have connected crypts with underground tunnels. We could look into it.' She looked up at Jonah. 'Are there specific times when he goes there?

'Yes. First week of March and same in October.'

This was looking good. It was the last week of September now. If luck was on our side—and we'd earned it by now—we might be on time.

'Can you point it out on a map of the cemetery?'

'I think so.'

'Then we have work to do.'


'BENEDICT.'

To me, my voice sounded as loud as a shout in the absolute silence of the mausoleum. The tone echoed off the cold stone and reverberated around the cave-like space.

It was cold. Not just the temperature, the ambiance, the atmosphere. Shivers ran up my arms. What is it with you humans that you're so obsessed with death. Why do you keep these crypts for those you want to remember. Surely you should cherish their life, not their death. I guess it has to do with your own fear of what is inevitable.

We live so long, we're basically immortal. Death is an exception with us, not the rule. Our fears are very different than yours. And if one of us does die, then we remember who they were. Not their dead husk.

Different perspective, I guess.

Anyway. The mausoleum was getting to me. I wanted to get this over with as soon as possible.

The archbishop stood up from his kneeling position and turned around. He scanned the room. The candlelight didn't reach the recesses, leaving lots of places to hide.

'Who's there?'

I stepped from the shadow of the corridor into the half-light.

If he was surprised to see me, he camouflaged it well. A slightly raised right eyebrow, that was it.

He carefully folded the bright red stole into a small package and placed it on the table next to him. Only then did he look up at me and take a step forward.

'Gabriel.' He looked me squarely in the eye. 'It's been a long time.'

I nodded. Not much more to add.

'What brings you here?'

'You.'

'I gathered that.'

We stood in silence. Eying each other. Neither one moving.

'You want to talk to me about something?'

'Not me. Someone else.'

He cocked his head in question.

'Please, follow me.' I turned and walked down the corridor I'd come from.

Benedict picked up a flashlight, pushed the on button and caught up with me quickly.

'You don't need light?'

'No. My eyes adapt better than yours.'

We moved towards a sarcophagus that stood at an angle to its pedestal. I disappeared behind the big stone box into a rough tunnel that led from this mausoleum to another thirty metres deeper into the cemetery. I waited for him to pass me at the entrance, then pulled the sarcophagus back to its normal position.

I turned and led him through the tunnel out into another equally dimly lit stone room. This one was smaller, more crowded, with plain stone caskets. More cramped, with a stale air.

The flashlight wavered when Benedict coughed at the clear stench of decomposing bodies. There was a recent body here somewhere. One in an inferior casket that didn't close off quite well. I continued towards a small alcove at the other end of the crypt and stopped about two metres before the opening.

The archbishop joined me, the flashlight moving over the solid rock face from left to right. He scanned the alcove, but the light hardly penetrated. As though something dark resided there. Something that sucked the light in and rendered it useless.

'Where is this mystery person?' I noticed irritation in Benedict's tone. He was losing patience.

I smiled and pointed my right hand to the alcove.

'Here.' A voice came from the dark.

Benedict literally took a step backwards. His eyes spread wide open, and his body pulled back from what was in front of him. He'd recognised Jonah's voice and acknowledged that it was impossible.

I had to give him credit. He pulled himself together and stood up straight, his stance one of strength.

'Jonah?'

The big man stepped out from the deep black into the light of the flash. The effect was eerie. The shadows in his features were more pronounced, the dark brows even more prominent.

Benedict's brow creased as the absence of tattoos and Jonah's violet eyes registered.

'You're not Jonah. You can't be. He died,' he stated resolutely.

'I did,' the big man answered. 'Then I came back.'

'And what is that supposed to mean?' Benedict's tone was harder than earlier.

'It's not a stretch. You know they reincarnate souls. Well, I'm one of them. I died and I came back. It's that simple.'

'Something tells me it isn't.'

He observed the big man in detail, his eyes going from Jonah's face down his body to the floor and back up again. He locked eyes and stared in them for what seemed like a long time. The tension in the air was heavy, robbing us of oxygen. It surpassed sound, everything. All attention was centred around what was happening.

The itch on my spine intensified. Would the archbishop believe this was his lost protege? I waited with bated breath.

Benedict held out his hand to Jonah. 'Whatever happened, I'm glad you're back. Good to see you again, Jonah.'

The big man's lips pulled up in a slight curl as he took the archbishop's hand and shook it.

I let out my pent-up breath. Looks like Benedict was on board.

Jonah pulled his mentor into a big bear hug. Obviously happy.

I wasn't so easily convinced. We still had the sensitive subject of betrayal to discuss. I decided to leave it to the big man.

Benedict stepped back. The smile on his face melted as his features became serious.

'You're not here for a reunion,' he stated.

'No.' Jonah's face darkened, the violet eyes hard and unforgiving. 'We came here because of Arizona.'

'What about Arizona?' Benedict looked surprised.

When Jonah stayed silent, the archbishop repeated his question. 'What happened in Arizona?'

Jonah looked to me; I nodded.

'We received information from you about an Establishment transport. Transponders. That and a list of recipients. Something we could use in our quest.'

He looked puzzled, then shook his head.

'We attacked the transport,' Jonah continued. 'It was a set-up.'

'I never sent you any information.'

We stayed silent.

He looked from Jonah to me and back again. 'You think I betrayed you.' He'd caught on to the reason for our visit.

'We do.' Jonah was blunt.

'I get that,' Benedict surprised me. 'It looks bad. I would come to the same conclusion.'

I cocked my head in agreement. That was exactly what we'd done.

'But that doesn't mean you're right,' the archbishop continued calmly.

'That message wasn't from me. Whoever sent it knows more about you than is comfortable. How did you get it?'

'Digital,' Jonah answered. 'It bounced off multiple addresses and was encrypted.'

'So you can't follow it back.' A statement. 'What convinced you it came from me? Did it name me?'

Silence. Good question too. One we couldn't really answer. We shook our heads in unison.

Jonah looked back to me. I shrugged. 'Maybe we just wanted it to be true,' I suggested. 'We were inactive and without any way forward.'

'Jonah, I get that you don't trust me. Or anyone for that matter. Especially not after what happened to you. You've gone through hell.'

'You have no idea.'

'No, I don't. It's probably much worse than I could imagine. And that's all the more reason for you to question everything. But you know me. Like I know you. We've been through rough times together. Deep in your heart you know the answer to your doubts.'

Jonah waited him out.

'If you have even a small doubt left. Then kill me. Be done with it.' Benedict leant back against the crypt behind him. Giving Jonah the space he needed to decide.

It was the big man's decision. Not mine. I would abide by his judgement.

Minutes went by, testing even my resolve. Then Jonah

stepped up to Benedict, his axe in his right hand, level with the archbishop's chest.

Benedict stayed put. He must have felt intimidated, but it didn't show. He continued to hold Jonah's eyes and wait for whatever would come.

Jonah stopped one step from his mentor, stared at him, then placed his left hand on the archbishop's shoulder.

No words were needed.

We were good.

## Chapter Thirty-Three

THE RELIEF WAS SHORT-LIVED.

Maybe two weeks.

Max.

Then Jonah was back up to his old reckless new self. This time it was a routine interception and information mission. One that should have been simple. With the big man around, nothing ever was.

The genius team—Ebony's wiz kids—came up with information about a production company involved in the promotional streams we found on the dark web. No matter how deep they'd tried to bury who was behind the clearly fundamentalist content, Ebony's team found them.

A shoot was planned for this weekend. One we would be gate-crashing. The plan was to go in and disrupt the shoot, grab any digital instruments we could find, including phones and computers, and bring it back to Ebs for analysis. It was kick ass, and maybe even have a bit of fun. Leave them alive but let off steam. Something we could all use.

The intel showed there would be nine people there. Five

I AM the Storm

cast members, three technicians and the producer. The location for the shoot was one of California's forty-seven thousand abandoned mines out in the desert.

Overlooking the mine was a ridge that effectively hid us from view. It offered us a vantage point to observe the preparations in the clearing in front of the mine entrance. The technicians milled about the set like busy ants, pushing wheeled containers of materials to their appointed positions around the clearing. Slowly a full movie set emerged from the back of the small truck.

Half an hour later two Ford-150 pick-ups rambled down the hard dirt track spitting up loose stones and dust. Three men and two women alighted from the vehicles and slowly walked over to the array of technical equipment. They were dressed in camouflage garb, though that of the women was strongly revealing in a very non-military manner. They didn't fit the soldier profile and looked more at home in a hip-hop music video. The guys were what we expected. In their late twenties, big, one heavily muscled, all strutting their stuff, very full of themselves.

It couldn't get more cliche.

They were met by what I presumed was the producer. A middle aged African American man in much too youthful garb, his screaming bright shirt opened low to a hairy chest covered in thick gold chains, one sporting a massive cross. The gold ring in his ear, the tight jeans and loud cowboy boots completed the look. He looked ridiculous, desperate to fit in.

The producer greeted the men with an intricate hand-shake routine. The girls were pulled close and kissed on the cheeks, his hand slipping down to the blonde's ass. She giggled and expressed mock shock. They all laughed, and he slapped her butt to more squeals.

This was bad in so many ways. I was looking forward to disrupting the party.

Almost an hour later, they were finally ready to start filming. The star stood in front of the mine, sporting an AK47 and the cliche ammunition belts over his muscled bare chest. The camouflage face paint threw hard lines over his face and body, accentuating the ripped physique.

The other two male actors had vanished into the mine with the women.

'Action!' the would-be producer shouted.

We heard a woman's screams coming from the entrance to the mine. The pseudo-Rambo moved centre stage, approached the darkness and shouted a challenge. He was rewarded with one of the men in cliche Arabian garb dragging the half-naked blond out into the open. He pulled her in front of him, using her as a shield, a large knife held to her neck, while he fondled her bare breast with his other hand. What was this? An adult rated version of a recruitment film?

The second "terrorist" pulled the equally scantily clothed and dishevelled brunette from the mine and screamed something almost intelligible.

The blond supposedly hit her tormentor and ducked to the side, opening him up for her saviour to mow him down. The brunette did the same and blanks went off in rapid staccato as the would-be Islamic terrorists flopped around in exaggerated and completely unbelievable death throes.

Finally, Rambo posed for the camera, flanked by the two women hanging on his thick arms. His studied speech centred around the perceived danger to Christian women from Islamic terrorists and the general decline of the American way-of-life as long as they were allowed to live in the US.

I looked sideways to Sly, disbelief in my features. Sly shrugged, as disgusted as I was with the quality of this would-be promotional junk. This production was so completely out of character to the quality the Establishment usually produced that it made me think these hanger-ons were still on the outside, desperately trying to make an impression on the real deal. Well, they'd failed miserably. This was rubbish.

We crept down the incline, staying low in the dry brush, all the time careful we stayed out of sight. We needn't have bothered. The actors and technicians were too preoccupied with the scantily dressed women who now proceeded to pull the ragged and torn camouflage clothes off, to pose for new takes in their Stars-and-Stripes minuscule bikinis.

Sly, Jonah, me and two others almost made it undetected to the set, until a loose stone from under Jonah's shoe clanged against one of the metal cases strewn about the circumference of the stage. One technician turned, saw the big man and raised the alarm.

Pure chaos reigned for the next minutes. The two supporting actors rushed back to the entrance of the mine, followed by the women. The technicians raced for the metal equipment cases and pulled out guns that were way too real to be props. The "producer" pulled a handgun from the back of his jeans and together they countered our failed stealth attack, as he backed into the mine shaft. Bullets rained down on us as we dove for cover.

We returned fire.

Resistance had not been expected. At least not in this measure. Sly motioned for us to circumvent the set and push in on all sides. I started to move left from one piece of cover to another when a tremendous war cry broke through the sound of the gunfire.

Jonah pulled his axe from the scabbard on his back, stood up and rushed headstrong through the rain of bullets towards the actor now wielding a real semi-automatic gun.

I saw at least one bullet hit my big friend, but he continued his head-on attack heedless of the pain. The actor's head left his shoulders in a spray of blood, hitting the floor after Jonah who proceeded on to the next gun man. Within seconds two more lay bleeding on the ground, the remaining man fled into the mine.

Jonah ran screaming into the unsafe cavernous entrance. I rushed in after him, stepping aside to let the terrified women leave the oppressing dark space and the bloodcurdling screams of their co-actor. I sped up, hoping I could at least stop him from killing them all.

I was too late.

Minutes later I exited the mine shaft, followed by the big man cleaning his axe on the tails of his t-shirt. His clothes were covered in both red and purple blood. I counted three splashes of deep purple where bullets had made their mark on his body. The bleeding slowed and finally stopped. He ignored it, waving away help from Sly. Instead, he went to a crate of water bottles and upended one over his head and hands, cleaning away the gore from his victims.

I wanted to scream at him. Berate him for his stupid headstrong actions that had cost us our mission. I took a step forward but was restrained by Sly's hand on my arm. I turned to him; he shook his head. Not now. Glancing back at Jonah I understood Sly's reasoning. The big man's eyes blazed with the blood lust. He was still spoiling for a fight.

Whatever I had to say could wait.

Until it was safer.

Sly interrogated the women, and—satisfied they were just hired wanna-be actresses struggling to escape their mundane day jobs and in no way involved in the actual fundamentalists—let them leave in one of the pickup trucks.

The rest were dead.

I came up empty with any information. The only computers we found were those connected to the cameras and sound equipment. Sly's men gathered all the phones, unplugged the computers and we left the dismal site.

I made sure I was in a different car than Jonah. I didn't trust myself to keep my mouth shut, my anger just barely contained. I wasn't the only one avoiding him. Jonah was alone in his vehicle.

We made our way back to base.

# Chapter Thirty-Four

'WHAT THE FUCK WERE YOU THINKING?'

I blew up.

Blame it on Jonah's recklessness during the past weeks cumulating in tonight. The idiot almost got himself killed and put us in big danger at the same time. His impulsive head-on attack through the rain of bullets was nothing short of suicide. I didn't know how he managed to survive that. And frankly, I didn't care. Jonah was out of control. Something had to be done.

'Leave it alone, Gabe.' The anger dripped off his words. Under normal circumstances, his demeanour would give me reason to rein in my own rage. But not this time. Who the fuck did he think he was? After all we went through to get him back.

'Hell no. Your actions are irresponsible, stupid. Reckless. You trying to get yourself killed or what?'

'I heal anyway. Stop moaning.' He ripped the remnants of his t-shirt off his torso and threw the bloodied material to the side.

'You won't survive for long the way you're treating your body. You're not immortal.' I followed him into the kitchen where he grabbed a bottle of vodka from the fridge and turned the cap. The bottle was upended as he took a massive slug of the strong alcohol.

He looked at me, his mouth a thin line of contempt. 'What do you care?' He took another drink directly from the bottle.

'Are you shitting me?' I yelled. 'After all we've been through to get you this second chance?'

His stare was cold, scary. 'I didn't ask you to,' he almost whispered. The silence in the room was total. Ebony and I were both stunned into silence.

'What?' I finally found my voice.

'You fought to come back. You said so yourself,' Ebony added.

He wouldn't look at us. His eyes were stuck to the bottle he held in both hands. 'I fought to get out of the void.' We had to strain to hear him. 'Not for this.'

I felt all the rage ebb out of me, replaced by disbelief and a profound sadness. I stared at him, unable to comprehend what he said.

'Aren't you happy to be alive?' I asked. 'It's a second chance.'

He huffed. 'Is that what you call this?'

I looked at Ebony. Her face showed she was as much in shock as I was. I'd never seen her so pale and overwhelmed.

'How would you describe it?' she whispered.

We descended into silence. Jonah—still holding the now half-empty bottle by its neck—walked to the sofa and dropped his bulk into the soft cushions. He stared at the empty fireplace, his mind a world away. Ebony joined him while I took a seat opposite the big man.

'You have no idea what it's like,' he broke the heavy silence.

'You're right. We don't.'

'So, tell us.' Ebony urged him.

Jonah was deflated. Every word cost him dearly. For the first time we truly saw what we had done.

'I'm a parasite in a body that is not my own,' Jonah whispered.

Ebony took his hand in hers. He glanced at her, and a faint smile flashed over his lips for a millisecond as his fingers curled around hers, dwarfing them.

Jonah turned to me. 'Every time I look in the mirror, an alien stares back at me. It's not me. The body moves when I want it to. It does what I tell it to do. I feel things it touches, but it's not me. It's like I'm steering a machine. And then the eyes, they're the worst. What I see are someone else's eyes staring back at me.'

'It is you,' I tried. 'What makes it you is your conscious-ness. That may be in a strange body. But it is your soul. You're the one steering you.'

'Am I.' He looked deep into me, sending goosebumps up my spine. This wasn't how it was supposed to be.

'It's your soul.'

He looked so very vulnerable.

'Then why do I feel like I'm not alone in this body?'

I was astounded. Not alone? What did he mean? I wanted to ask him but was afraid of the answer.

'I bleed purple,' he continued. 'There's a constant echo to my heartbeat. Like someone else is there.' He took another deep slug of the vodka before he continued. 'My body doesn't even look like me. Oh sure, the size is the same, and the facial features look like my real ones. But it's a blank slate. No scars, no tattoos, no history. Nothing. Like I never existed.'

I had no answer to that.

'I feel like I'm in a nightmare. One that doesn't end.'

A block of something hard and heavy settled in my gut, inhabiting my breathing.

'I don't feel alive. I go through the motions. Eat, sleep, even love.' He looked apologetically to Ebony who smiled and squeezed his hand in sympathy. 'But it's not real. Like a movie I'm watching. Or an avatar in virtual reality, only I can't take off the goggles. I'm stuck in a sick video game. The only time I feel anything is when I hurt. The pain brings back feelings and I can relate to the ache. But even that doesn't last long. This stupid body takes that last bit of contact away by rapid healing. Other than that, I feel nothing.'

There was nothing I could say. I was perplexed. I never thought what we had done could be wrong. I was just too happy it worked, and we got the big man back. I assumed he would feel the same. I never contemplated it could in any way be negative.

I sat back in the chair, deflated.

Ebony continued to hold Jonah's hand. She was as much at a loss for words as I was.

'I didn't know,' I tried. 'I never imagined it could feel so bad for you. Not like this.'

Jonah nodded.

'There's more.' Jonah broke the silence.

I looked up, surprised.

'Sometimes I black out. Not like losing consciousness. More like losing control. Like I'm locked in another room for a moment and can't access my body. It's frightening. I never know when it will happen. Or how long it will last. It just comes out of the blue.'

'Has this happened from day one?' I asked.

'No, just the past weeks. Initially, there was nothing wrong.'

'And is the frequency increasing?' Dread took hold of my hearts, its cold icy hands squeezing.

He shook his head. 'Not really. It happens once or twice a week. But it's petrifying. I don't get a warning. No strange feelings beforehand or anything like that. It just happens.'

This was a very bad development. Naive as I had been, I hadn't expected any problems to using a replacement body. It dawned on me how little I knew about the whole process of reincarnation and what happened after that. Not for the first time, I cursed my previous indifference to what my family was doing to humans. And even now, the extent of the damage we had done surprised and frightened me.

'When did they start?' Ebony asked. 'Exactly.'

Jonah shook his head and pouted his lips. 'Not sure. I think about four weeks ago.'

'Was that after or before the issue in Seattle?'

'After.'

'Is it possible it's the result of the head injury you sustained then?'

'Could be. But it doesn't explain everything. Maybe the black outs. But not the voices.'

Come again? 'What voices?'

'I hear voices in my head,' he explained. 'Sometimes it's like an echo to what someone is saying. Other times the words are not the same.'

What started out as an argument about recklessness was quickly developing into a very unsettling revelation. Blackouts. Voices. What the hell was going on?'

'When do you hear them?' Ebony urged the big man on.

'I don't really know. It's not the whole time. I can't pinpoint exact moments or causes.'

'What about now?' I chimed in.

He cocked his head in question.

'Are you hearing any voices now?'

Jonah concentrated. He slowly shook his head, then stopped. 'There.' He pointed to me. 'I heard a voice like yours.'

'What was it saying?'

Dread crept up my spine, leaving goosebumps and tremors in its wake. This was truly frightening.

'Something about the blackouts,' he answered looking me in the eye. 'I couldn't make out the rest. Most of the voices aren't clear. Like an incessant hum in the background. Occasionally I make out a single word or if I concentrate, maybe half a sentence.'

'Do you know who's voices they are?' Ebony probed. Jonah turned to her and shook his head.

'Not always. Sometimes it's clear, but mostly impossible to single out a specific person.'

'Can you stop them?'

He held up the bottle. 'This helps.' He even attempted a strained smile. 'And when I concentrate on something else. If I'm tired, it gets worse.'

The silence felt like a thousand pounds of concrete pressing on our shoulders. There was nothing I could say. No words formed, just random thoughts, all compounding the feelings of complete futility that filled my mind.

'How can we help?' Ebony asked, breaking the silence, a slight tremor in her voice.

Jonah looked up at her and smiled. 'Thanks. I appreciate it. But I don't think there's anything you can do.'

'I'd still like you to see Dr Patil,' Ebony insisted.

Jonah nodded. 'Not sure what he could find though. It's not like he's an expert on borrowed bodies.'

Ebony turned to me. 'You could ask Aaliyah next time you see her?' It was a question, but in her friendly--don't refuse--way. I smiled and nodded my agreement.

It was the least I could do.

That Aaliyah and I could do. This whole mess was fundamentally my people's fault. The result of our greed.

# Chapter Thirty-Five

'YOU LOOK WORRIED?'

'I am,' Dr Patil answered.

Shit. Not what I wanted to hear.

We were in Patil's lab in his town clinic. It was after hours and there was no one else in the stark-white, modern building. The subdued lighting made it seem a lot smaller than it was, and less clinical. I'd entered through the back door, making sure my car was parked at least two blocks away at a restaurant where it wouldn't attract any attention. Patil was Ebony's medical advisor, and this clinic was a beautiful working front to what could only be called his less than legal activities.

This place, and the out-of-town spa, were both owned by Patil. He had legitimate clients who greatly appreciated the one-stop full-body diagnosis and treatment centres. The back door was used by Ebony's team whenever patching-up was needed. Why she trusted him so fully and what her hold was on him, was a complete puzzle to me. But trust him she did. And I followed her lead. Besides, this was the only place where we could run any kind of tests on Jonah's alien body without getting shipped off to "Area 51" as the find of the century.

Patil had performed all the tests he could think of. Scans, blood tests, anything. He'd put Jonah through his paces with stamina tests, checked his heart rates, oxygen saturation. He'd thrown the book against it. Only issue was, it was the human test book. And Jonah wasn't human anymore.

What he did have, was a comparison. When Jonah came back, Patil had run the same tests to form a baseline. Just in case we needed to monitor changes. I'd never expected it to be necessary, but it was.

'I'm not sure what help this will be,' Patil said two days ago after he completed all the tests on Jonah. 'The only reference I have is the earlier data and that was from when he arrived. Not exactly a stress-free period.'

'How about me?' I suggested. 'Why not run the same tests on me. I can't guarantee I'm one-hundred percent healthy, but you would have more data.'

'That's a good idea,' he replied. 'At least it will give me more insight into what's considered normal in your world.'

'Not sure I'm normal,' I joked. But the humour was lost on the ever-serious doctor.

One day later I regretted my impulsive suggestion. I'd been through the wringer. Every conceivable test had been done, and I felt prodded, punctured and very, very tired.

A phone call from Patil brought me here after-hours.

'The news isn't good,' he said.

I'd guessed that, the way he only called me over.

'Your stats were very helpful,' he continued when I nodded.

He keyed some information into the computer and a list

of test results came up on the left screen. He swiped the screen, and the information moved to the right screen as he pulled up more information on the left.

'See this?' He pointed to the left screen. 'These are the results from your test.' Then he moved his finger to the right one. 'These are Jonah's.'

I leaned in closer to look at both screens in turn. The results didn't say much to me, but even I saw that they were very different.

'These values show the oxygen saturation of your blood. You can see Jonah's are much lower. That could explain the blackouts. Temporary shortage of oxygen to the brain will do that.'

He changed the data on the screens and continued his explanation.

'This is a graph of Jonah's brain activity while he slept.'

I was astounded. 'Asleep?' The graph showed dramatic spikes and angry looking scratches. 'Is this normal when someone sleeps?'

'No. It isn't. Some activity is to be expected. Especially once the subject achieves rem sleep, but this is extreme. If you compare it with your brain activity during the MRI, it becomes even more apparent.'

Another graph came up on the second screen. There, the undulations were less extreme. Their heights and dips not even half of Jonah's.

'And you were awake then, though very relaxed.'

'And when someone is awake it's generally higher than during rest or sleep?' I asked just to be sure.

Patil nodded.

He brought up a third graph next to Jonah's. 'This one was from when he arrived back. The changes are slightly more erratic compared with yours, but nowhere near what Thursday's results show.'

Apprehension started to make its way up my spine. I felt the tell-tale dull ache in the back of my head. There was more bad news. I knew it.

Patil changed the content of the screens again. Now I saw the slowly moving images of the MRI scans. Mine again on the left, and the big man's on the right. The difference in body size was apparent. But that wasn't all.

Patil timed the two screens so that they moved through the body at the same acceleration. He stopped them halfway through the chest area.

'Look at the left heart in each picture,' he suggested.

I did. There was a distinct disparity in the two images. Mine—which I sincerely hoped was the healthier one—was clear with smooth lines on the periphery. The one on the right was smaller with one side almost pushed in. The form of the organ was dented and ragged. Patil slowly moved both screens through the following images and I saw that the damage to Jonah's heart was structural. It looked withered. As though it had sustained enormous damage and not rebounded. How was that possible? Our bodies healed. The extent of the deterioration was unheard of for my kind.

'If we move up the body, you can see that the scarring is more widespread.' Patil pointed out a ragged break in a rib bone. It had healed, but not well.

I studied the image. The skin and first layer of muscle was intact where I knew Jonah had been wounded. Anything under that looked in bad shape. His healing was literally only skin-deep.

That shocked me. I glanced back to my MRI and homed in on a spot where I knew I had been wounded before. Nothing. The skin and everything below were pristine. No scarring. Nothing. This was how Jonah's body should look. I know the grunt's bodies were not completely up to par. They were not meant for durability. But healing capabilities were essential. The work they did was dangerous, and accidents were common. The body had to heal itself from that, otherwise the grunts wouldn't even last the short ten years they were designed for. To be absolutely blunt, they wouldn't sell without that basic functionality.

'His body is deteriorating rapidly,' Dr Patil voiced my conclusion.

'How is that possible?'

'I have no idea. But then again, I am not skilled on your physiology. I was hoping you could shine a light on these results.'

'I wish I could,' I answered sincerely. 'But I'm no expert either. I'm more of a technical guy.'

'Is there any way you can get hold of other data? Maybe from your home dimension. Then I can educate myself and determine a way forward. We need to do something to stop the degradation, or he may not live much longer.'

'I don't see how I could,' I answered with a heavy heart.

I shuddered. The news was much worse than I could have imagined.

'Can your kind live with just one heart?'

'I don't know. I haven't heard of anyone who did. But that's not to say it's impossible. I mean you do.' I was holding on to straws now. 'What about the rest of his body? I saw scars in the muscles and organs that shouldn't be there.'

I pointed to the screen where my scan showed my chest. 'I was wounded a few years ago. My body has completely healed. Both internally and externally.' I moved my attention to Jonah's scan. 'These deep scars don't seem to be healing at all.'

'It's early days yet,' he tried to reassure me. 'The body is less than a year old, while your wounds were older, right?'

I nodded, ready to hold on to every smidgen of hope I could get. But the voice at the back of my head—you know, the one that cuts through all the bullshit—coldly informed me it would not improve.

'We will have to do a new scan in a few months' time,' the doctor continued. 'Then we will be able to see what the trend is.'

There was nothing else to say. I stared at the screens, very aware that mine was so much better than Jonah's. I racked my brain how I could get hold of more data. Anything that could help us save the big man.

Again.

'Do you want me to tell Jonah?' Patil brought me back from my reverie.

'No. At least, not all of it. Just the part about the blackouts. I don't want to unnerve him any more than necessary.'

'Lady E has been informed.'

I nodded. Of course. Dr Patil's first loyalty lay with Ebony. He would have informed her first. The fact that he'd asked me here alone strengthened my decision not to tell Jonah everything. I deduced Ebony had come to the same conclusion.

I would have to talk to her.

Make a plan.

Though what that would be, completely eluded me.

# Chapter Thirty-Six

'DR PATIL TOLD YOU?' It wasn't really a question.

Ebony knew the answer. She'd heard from Patil, but even that wasn't necessary. She could read it straight off my expression.

I hadn't slept since I got the news. This, combined with Jonah's earlier revelation of his feelings about his life, kept me awake. I fully blamed myself. If I hadn't brought him back, then he wouldn't be in this hopeless situation. If Aaliyah and I hadn't doped him up with the nanos, he might be in a better place.

Yeah, and he would probably have been in a worse one.

I could beat myself up as much as I wanted, it wouldn't help. Or change anything. We had to deal with the cards we had now. Bad hand that it was.

I nodded.

'Patil said that Jonah wasn't aware of everything.'

'I thought it wouldn't be a good idea at this time,' Ebony explained. 'Not with his revelations last week. I don't want to depress him anymore than strictly necessary. Not till we've looked at all the options.'

'Yeah.' I didn't sound optimistic. Exactly how I felt.

'What does he know?'

'Patil told him the blackouts were probably the result of sporadic oxygen deprivation, and that he was working on a possible solution. Maybe some meds that could improve the saturation.'

I nodded. It sounded plausible. 'How did he react to that?'

'No real reaction at all. That concerned me more than if he'd blown up.'

'Same here.'

We knew how to deal with Jonah's direct reactions. A thoughtful big man was new, and not something I knew how to handle. I didn't relish trying to figure out what he would do.

'What are our options?' Ebony asked.

I shrugged. 'To be absolutely honest, I have no idea.'

'No previous experience with what's going on in his body?'

'No. None.'

For a moment, she looked disappointed. But that disappeared quickly, and the ever-pragmatic Ebony came back.

'Dr Patil is looking into what's wrong with his blood. He has yours as a comparison. Do you have different blood types in your dimension?'

'No, just the one.'

'That simplifies it then. Yours will be the benchmark. It will mean that you may be needed for more tests.'

'Whatever it takes.'

A faint smile. I really needed that. Things were so gloomy at the moment that I couldn't bring myself to think of solutions. I know. I'd all but given up. Thank goodness for Ebony's tenacity.

'He has a friend he trusts who will help with further analysis. Together they will try to determine why Jonah's body is deteriorating so rapidly. And hopefully once we know that they can find a solution.'

I felt there was something more. Something she wasn't telling me. I cocked my head, but she ignored my unspoken question.

'Is there any way you can get more information about the physiology from your dimension?'

I shook my head. 'Not without going there, and that's not an option at the moment. Maybe we could ask Aaliyah next time we see her. After all, the body was grown in one of her family's facilities. There are small differences in the techniques Arand's people use and my family's. I'm not familiar with the details, but I do know that dad and Michael were dedicated to find out more about Arand's technology. I expect it was—is—more advanced. They have better scientists than we do.'

'Okay, that's an option. She can move more freely between the dimensions, so maybe she could find out some details that are important. Is there any way you can contact her?'

'No. Not really. The only way I know how is through Jonah, and that's not really an option now.'

'Then we'll just have to wait until she shows up again. I expect she won't stay away for too long.'

The last comment had an edge. Aaliyah and Ebony had a very strained relationship, the reason being Jonah. Both had a stake in the big man. He didn't necessarily play them, but he didn't choose either.

His final words before he died were that he loved Ebony.

Death seemed to have fuddled that memory. Maybe it had something to do with what happened back home in my dimension. Neither he nor Aaliyah would tell me what that was.

## Chapter Thirty-Seven

'WHAT'S GOING ON HERE?' Ebony's voice stopped the fight.

Jonah let go of Sly and pushed him back. Ebony's bodyguard reeled from the force and came up against the wall. He sank slowly to the floor, his face a mass of bruises and cuts.

Jonah wasn't unscathed. Purple blood seeped through his long hair and stained his t-shirt. A cut above his eye and another on his ear started to heal slowly, the edges closing.

He stretched his left arm and rotated the shoulder. Obviously, a sensitive spot. I walked over to him and cocked my head in question. He shrugged and turned away.

'Again. What the hell is going on here?' Ebony repeated, her tone hard and unforgiving. 'Sly?'

'We had an altercation, Lady E. Nothing major.'

'About what?'

Sly lowered his eyes and stared at a spot on the floor in front of him.

Ebony turned to the big man. 'Jonah?'

He looked up and shrugged again, not offering any further explanation.

Ebony cocked her head at Sly and her bodyguard left the room to tend to his rapidly swelling face. He was joined by the others in the room. Only Jonah, Ebony and I remained.

'Gabe? You going to tell me what this is about?'

'I came in just before you,' I answered, slightly intimidated by the way she stared at me. 'They were already at each other's throats.'

She walked over to Jonah and placed a hand on his arm. 'Big man. I can't help you if you won't let me.'

'You don't have to help,' he rebuffed.

'I think I do. You and Sly have always gotten on well, what's changed?'

'Nothing,'

'Didn't look like nothing to me.'

'He said I was losing it,' Jonah finally explained. 'I was crazy. A danger to you.' Jonah looked up at Ebony and his features softened. 'I'd never hurt you. You know that, right?'

'I do.' She wiped the bloody hair from his face. 'And so does Sly.'

'I'm not crazy Ebs, I heard him. Loud and clear.'

'I'll talk to him, big man. What else?'

He was about to contradict her but thought better of it.

'He's not the only one. I hear them all talk about me. They do it while I'm there. As though they can't see me or just don't give a fuck.'

'I'll look into it, Jonah. Now please, go clean yourself up and meet me back here.'

Jonah left the room, pulling the blood-soaked t-shirt over his head as he crossed the threshold.

Ebony joined me and quizzed me about what I'd heard.

'Most of what I heard was Jonah shouting at Sly.'

'How did Sly respond?'

'He denied that he's said anything. That more or less pushed Jonah over the edge again. He went for Sly shouting that he wasn't crazy. That he knew what he heard.'


EBONY LEFT to check up on Sly and hear his side of the story.

These altercations were becoming more common. All of them centred around comments that didn't go down well with Jonah. As one, the perpetrators denied all his accusations. A trend was starting to evolve. One that was extremely disturbing. I remembered the earlier conversation we had months ago when Jonah mentioned the voices he heard in his head.

His actions bordered on paranoia.

Ebony returned and walked over to me.

'Sly repudiated the accusations,' she informed me. I nodded. It fit the pattern. 'He did say one thing that I found quite strange.' I was all ears.

'He agreed he's entertained the idea, but swore he'd never said it out loud.'

I scrunched my brow. What did that mean? 'He thought about it, but didn't say it?'

'Exactly.'

'How did Jonah pick up on it then?'

'Good question.'

# Chapter Thirty-Eight

'DON'T FREAK OUT, Gabe, but I've been thinking of something.'

I turned to look at Ebony. She seemed uncharacteristically meek. Apologetic even. I wondered what this was about. In the past few months, she'd changed from her positive self to a serious and sometimes even morose person. Not a change I welcomed. Especially not with all the crap we were having with Jonah.

Come to think of it, her transformation started about a month after he came back. Were the two connected? Probably. The big guy was hard to handle.

She sat down next to me on the fallen tree, lost in thought, her gaze turned to her fidgeting hands. This was definitely not right.

The fresh breeze between the trees was welcome and I imagined it blew the cobwebs out of my mind. Out here in the forest, the world seemed almost peaceful. A far stretch from what was going on only sixty miles away.

Ebony must have felt my gaze, she looked up, a tear in the corner of her eyes. I took her hands in mine.

'What's eating you Ebs?' I asked softly. 'You can tell me.'

'Can I?'

'Of course you can. We've been through so much together; there's nothing you can't tell me.' I tried a smile. She returned it half-heartedly. But it was a start.

'Jonah,' she finally burst out. 'It's to do with him.' I nodded. No surprise there.

'You know how I feel about him, Gabe?' Again, I nodded. 'Since he came back, he's not been the same.' I squeezed her hands in support.

'I don't know what he went through, it must have been terrible, but I don't know him anymore.' The tears made their way down the side of her cheeks and dripped off her chin onto our hands.

'He's not the Jonah I know, and love.'

'He's been through a lot, Ebony,' I tried softly. 'He died and came back. That would rock anyone's world.'

'Yes,' she agreed. 'I know, but it's too much. He's too different. I look at him and he looks like the same big lug I knew. He talks with the same voice. Walks the same way. Even eats as much as before.' We both smiled at that. 'But it's not him.'

The revelation had an enormous strain on her. She suddenly looked small. Not the powerhouse I was used to and had come to love and value so much.

'He is different,' I agreed with her. I heard a big sigh of relief. 'I think what happened to him would change anyone.'

'I guess,' she was hesitant. I cocked my head and squeezed her hands again to encourage her onwards.

'He's not here,' she declared. 'I don't know where his

mind is, but it's not here. He's so distant. He goes through the motions. Even in bed.' Ebony looked up to me and I saw a new flood of tears push at the edges of her eyes and roll down her cheeks. I brushed them away softly with my hand.

'You're right,' I acknowledged. 'Even though he looks almost happy enough sometimes, he seems removed from everything round him. From us, from the quest. everything.'

She nodded.

'Maybe it's PTSD?' I suggested.

'Could be, but then how do we help him?'

'I don't know. Have you tried to talk to him about this?'

'I did. He just smiled, kissed me and left. I'm not sure anything I said registered at all.'

My turn to sigh. I had no idea how to approach this. Sure, I'd noticed changes in the big man, but I'd put them down to the trauma he experienced. Now I was not so sure.

'No one ever came back, did they?' Ebony asked. I shook my head.

'Not that I know of. So, we have no comparison. Humans aren't supposed to come back after they died. It's possible that the whole experience could have a massive impact on his personality.'

'Something has been bothering me that I want to ask you.'

I nodded and cocked my head in surprise.

'When your dimension reincarnates the souls, they build the body based on the DNA. On the building blocks.'

I nodded again. She knew all this. Where was she going with her questions?

'But there are differences. Things your scientists couldn't know. The nurture part, but also any discrepancies or errors in the original?'

'The procedure takes out any weaknesses or genetic

abnormalities they can identify. The bodies have to be as strong and healthy as possible.'

'So it's not a complete reincarnation? Not an exact copy?'

My brow creased as I shook my head.

'You don't rebuild everything as it was,' she continued her probe.

'No, we don't. Besides the obvious of the two hearts and violet irises, we don't know exactly how the person was, and usually we take away the reason they died in the first place,' I continued, unsure where she was taking this. 'We use the blueprint in the DNA and the images of that person in their essence. So differences are possible.'

'Does that mean the body is actually fake?'

'I guess you could see it that way. It's no more than a vessel for the soul, or essence, whatever you want to call it. Because we want to avoid mental conflicts, we try to make the body as close to the original as possible.'

'But it is completely artificial.'

'Yes.'

'We tried to reincarnate the souls into a standard body that suited the needs of the customers, but that backfired. There was no cohesive whole. Basically, it didn't fit. '

'So, you copy what you think they looked like in their previous life?' The emphasis was on the "you" part.

'Yes.'

Where was this going to? The questions Ebony was asking were all geared towards getting my mind in a certain place. She knew the answers. Why was she manipulating me this way? I observed her nervous fidgeting, something I would never have believed possible.

'I miss the old Jonah. The one with the tattoos and scars.' Ebony pulled me out of my reverie.

I cocked my head. 'So do I, but this is the one we have. There's no going back.'

She hesitated and turned her gaze to the forest floor, pulling her hands from mine.

'What?' I asked.

'What if we could go back?' She locked eyes with me. Small tears slid down her cheeks.

My brow creased. 'Could what?'

'Reunite him with his old body.' A small spark of hope shone in her eyes.

I shook my head, confusion apparent. 'We can't, I watched it burn. It was cremated.'

She took a deep breath and looked me in the eye. 'Actually, you watched the coffin burn. Not his body.'

I was in shock.

Where is his body?' I whispered.

'It's in cryo.'

The hope she'd ignited was swamped by doubts as soon as I pondered the enormity of what Ebony had just revealed to me. I placed both of my hands on the tree trunk beside my hips and let all of the emotions swarm over me.

Relief—that we might have a way of saving Jonah—but equally respondent dread that it would not work. How could it? Jonah had been mortally wounded in the fight. No matter that it was on cryo. Freezing it wouldn't repair the excessive damage that had resulted in his death.

'Even if we were able to put his essence back in his original body, there's no use. The wounds he had were terminal. He would just die all over again.'

She was silent. I glanced to the side. She bit her underlip and swallowed hard.

'What did you do?' I asked carefully.

'Before we froze him, we put his body on life support to heal it. We couldn't repair it completely, but most of it.'

'How did you do that?' I was amazed.

Her tone was accusatory. 'Your dimension is not the only one to use nanos, you know? Only we use them to heal people. Not enslave them.'

Touché.

'So, you have his original body on ice, waiting for his essence?' A small flicker of hope started to grow in my hearts, the emotion filled me with warmth.

'Yes.'

'Is it possible?'

I shrugged. 'I don't know. Nothing like this has ever been done before. You would effectively be resurrecting an actual body from the dead.'

She nodded.

'We have no way of knowing what the effect of that would be.'

'Could he become a kind of zombie?'

I pulled up my shoulders. Her guess was as good as mine.

'But what about your kind?'

'What do you mean?'

'Well, if anyone from your dimension dies here, don't they take the bodies back?'

'Yes, they do. Most of the time.' My mind drifted for a moment.'

'Most of the time?'

'I'll tell you some day.'

She raised an eyebrow.

'Okay. You said it didn't make any difference if you killed your brother Michael here, because he would be

269

resurrected anyway. So, do they use the old body or make a new one?

Good point.

'They often use the old one, unless it's too damaged. If they can get it.' My mind wandered back to Rafael. He would never be reincarnated. He was completely gone.

'But didn't they die? I mean they sustained mortal wounds. You fix those then, didn't you?'

'We do.' I understood how her mind was working.

'So, can't we do that with Jonah?'

'I don't know.'

'Besides, it's moot,' I crashed her hopes. I had to.

'Why?' She asked angrily.

'Because we would have to transport the body to my dimension and then back again when—if—it worked.'

'And why is that a problem?'

'Transportation is a very invasive procedure. It makes me sick every single time, and my body is used to it. I don't think your physiology would be up to it. It takes an enormous strain on the heart and other organs.'

'And your kind can do it because you have two hearts?'

'Probably, yes.'

'Is that one of the reasons you never take the human bodies, just the souls?'

'Yes. But we also don't want to call attention to us. Missing bodies would.'

'I can see that.'

'But what if we could?' She wouldn't let it go.

'Ebony. I want to believe it would be possible. But there's no way we can. We can't just go over and resurrect him. They wouldn't let us.'

Ebony stood up and paced the small clearing in front of me. The stubbornness in her stance made me smile.

She stopped and looked at me. 'But we might be able to copy your technology here. If you can get the blueprints. I can build it.'

She was tenacious.

I didn't want to dash her hopes, but we had to be realistic, even if I didn't know what that was right now.

'How would we get them? I'm not exactly on speaking terms with my family. I can't just show up there and ask them, for the design.'

I wasn't just disappointing her, my own emotions screamed at me to stop trashing what I wanted to be a real option.

'No. But Aaliyah can.' The flash in her eyes dared me to contradict her. The old Ebony was back, with a vengeance.

I raised my eyebrows. 'You want to ask Aaliyah's help?'

She nodded.

'I thought you two didn't get along,'

She pursed her lips. 'We don't. Well, we could. If she would lay off Jonah.'

I laughed. 'The new Jonah.'

She nodded again.

'And now you want her help in getting the old one back?' Ebony stayed silent. 'Why would she help you? She doesn't really have a stake in the old one, does she?'

'If you ask her, she might help us.'

'There is another problem though,' I commented.

'What?'

'Even if we found a way to move Jonah's essence from his current body to the original. Who says he would want that?' An icy hand gripped my hearts.

'After this past experience, he might veto the whole thing.'

271

# Chapter Thirty-Nine

'HE'S GETTING WORSE,' Patil voiced what we already knew.

Jonah's blackouts were more frequent. And if that wasn't enough, his body bled more profusely and for longer with every callous, unnecessary wound he amassed. Healing drained his energy, took longer and left scars.

There was no avoiding the obvious. We were going to lose our big friend again.

I glanced at Ebony. She was keeping up a good face, strong and as decisive as always, but her eyes were sad. There were constant worry lines on her forehead. Sometimes she even seemed distracted, unable to fully concentrate on her work. I was worried for her.

'Is there anything you can do, doctor?' she asked, already knowing the answer.

Patil shook his head. 'No. Nothing other than sedating him which might slow the process down a bit. He's pushing his body to its extremes and further. This only accelerates the deterioration. Frankly, he's killing himself in a hurry.'

'Thank you doctor, we'll talk to him.'

'Good luck with that.'

That brought a small smile to my lips. We would be in for a struggle if we wanted the big man to slow down and take care of his body.

The doctor packed his tablet and nodded his goodbye. He left us alone in Ebony's comfortable office.

I looked around, as much to stall the discussion we were going to have, as anything else.

The office was beautifully decorated in warm tones and white, the combination offered a clean almost minimalistic effect, offset with earth tones. It was a perfect marriage between styles, resulting in a warm, simple work environment.

The banks of computers I was used to were missing, substituted by a single screen that now disappeared back down into its slot at the head of the desk, taking the projected virtual keyboard with it and leaving the desktop pristine and clear.

The seats were comfortable but simple. Not ostentatious in any way. The place breathed style and an undertone of wealth, not so much by what was there, more by what wasn't.

'We're going to have to discuss the options with Jonah,' Ebony broke the silence. I wanted to ignore her, stay in this relatively peaceful contemplation. But it wasn't fair. And it wouldn't help.

I turned back to my friend and nodded.

'You're right. I'm just not looking forward to it.'

That elicited a smile. One I had missed for a long time. It mirrored mine.

'He might be positive, you know,' I tried.

Ebony raised an eyebrow. 'Really?'

'Well, he doesn't like this body. He keeps saying he wants the old one back.' I attempted to lighten the dark mood.

'That's not the part I'm worried about,' she answered forcing a faint smile. I nodded.

'Will the reincarnation into his real body be as invasive as the last one?'

I shrugged. 'I don't know. No one has ever done it before with a human body.'

'What about you? Have you ever been reincarnated yourself? You said that sometimes your people are reincarnated into their old bodies.'

'I've never experienced it myself.' I raked my brain for an answer. 'I vaguely remember something about an uncle. I was a child then. A long time ago. My mother's brother. He died during what we called the "harvests", and they brought his body back.' I looked at her sheepishly.

'Harvest?' her voice was harder.

I sighed. 'It's what we used to call the battles my family started here on earth to collect souls before the Establishment was set up. It was very brutal then. Direct. Large teams came from our dimension and basically massacred whole towns or villages. Dousing them with nanos when they died.'

'Like with Jonah?'

'I guess.' I'd never thought of it that way. 'It was very primitive and brutal. As you can imagine, there were bloody battles. Lots of casualties on both sides. My uncle was killed during one specific fight and reincarnated back in our dimension.'

I didn't really want to go into any more details. 'But that was a long time ago, the technology is much better now.'

No such luck. Ebony saw right through my lame excuses.

'Jonah's reincarnation was the state-of-the art technology, at least for your family.'

I shrugged my shoulders in defeat. She was right.

She added, 'the only thing he'll focus on is the reincarnation itself. The terrible torment he went through last time.'

I sat down, all energy leaving my body.

'We don't have an alternative,' I said dejected. 'It's this or we lose the big man for good.'

'Sometimes I think that's what he would prefer.'

Ebony's words chilled me to the bone. She was right. Any plans we made could easily be vetoed by Jonah. It was his life, crappy as it was. He had to decide.

'He's never been good with bad news.'

'No, he hasn't. And something tells me this one will not be a doozy.'

Ebony's lips pulled tightly again. Seriousness returning. 'He still hates the last reincarnation. No way he'll embrace a new one.'

'Not immediately.' I had to stay positive. If I didn't have that then there was no use. 'This is his own body. That should count for something.'

Ebony sighed. 'Don't hold your breath. I sincerely doubt he will accept anything we suggest. Not the way he is now.'

'You're right. He won't. Not straight off. But even he has to acknowledge that he's on a dead end here.' I immediately regretted my choice of words.

'He won't.'

'Ebs.' I took her hand in mine. 'We have to believe he will wake up to what's basically his only chance.'

She avoided my eyes. I cupped her chin in my hand and softly turned her to face me.

'We all want the old Jonah back. You, me and even the big man.'

Tears formed at the edge of her eyes. I saw hope desperately trying to push through the desolation and pain. Ebony hurt. To her core. And I felt for her.

Nothing would make me happier than to solve everything in the blink of an eye. But I couldn't. It wasn't up to only me. Jonah had a role to play in this. A big one. I had to find a way to convince him.

For his sake.

…And for ours.


'WE STILL NEED THE TECHNOLOGY.' Ebony's words brought me back from my musing. She was right.

'How far are you?'

'Just scratching the surface. We need to get more information from your world.'

I swallowed hard. This conversation was quickly moving in a direction I definitely didn't want to go in.

'Have you heard from Aaliyah?'

I shook my head. 'Nothing.'

'We can't just wait until she shows up.'

It was getting harder to breath, or was that just me? It was me.

My anxiety was coming back again with a vengeance. I pushed it to the background, berating myself. It was time for me to grow a spine. Quit all my useless self-pity. It was pathetic and it wasn't getting us anywhere.

If I had to go back to my home dimension to help the big man. Then that was what I would do.

Yeah, now the only one I had to convince was my cowardly self.

'I'll go back.' I blurted out.

Ebony just nodded. It wasn't debatable. It was the only —very slim—chance we still had.

'Is that possible?'

'It will have to be. There's no other way. It could take weeks, or even months before Aalyiah returns. We don't have that kind of time. I'll go there. Find her, somehow. We know the coordinates from where she transported last time. I'll start looking there.'

'I can get you those.'

'Then that's what we'll do. I'm transporting into Arand's territory. They won't expect that. Hopefully no one will recognise me. They shouldn't. Not if I'm careful.'

'When will you go?'

'As soon as we key the coordinates into my transporter, and I get some appropriate clothes. I need to blend in.'

'Just tell Sly what you need. He'll get it.'

I nodded. It felt good to be active. Finally, we were taking the initiative. Even if it was a dangerous one.

I was going home.

…Kind of.

# Chapter Forty

I FOUND AALIYAH.

Not that she was happy about it.

We were in the back room of the restaurant where I caught up with her. When she spied me, she pushed her food away and gestured me to follow her through the kitchen to a cosy, small room no bigger than a pantry. There she tore into me.

'You idiot. Do you have any idea what will happen to you if they find you here? Or me for that matter. My brother would have a field day.'

'I had to come,' I tried to get a word in.

'What the hell are you here for anyway?' Her anger was palatable.

'Last time we spoke, you said your family had radically improved the reincarnation technology and that you could expand your reach.'

She threw up her hands in desperation. 'You're here for industrial espionage? You have to be kidding me.'

'No. Nothing like that.' I tried to calm her down before

someone else heard her ranting. 'But I do need to know what improvements your technicians made. I got the impression reincarnation had become more mobile.'

She hesitated and looked at me intently. I was just happy she wasn't shouting anymore. The walls didn't seem thick or soundproof.

'What if it is?'

'We have a problem.' I used the trump card. 'Jonah has a problem. And your technical innovations might help him.'

That got her attention.

'His body is deteriorating rapidly. More than triple what would happen here. I think it has something to do with the teleportation. The bodies were never made for that.'

'What's happening?' Concern quickly pushed anger to the background.

'His hearts are eroding fast. One is already failing, and he blacks out.'

'How long does he have?' The fear in her eyes was genuine.

'I don't know. Maybe just months.'

'And you want to do what? Put him in another body?'

I nodded.

'But wouldn't that have the same effect? Wouldn't that body just deteriorate as quickly as this one?'

'Not if it was a human body.'

She looked at me incredulously. 'You're going to kill someone to give him another body?'

I shook my head vigorously. 'No. No. His old body.'

She was taken back by that. 'Say what?'

I motioned us to sit down on some crates. I leant in closer to whisper. 'Ebony took his body after he died and put it on life support until the wounds healed. Then she had him frozen using Cryogenics.'

Aaliyah raised an eyebrow. 'What's that?'

'The body is frozen at one-hundred-and-thirty degrees below zero,' I explained.

'Why?'

'To revive it at a later date in the hope any illness or damage can be reversed, and the human can come back to life.'

He thought on it for a moment. 'Wouldn't the brain be damaged beyond repair?'

I cocked my head. It had crossed my mind as well. 'They believe it wouldn't.'

'Believe?'

I shrugged. 'No one's come back yet.'

'And Ebony did this to Jonah's body?'

I nodded.

'And now you want to reincarnate his soul back into the frozen husk.'

'Well, defrost it first.' I tried a little banter to lighten the mood. It didn't work.

'You think?' she answered sarcastically. 'That's a long shot.'

'It is.' I conceded. 'But the only one we have.'

'What does the big man say?'

Ahh, I had been dreading that question. 'He doesn't know,' I said sheepishly.

She raised her eyebrow. 'You're doing this without his knowledge?'

'For now. He has enough to worry about, without all of this.' I tried to salvage what I could.

'Does he know about the degeneration?' The other question I wanted to avoid.

I shook my head. 'Not all the details.'

'Don't you think he has a right to?'

'He's changed. He's not the same man we knew before.'

She shrugged. 'Understandable. He died and came back. Not an everyday experience.'

'He's intense. More than he was. There are depths to him now that are dark and dangerous.'

'He was always dangerous.' Her arms were crossed over her chest, and she looked down on me, her eyes blazing.

'He was. But that has grown exponentially. He seems to have talents he didn't have in his previous life.'

That got her attention. 'Like what?'

'Like mind reading. Psychic powers.'

Aaliyah raised an eyebrow and pulled her lips in a sarcastic smile. 'And you still think he doesn't know?'

She had a point.

'Will you help me get either the equipment or the designs. Ebony can replicate the technology if she has the design.'

She mused over it for a few very, very long moments. 'Then you'll go back?'

'Yes,' I assured her. 'Believe me, I don't want to be here a moment longer than absolutely necessary.'

## Chapter Forty-One

SHE WAS in a hurry to get me out of this dimension. I couldn't blame her. My presence was a major risk. For me, and also for her.

'Did you get them?' I asked when she finally returned.

'I wouldn't be here if I hadn't.' Her tone bordered on the patronising. Sure, I'd never been her favourite person, and whatever minute positive I had going for me, disappeared as soon as I set foot here. This was her home. Her family. And any help she gave me would put all that on the line.

WE WERE in one of the hundreds of rooms in the palace.

The place was vast. It covered at least one square mile. The whole complex was surrounded by a high metre-thick stone wall interspersed with tall narrow archery holes. Massive gates stood on opposite sides of the monumental courtyard.

The palace itself was situated at the far end of the

construction; a two-story stucco building with single-story wings to both sides. Countless archways and minarets gave it a distinct Arabian appearance. The sand colour mimicked the sandy earth desert, which in itself was a completely foreign concept in this dimension. We didn't have sand. This was all the result of Arand's megalomaniacal delusions. He—like my father—was so completely in his chosen role that he believed himself the Islamic deity.

Aaliyah snuck me in here from the restaurant. As Arand's daughter she was exempt from the strict security at the gates. The guards didn't dare search her vehicle. They waved her through after a cursory visual check. I held my breath crouched under the flimsy layer of clothing and shopping she had layered haphazardly over the back seat.

Parking at the rear of the building, she almost dragged me through the back entrance to the left wing of the palace and deposited me in one of the many rooms. Judging by the thick level of dust, this particular one hadn't been used in a long time. I'd huddled down to wait it out.

FIVE AGONISING HOURS LATER, she returned holding a cloth bag containing papers and charts. During the long wait, I'd convinced myself she wasn't going to return. My desperate attempts to think of another way out of this mess were useless and I was close to giving up. Transporting out of the palace wasn't an option, Aaliyah had dropped that small gem of information as soon as we set foot in the complex. No matter how medieval the palace looked on the outside, it was protected by start-of-the art technology that monitored any clandestine transportations.

This was Arand's official home. His business had brought prosperity for most of the people in this town, but he still had enemies. My father being one of them. There was no such thing as too much security.

'These are all I could get,' Aaliyah pushed the bag into my hands.

'Thank you,' I answered with sincerity. 'I know how much trouble you could get into to by doing this.' She stared at me, gauging whether I actually meant it.

'It's not for you,' she tried to downplay what she'd done. 'It's for the big man.'

I nodded and smiled. Whatever the reason, she'd come through.

'I'm not sure it's enough,' she continued. 'I couldn't find more.'

'Ebony will be able to fill in any gaps,' I assured her. 'And maybe I can help a bit. I'm far from a technician, but not a novice either.'

Her smile was tentative.

'You have to leave. I can't get you out of the palace, my father is expecting me any minute. You'll have to do it on your own.'

My heart sank. I'd counted on getting out the same way I came in. Damn.

'What's the best way?'

'Try to blend in with the people here. Get some bags of shopping or something like that. As though you'd been to the market. Then join the crowd moving out of the central gate.'

'There are no other exits?'

She shook her head. 'The second gate is locked and heavily guarded.'

'Okay, the central gate it is.' I had no choice. I had to get out to be able to transport. But that meant passing the guards. My gut churned at the prospect. There was a very definite possibility I would not make it out of here in one piece. If push came to shove, I couldn't let them catch me. I'd have to chance a transportation or die trying.

'Good luck.' Her words brought me back from my dark thoughts. Yeah, luck. I'd need that.

I half smiled, not trusting myself to say anything that wouldn't come out wrong.

Aaliyah made her way to the door and opened it slightly to peer out into the corridor. It was quiet. She slipped through and left me alone in the small dusty space again to gather my wits about me.

I racked my brain for any bright ideas. Nope, there was no other option. I'd have to pull myself together, do my best acting and chance it. I pulled the cowl up over my head, my cloak around my shoulders and headed for the door.

Outside, I shuffled slowly along the corridor, pretending old age and physical restrictions. I made my way to the end of the corridor, staying in the shadows as much as possible without attracting attention. Thankfully there were few people around.

I was about to move into the open when a door in the corridor up ahead opened and my worst fear came true.

# Chapter Forty-Two

MY BREATH CAUGHT in my throat, and I froze.

Every cell of my body screamed at me to run, now! But I couldn't move. My muscles refused to act.

There, no more than fifty metres from me, stood Ibrahim. I was sure it was him. There was no mistaking the angry visage of my almost-nemesis. The dark stare and thin lips sent shivers up and down my spine. The obvious position of power, emphasised by the black robes bordered with gold thread, only enhanced the threat he posed.

I'd never entertained the idea of him being reincarnated. Stupid, I know. I should have known. Aaliyah may have taken care of his ticket-to-heaven, but we'd forgotten about the nanos. Ibrahim was a recruit. It made sense that he'd been administered nanos, or maybe even taken them himself. He knew about reincarnation and would have definitely been in line for that.

But recruits ended up in slavery. He should have been one of the anonymous grunts sold into a short life of unbelievable horror and pain. How was he able to get out of that? The quality of his robes and the wicked curved sword put him squarely in the higher ranks of the Hashta in this world.

Whatever, he was a threat. If he remembered anything about earth, he could expose me. And not just me, what about Aaliyah.

A thought occurred to me, if he did remember, why hadn't he exposed her?

Whatever, I had to get out of here now. I couldn't run the risk of discovery. Not with what I had in the bag at my feet.

I moved back into the shadows of the alcove, thankful the building had so many corridors and blind spots.

Pulling the cowl further over my head and hugging the walls, I made my way out of the central construction into the bazaar-like market. I still had to get through the gates. The stone walls encircling the square looked insurmountable and were—as said—no option.

The atmosphere was oppressing. Interspersed between the buyers were a multitude of guards, all armed with the curved swords I'd become used to here and a backup automatic weapon for the more practical law enforcement. As one, they sported hard visages as they pushed their way through the throngs of people. There was nothing subtle about it. They were in charge. The market visitors moved out of their way, their heads held down, not risking eye contact.

I hunched my body and made myself smaller as I carefully shuffled through the stalls. I avoided the guards like the plague, slowly moving closer to the gates. I joined the flow of people leaving the courtyard and held on to a wagon as though it was something I was connected to.

The sharp pains in my neck and skull screamed my

anxiety. With every step I took, I expected a hand on my shoulder, or a sword through my back. I couldn't look behind me. It would be suspicious, and people were watching, I had to stay focussed on the gate.

There were three guards at the gate, two on the left and one on the right. All three scanned the crowd that entered or exited the bazaar. I trudged onwards, hoping I wouldn't stand out.

Shouts caught my attention. One of the guards on the left side was gesturing angrily at a trio of women who wanted to come into the square. I dared raise my head just enough that I could see what was going on.

The three women were engaged in heated argument with the guards who pointed to their clothing: casual blouses and our version of jeans. Obviously, they didn't approve and refused to let the women into the enclosed space. The shouting intensified as the discussions became more heated. One guard grabbed the red-headed woman by the arm and tried to pull her back out of the gate. Her two friends pulled at him and attempted to free their companion. The second guard joined in the melee.

In the meantime, the row of people exiting the courtyard kept up a steady pace out through the gate. The guard there waved them through, distracted by the argument of his colleagues. Everyone turned to watch what was happening, the screams of the women pulling others into the discussions. The original guard now had his charge in a neck hold and she screamed she couldn't breathe.

I was a metre from the guard on my side of the gate when he left his post to push through the throng and help his fellow guards. I moved to the right and circumvented the onlookers, quickly taking advantage of the lull in security. As I slipped through the gate, I saw other guards move towards the noise and hard-handily push civilians out of the way.

The shouts and screams intensified as I pushed onwards, not looking back. Thankful for my windfall, but sorry for the three women who would no doubt pay for what the guards determined was unwanted clothing choices and resistance to their expulsion.

Part of me felt guilty that I had not been able to contact Aaliyah and warn her about Ibrahim, but there was nothing I could have done.

As soon as I got back to earth, I would get the message to her, somehow.

I hurried onwards past the steady flow of people entering the palace.

# Chapter Forty-Three

'CAN you make anything out of these designs?' I asked Ebony.

'I'm not sure. The language doesn't help,' she remarked.

'I can help with that,' I suggested.

'No, I'm good. Jonah taught me the basics and I should be able to decipher it.'

Of course, Jonah would have had some understanding of the language implanted because he was reincarnated there. Arand's teams obviously equipped their recruits with the foundation of the language as we did. It made them easier to control.

'If you need me, just call,' I answered. 'I have a passing knowledge of physics as well.'

She mumbled something unintelligible that I took as a dismissal. That wasn't fair. She was engrossed in the material I'd given her. The real nerd in her character was showing. That brought a smile to my lips.

I decided to find the big man. See how he was doing.

He was in the gym. No surprise there. Jonah was

constantly pushing his body to new highs. It was the only thing that gave him any fulfilment. And even that was fleeting.

Tyrone and another man were spotting him at the bench press. The Olympian barbell was bent under the weights on either side, the green fifty kilo plates the most prevalent on each side. Jonah strained under the ridiculous total weight, the two spotters positioned with their hands under the weight stacks to intervene in case he was unable to compete the press.

He grunted under the strain. Took another breath. Clenched his teeth and pushed with the exhale. The barbell moved slowly but surely up until Jonah's arms locked. He shouted out his triumph.

The spotters assisted in moving the barbell back up over the uprights and dropped the bar back onto the bench, freeing them all from the weight. There was a collective sigh of relief.

I was used to my dimension's strength. But even with that in mind, Jonah broke any and all records. As impressive as it was. I saw the strain it put on him. His breath came in short bursts, His shoulders and arms shook slightly. Sweat dripped off his brow onto the towel he held in his hands. He didn't dry it off, just waited until the trembles stopped.

These—outwardly small—signs of fatigue were what scared me. In a normal person, I would brush them off as normal. Not with Jonah. Two months ago, these weights would have been a breeze. Barely enough to break out a sweat.

He glanced up at me from under his thick brows. There was pain in his eyes, and something else. Reproach. Where did that come from? I hadn't said a word. But then again, I didn't have to anymore. Just thinking was sometimes enough around the big man.

He wiped the sweat from his face and turned to the others. 'Thanks, guys.'

They both smiled and nodded. It was a dismissal, but one they took without question.

The silence was heavy once the door closed behind them. Jonah drank deeply from his water bottle. I waited, not sure what to do. The tension in the air was palatable and I had no idea why.

He stared at me again. Anger in his eyes. His lips pulled tight.

He stood up. 'I don't need your pity.' He spat out the words and stalked off.

'Concern, not pity,' I tried.

'Same thing,' he called back without even turning to address me.

'No. It isn't.' My turn to get mad. 'It's much more difficult. Especially with you.'

Jonah turned; his face contorted in anger. Well, tough. I'd had enough of this shit.

'You may think you knew what I'm thinking Jonah. But you're wrong. You get snatches maybe. But never the whole story. That's making you paranoid and honestly, impossible to live with.'

'So leave.' He took a few steps back in my direction.

'I just might.'

'What's stopping you?'

I stared at him. 'Ebony.'

He blushed; the anger replaced by shame. I'd hit a nerve. Instead of letting him digest it, I just had to have the last word.

'You're killing her, behaving like this.'

Jonah closed his eyes and put his head in his hands as he leant against the coffee bar. I saw his shoulders sag and the otherwise strong aura diminish spectacularly. I almost felt sorry for him.

'Pull yourself together, Jonah. I know it's shitty now, but you're just making it worse.' Trust me to rub it in. I should have stopped while I was ahead.

'Fuck off, Gabe.'

Why didn't I take the hint.'

'That's your answer to everything. "Fuck Off." Leave me alone.' I walked up closer to him. Crowding his space, but I was sick of his pathetic attitude and constant reproach.

'Don't push your luck, Gabriel.'

I ignored the danger in the tone, full of my own righteous indignity.

'Luck? Is that what you call this? Luck, being partnered with you?'

'No one asked you to. And I don't need you now. All you've done is get me killed.'

I exploded. 'Got you killed? If I hadn't been here, you would have done that yourself years ago. I'm the only reason you're alive!' I shouted, almost in an exact repetition of an earlier conversation. We were stuck in a repeating circle. A downward one.

From the corner of my eye, I saw the door open. Sly glanced in the room, thought better of it and retreated immediately, closing the door behind him.

'You're the reason I'm dead,' Jonah bit back.

'Oh, get over it will you. You're like a broken record. I know things didn't turn out as anyone hoped. But we tried. We risked a lot to get you back and to help you.'

'Well stop. I never asked you to.'

'We didn't want to lose you.'

'It's not your choice.'

'No. It isn't, and you've made that very clear. You're an ungrateful bastard, Jonah.'

'Have you looked at yourself recently? You're a class act, Gabe. A typical spoiled, poor, little, rich kid with a daddy complex. You're good at standing in the shadow of those who actually take the risks. What the fuck have you ever done for anyone other than yourself.'

We were in a shouting match now. Emotions running wild, cumulating in this volcano of spite and pain.

'You're a parasite, Gabe. And the whole "I hate daddy" routine is getting stale. This has been nothing more than an adventure for you. You're hiding behind this cause you latched on to for excitement and fun. It's not your ideal. It's just a way to stick it to your dad. You're still trying to get his attention, and you don't care who pays for it. Me, Ebony, all of us mere humans.'

I was dumbfounded. Was this really how he viewed me?'

'This is not about my relationship with my father. I believe in what we are doing. I want—no, I need—to stop the Establishment. That's why I'm in this. You know that.'

'No. I don't. I just see a spoiled brat who didn't get his father's love and is rebelling to get attention.'

His words cut me to the bone. I knew it was spite and should have pushed it aside in the knowledge that Jonah wasn't himself. I kept saying that to myself. Well, what if he was? What if he really meant this?

'Well, we don't need you. You're not even human. How can you fight for us?'

I spat back. 'Neither are you.'

The weight disc caught me completely by surprise. It hit me squarely in the abdomen and knocked the air out of me.

I fell backwards hard onto the floor, banging my hip violently on the hardwood surface. My breath came in gasps and my hearts were raging. Not just from the trauma, as much from pure rage. What the fuck?

I pushed my body up from the floor onto all fours, my head low to stop the vomit before it filled my mouth. With clenched lips I forced the bile down, struggling to swallow the vile liquid.

The floor spun underneath me, and I closed my eyes, willing my body to come back under my control. It rebuffed my efforts, but slowly I regained some form of mastery over my limbs. Carefully, I sat back on my haunches. I took deep breaths through my nose, not daring to open my mouth in case I lost my battle with the bile.

Anger pushed the pain away. My indignation at the abuse I perceived as senseless and totally inappropriate, increased.

'I have endured enough debasement from you, Jonah. You've won. I'm out of here. I'll take down the Establishment without you. It will be a lot easier. And less dangerous.'

'Dangerous? You get yourself into a tight spot by your own incompetence. I'm glad you're leaving. You're a burden to us. We have to constantly bail you out. How many times have we saved your life?' Jonah replied with venom in his tone.

'About as many times as I have yours.'

'You've never done anything for me. Not if it wasn't in your own interest.'

'I risked everything for you.' I shouted back, no longer caring what I told him. 'I was almost captured just to get you a last chance at a real life.'

The silence pushed home what I had blurted out. Jonah looked at me and cocked his head in query.

'What do you mean? My last chance?'

'Forget it,' I tried.

Jonah's tone had changed. The anger was gone, replaced by what was it? Concern?

'What did you mean, Gabriel? And what's this about my old body?'

Shit, I'd forgotten he could pick occasional words out of thin air, or my mind in this case.

I stayed silent. Hopelessly attempting to stop my thoughts from going to my last visit to Arand's palace, from Jonah's condition.

'What condition?'

'Leave it, Jonah. You don't want to know.'

His voice hardened again. 'That's not up to you. I decide what I do and don't want to know.'

Silence.

'What condition?' he repeated.

I looked up at him. Worry dominated his features. The anger was gone, replaced by a creased brow and wide-open eyes.

'Please, Gabriel. You're concerned about whatever my condition is. I can sense it. I hear it in your thoughts. I need to know.'

I sighed and pulled a bar stool closer and sat down. This was not how I'd envisioned our conversation. I wanted to bring the bad news carefully. With compassion. And here I was, blurting it out almost in spite. That was the effect the big man had on me sometimes. I regretted this was one of them.

I looked up. He was still staring at me. Willing me to tell him about what he had caught scraps of from my mind. How bad was it? He was worried. Despite all his bravura about hating this life, he was reluctant to give it up.

I sighed, closed my eyes tightly and pushed the pain in my gut back to the internal compartment where it was closed off. When I opened my eyes again, I'd reached some kind of peace.

'It's bad news, Jonah,' I said in what I hoped was a friendly voice.

'I gathered that.'

'Your body,' I continued. 'It's deteriorating at a much faster pace than we ever imagined.'

He nodded me onwards.

'The grunt bodies—and your body—are not made for longevity. They are strong but not made to last.' I looked him in the eye, no longer recoiling from the responsibility.

'In my dimension, they generally endure for ten years. I expected yours to last longer because you are not subjected to hard labour. But the tests show that the opposite is the case.'

'How bad is it?'

The delay in my answer said it all.

'That bad, huh?' He tried a smile. It didn't reach his eyes. They were sad.

'Yes. Bad.'

'The black outs? The healing? That's all related to this?'

I nodded reluctantly. 'Your body is deteriorating. Your healing abilities are only skin deep. The internal wounds heal badly, leaving scars. One of your hearts is shutting down.'

'Can I live with one?'

I hesitated, but there was no going back. 'We don't know.'

He shrugged, holding on to that straw. I hated to do it, but now was the time to be brutally honest.

'Your heart is not the only thing. Your organs are wasting away. I'm sorry Jonah.'

He nodded. 'Not your fault.'

He took a moment to digest the information. I stayed silent. Giving him space for what must be devastating.

'I guess I knew,' he finally said. 'The things I feel. The pain. The restrictions.' He sighed, his features slack and soft. 'So how long do I have?'

I shrugged. 'We don't know.'

'Educated guess?'

'Months. Maybe weeks.' It literally hurt me to deliver the news.

He raised his right eyebrow, then sighed.

Jonah sat back against the bench. He stared at the ceiling; his hands clenched in his lap.

'And this is irreversible?'

'For this body, yes.'

We were silent. What more was there to say at this time? I felt absolutely terrible. Don't shoot the messenger? Well, this messenger wanted to shoot himself at that moment.

Jonah broke the silence. 'What do you mean, this body?'

I had to be very careful. 'There might be something we can do. A small chance.'

That got his attention.

'What kind of chance?'

'You will have to be openminded.'

He laughed. 'I died, came back and now I'm dying again. I've experienced enough to be more than open minded.'

Yet still I wasn't convinced he was ready for the news.

'I am,' he answered my unspoken question.

'Ebony, might have a way to reunite you with your old body.' There, I'd said it. I expected him to erupt, call me all kinds of terrible names. Or laugh hysterically at the mere idea.

He didn't.

'Is that possible?'

'It might be.'

'How? I thought my body had been cremated.'

'So did I. But Ebony kept it alive, healed it and put it on Cryo.'

'It's on ice?'

I nodded.

I looked up at my big friend. There was a smile on his lips. A distant sparkle in his eyes. 'She kept my body?'

'She did. Thankfully.'

'And you think what? That you can put my soul back into it?'

'Maybe,' I said carefully.

'That's a very big maybe.'

I had to agree with him.

'How would you do that?'

'We have the technology from my dimension,' I started.

'How did you get that?' He cocked his head, maybe half expecting my answer.

I hadn't wanted to tell him. 'Aaliyah came through and gave us the blueprints. Ebony took it from there.'

'She brought them here?'

'Not exactly.'

His raised eyebrow and asked the question without words.

'I went back and got them.' I whispered.

'You went to your dimension?' The surprise was genuine.

I nodded.

'Home?'

'Not exactly. I went to Arand's complex.'

His eyes opened wide. He realised what I had done, what I had risked.

'You did that for me?' His words were almost whispered.

I just nodded. An answer would have just made him feel more uncomfortable. It wouldn't add anything.

I didn't have to read his mind to know that he'd finally realised what we—I— would do to save him.

I felt he needed to be alone. I stood up and walked towards him. I squeezed his shoulder. 'Think about it Jonah. You don't have to decide now. We still have some time.'

He nodded. His head down as he stared at his hands.

I left the gym with mixed feelings. It had been hell, but maybe, just maybe, we might have a sliver of hope.

# Chapter Forty-Four

JONAH ALTERNATED between optimistic highs and moody, morose bouts during the next five days.

Today was one of the bad days.

'You want to kill me again?'

We all convened in the big living room after Jonah indicated he wanted to talk. We'd been attempting a conversation for half an hour. To no avail. The resentment was still close to the surface. Jonah took all our words literally and it was tiresome just trying to keep the discussion going.

'We didn't kill you the first time.' Not a good idea to contradict him with his current fragile mood.

'Okay.' His features contorted in a scowl. 'Let me rephrase. You want me to die again.'

I thought about pointing out that we hadn't wanted him to die the first time but swallowed the comment when I saw the daggers in his eyes. He was daring me to. I decided I wouldn't call his bluff this time.

'You are already dying.' I declared, the hardness probably overdone. 'It's just a question of time before this body is worn out. It was never made for longitude.'

'You said ten years.'

'Under normal circumstances in my dimension, yes. You transported. You have been abusing it as though you're indestructible. And it wasn't made for earth.'

'Neither were you,' he spat back.

'No. But I wasn't created in a lab. My body is different from yours.'

'You tell me I'm dying. Again. Then you throw me a lifeline with an experimental process you "think" you have worked out. And you expect me to what? Jump at the opportunity?' His obnoxious paranoia was back again with a vengeance.

Silence reigned. His words cut me deeply. He said out loud exactly what the voice in my head had been telling me for the past week.

'It's your own body,' Ebony tried. 'It's you.'

'It's dead.'

She disagreed. 'No. It was in limbo for ten minutes before we put it on life support.'

'Then you did what?' Everything he said sounded like an accusation.

'We healed it.' Ebony wouldn't let it go that easily.

'And killed it again.'

'Not killed it. Put it in cryo.'

He spat out his words. 'This isn't a semantics thing. You stopped the heart. Stopped the breathing. What do you want to call that if not death?'

'Your heart wasn't pumping. The life support was doing that. Breathing was the same. We stopped the artificial movements in your body and let it rest.'

302

'Rest?' He huffed in disgust. 'You make it all sound so clinical.'

I had to intervene. 'Jonah. Ebony is trying to help you. The least you could do is hear her out.'

'That's exactly what the problem is. Your help is my Hell.'

'I'm sick of you all trying to control my life.' He paced the room in angry steps.

'We're not.' I contradicted him.

'Yes, you are. You bring me back from the dead. Then transport me to earth in a strange body, expecting me to just continue as though nothing happened. And now you want to see if you can get me back in my old, DEAD, body.' He had to have the last word.

I sighed. 'We've had these discussions, Jonah. It's time to let them go. Blaming us for all your problems doesn't help anyone, least of all you.'

'That's easy for you to say. It's not about you. It's me. My life. My choice.'

The big man was looming close. Too close for comfort in this mood. His and mine. But I didn't care. This battle of wills was tedious, and I was sick of it. The constant reproach, the thinly veiled condemnation for his predicament was aimed at me all the time.

I glanced at Ebony. Her creased forehead and the thinly pulled lips showed she wasn't in a much better place than me. She took a deep breath to calm down.

I followed her example, breathed deeply and splayed the fingers in my clenched hands, relaxing the muscles. 'No one is contradicting that,' I answered, barely keeping the irritation out of my voice. 'It's your life. You decide. But we care. We don't want to lose you.'

'That's not up to you.'

'I just said it wasn't.' I threw up my hands. What was the use? He wasn't listening to a word I said.

'If you really cared, you wouldn't have brought me back,' he shouted.

'Not again.' My anger won; I felt the heat rise from my neck up to flush my face. My muscles tensed and I leant forward to emphasise my rage. 'Cut the crap, Jonah. Stop wallowing in your stupid childish blame game. We didn't kill you.'

'Your brother did.' Low blow. Very low.

'Yeah, and I killed him for it,' I snapped back, reeling from the mental blow. One thing was for sure he still knew how to push my buttons. I wanted to jump him. Smash that stupid, mean grin off his face. He was close enough.

Instead, I forced myself to take another deep breath. 'We didn't force you to come back. You did that yourself. You fought to be here. To live.' And big mouth that I have, I had to throw out that last sentence. 'Why don't you stop bitching and start doing something positive. This is beneath even you.'

I didn't see the fist coming.

Jonah hit me squarely in the face.

Again. This was becoming a habit.

I heard the crunch as the cartilage in my nose broke and felt the spray of blood coming from the split skin of the damaged appendage. My back hit the floor hard from the force of the punch. I struck the table first and slammed the breath out of my body. I instinctively closed my eyes, wrapped my head in my arms, and curled up into a ball. The rush of air and accompanying blows I expected remained absent.

The sound of a scuffle and Jonah's violent swearing answered my unspoken question. He was restrained—only just—by Sly and two more of Ebony's guards that came running to her call. Carefully, I peered through my half-closed eyes to see what was happening. The big man sat in the armchair, flanked by Sly and another man. Ebony was on one knee in front of him, her hand on his, softly talking to him. I couldn't make out the words, but they had the desired effect and slowly the deep red in Jonah's face faded to a more normal colour as his rage dissipated.

I pushed my hands onto the floor and scooted backwards until I felt the wall. I rested my torso against the cool concrete and took stock of the damage. My nose was broken. Shit.

With my left palm against the upper part of my nose, I pushed the bottom half hard with my right, realigning the cartilage before it healed. Bright stars bloomed on the inside of my closed eyes as the pain hit me again. Tears collected at the side of my eyes and ran down to mix with the blood that seeped down my chin onto what had been a clean t-shirt. Now it was bright purple.

I continued to assess the damage to my face. The inside of my right eye socket hurt, indicating a fracture. That would heal. Nothing to worry about there. Other than my nose, eye socket and the massive bump on the back of my skull where I'd hit the floor, my head was still reasonably in order. I stretched the muscles of my back where I'd made contact with the table before hitting the ground. A bad bruise, possible fractured ribs. No bleeding.

My head hurt. Sharp stabs moved from my injured nose, behind my eyes into my brain, causing me to close my eyes again. It didn't help. I took a deep breath and rested my head against the wall.

Someone offered me an ice pack and a glass of water. I

accepted both, relishing in the cold relief of the ice on my damaged face.

The icepack would at least numb the pain. A soft crunching noise and the pull of the soft tissue in my face informed me I was already well on the way to full facial repair. The recovery of my ego would take a while longer. It wasn't the first fight I'd been in with Jonah. But this one was different. I was trying to help.

Rage pushed up from my torso and flushed my face. "Who the fuck did he think…" then it dissipated as quickly as it had risen. One glance at Jonah was enough.

His eyes were empty. The sparkle of life and hope was gone. His shoulders hung listlessly. His back was curved, and his torso leant forward in the chair. He looked defeated. The shock took me back. I'd never seen the big man look so small. So broken. Not even when the last breath left his body on the fateful day months ago.

Ebony held his hand and softly stroked the side of his face as she continued to talk to him.

I felt bad.

I'd never seen my friend look so dejected. So utterly lost. I knew it wasn't my fault, but I still felt guilty in some way. Ultimately Aaliyah and I had been instrumental in administering the nanos, so I guess we were—at least partially—the reason he was in this mess. I had to keep reminding myself that our actions had been motivated by compassion and love. Nothing else. We simply didn't want to lose him. We saw a way out and we took it, without debating the possible outcome. How could we? There was no time. We had to act fast. Besides, we had no idea of the fallout. No inkling of what it would mean for Jonah.

And now we were here.

In this mess.

Sly left Jonah's side and came back with a large bottle of whisky and a tray of glasses. He poured a generous amount and offered it to Jonah. Without looking up the big man murmured a thank you and accepted the glass.

I did the same, happy to numb the feelings of inadequacy that were pushing into my mind. If I… If only… and all that useless meandering.

We sat in silence for what must have been at least ten minutes.

My nose had healed, and I dabbed away the blood from my face with a wet cloth Sly handed me. Slowly I started to feel whole again.

I glanced at Jonah. He raised his head and attempted an apologetical smile. I nodded. No more needed to be said about it. No use piling more misery on his head now.

Five minutes later Jonah finally broke the silence. 'This machine you built. How do you know it will work?' His voice wavered, the tone dejected and submissive.

'We don't. Not for sure.' I answered. We had to be brutally honest. Time was running out.

'We've followed the blueprints. Gabriel helped with his knowledge of their science. Technically it should work,' Ebony added softly.

Jonah took a sip of the whisky, swallowing with effort. 'A stolen blueprint. Grabbed by an amateur who has no prior knowledge of what she was actually looking for. An alien science. Something that has never been attempted before. Why doesn't that make me feel any better?'

His attempt to pass it off as humorous didn't work. It was much too close to the truth.

Jonah sat back in the sofa, sighed and pulled himself together. 'Okay. Just for argument's sake. What are the biggest challenges?' He was back again.

'Your body for one. As far as we know, a human body has never been reincarnated. The soul has always been encapsulated in a fabricated vessel.' Ebony jumped onto the small window we'd been given.

I added my reading of the risk. 'We don't know how your human body will react to the soul returning. The procedure is extremely invasive, as you know.'

He nodded. 'You think?' The smile now was warmer, with more depth.

There was one more hurdle to overcome. 'And the last challenge is you.'

'What do you mean, me?' Jonah's eyebrow was raised in surprise.

'You have to want it. You have to fight. What you experienced the first time will probably be repeated, maybe even expanded. Your will, your push, will be the determining factor. If you do not have that drive, that dedication, then you won't come back.'

I let it sink in. 'You need to want to live.'

'And you don't at the moment.' Ebony whispered, tears in her eyes.

'So, what do you want to do?'

'How the hell am I supposed to know?' He answered, truly clueless.

'You're the only one who can.'

# Chapter Forty-Five

'CAN WE GET A MESSAGE TO AALIYAH?' Jonah asked. 'She needs to know about Ibrahim.'

I agreed with him whole heartedly. 'She's in much more danger with him around. She's done for if he remembers what happened.'

'Isn't that a given?'

'Not necessarily. I mean, you didn't at first. And if he does recall his previous life, then why hasn't he snitched on Aaliyah already? When I was there, it looked as though he was completely at home, like he belonged. He died months ago. If his memory was coming back. It should have by now.'

'Still, it's a big risk,' Ebony interjected.

'It is.' I nodded.

'No answer from the phone?'

Jonah shook his head. 'No reach, so I conclude she's not in this dimension.'

We agreed.

'What about the mosque?' Jonah asked, the worry clear in his lines.

'I can't show my face there anymore,' I shook my head.

'And I very much doubt that she would be anywhere near there either,' Ebs came to my rescue. 'The mosque is a hot spot now after the Anti-Terrorism raided it. She wouldn't want to run the risk of being identified by them. They'd have a field day with an alien.'

We both nodded.

'There has to be something we can do.' The big man was becoming anxious. I felt for him. And for Aaliyah. She'd helped us and we owed her. Not only that, I reluctantly had to admit that she was growing on me. I almost liked her.

Almost.

'Other than going back again, I don't know how to warn her.'

'Could you go back?'

'I'm not sure,' I answered honestly. 'I got away with it last time, but there's no guarantee it will happen that way again. I'd have to make sure no one could recognise me. Including preferably Ibrahim.'

'It would be dicey,' even Jonah agreed.

'Yes. But we owe her that.' I answered. 'I owe her to at least try.'

'We'll get a make-up artist in here,' Ebony suggested. 'Maybe someone with extreme restyling experience. From the film industry. They can make you unrecognisable.'

'Good idea. I'm not comfortable going like this.' I pointed to my clean-shaven face. Since the last visit I'd gone back to my more familiar look. Clean shaven, shorter hair and semi-casual designer suits. Much more comfortable, but immediately discernible as an enemy in Arand's camp. I don't think there would be anyone in the palace who wouldn't single out their main enemy's estranged son. We didn't have time for me to grow a beard again, so make-up was the way to go.

'I'll make a call.' Ebony left the room.

'Thanks,' Jonah said.

I smiled. 'I have to do this. At least try.'

'Be careful. We can't lose you either.'

I laughed. 'A few days ago, you were all too happy to get rid of me.'

He joined me in my amusement.

'Yeah. I was quite obnoxious.'

I cocked my head in answer and smiled again. More wasn't needed. 'You're going through a lot.'

'Still no excuse.'

'No worries, Jonah. We're partners in this.'

'We are.' He nodded, then stood up and left the room.

I was alone. Goosebumps ran up and down my arms. Sweat trickled down my spine. The familiar dull ache of anxiety started at the base of my skull.

Yes, I owed her. Big time. And I would go. But it didn't mean I was comfortable doing it. Just the idea of returning scared the shit out of me. Especially now I knew I might encounter Ibrahim. He might not recognise Aaliyah, but my gut had no doubt whatsoever that he would identify me in the blink of an eye.

Ebony's make-up artist came early the next day lugging a big rolling case full of prosthetics and more tubes, pots and boxes of makeup than I'd ever seen in one place.

He was an eccentric person, dressed in colourful, bohemian clothes, sporting a black goatee and pink hair which brought a smile to my lips. Creativity would be needed here, he seemed like the right person.

We discussed what the general image should project and the options he could do. An hour later I sat in a chair with cheek prosthetics, a half bald head and a full grey beard. A padded body suite would add the illusion of another fifty pounds to my silhouette.

Three hours into the makeover and even my mother wouldn't recognise me anymore, and that was the general idea. I started to feel better.

I PUSHED the nausea down as soon as I materialised in the dense forest two kilometres outside of the city. This was the safest place. Even if people here were used to transportation, it would put a spotlight on me, and I didn't want to push my luck. Back home in my family's part of this dimension, transportation was solely through the central stations. Thank goodness Arand's technology was much more advanced. Ebony had adjusted my old transporter to use the new technology, enabling me to appear wherever I wanted.

There was no one around. Great.

Now all I had to do was return to the tavern where I'd found Aaliyah last time and hope she still frequented it.

She did, though not every day. I hung around for thirty-six hours before she turned up. I wasn't in the tavern all that time, that would have been too suspicious. But nearby. Far enough not to stand out, close enough to see her finally walk through the door with a man in tow.

Hunched over like the old man I portrayed, I entered the dim tavern. It was half full. Not as busy as last time I was in this dimension, but still enough people to make me feel uncomfortable. I glanced to the side, to a dirty mirror and marvelled at the stranger who looked back at me. No one would recognise me here. Probably not even Aaliyah. But I'd cross that bridge when I got there.

Aaliyah and her companion sat in a small alcove to the right side of the bar. It was private, something I think they needed by the way they huddled together in an animated discussion.

I pulled a bar chair back and pretended to struggle onto it. The bar keeper hardly glanced my way, sure I wasn't a big spender.

A bar maid finally took my order, and I huddled over the glass, full into my new persona. It also allowed me to clandestinely observe my surroundings. Small groups of people laughed and talked at the bar between me and the alcove where Aaliyah was. Others came up to the bar, ordered and left with their drinks, none giving me as much as a glance. As far as they were concerned, I was just another old, lonely drunk.

Now I just had to get Aaliyah's attention without alerting anyone else.

My chance came when she approached to order a new round of drinks. She stood just a metre from me leaning on the wooden bar. I coughed softly. No reaction. Louder, still nothing. The bar keeper was almost back with her drinks. It was now or never.

I fumbled with my glass, feigning clumsiness and the container toppled, spilling the contents over the bar and soaking Aaliyah's elbow. She turned to me, anger in her violet eyes.

'Watch what you're doing, old man,' she admonished me.

'My apologies, my lady,' I stuttered, taking my scarf and mopping up the liquid and dabbing at her sleeve. That angered her even more and she grabbed my wrist.

'Keep you hand off me unless you want to lose it,' she hissed.

'That wouldn't do, I need it for our quest,' I answered softly in my own voice. She looked at me intently, suddenly interested.

'What did you say?' Her voice was subdued, excluding anyone but me.

'Our quest would be hampered if I lost any limbs, Aaliyah.'

She looked me up and down. Tested my strength in the wrist she held. 'Gabe?' she whispered.

I smiled.

'What the hell are you doing here?' She was annoyed. Then worry clouded her features. 'Is the big man okay?'

'He is. I'm not here for him,' I whispered. She raised her eyebrow in question until I added, 'I'm here for you.'

The bar keeper returned with her drinks. 'Is this bum bothering you, my lady?'

'No, Hassan. He's an old acquaintance. One I haven't seen in a long time. He spilled his drink, please provide a refill.'

When my new beverage appeared, she paid the bar keeper and turned back to me. 'Join us at my table.' Aaliyah pointed to the alcove. Sure, it was private, but there was someone else there. I couldn't hesitate too much. The barkeeper was watching me.

'Thank you, my lady.' I picked up my drink, and unsteadily followed her to where her companion sat.

Aaliyah gestured I sit on the right of her, with my back to the door. It wasn't my favourite seating arrangement; I couldn't keep an eye on who came into the tavern. Aaliyah could. I would have to trust her.

The man she'd come in with looked as uncomfortable as

I was. He looked me up and down, pulling up his nose at the somewhat stale smell I'd cultivated in the past thirty-six hours. He cocked his head in question to Aaliyah.

'Who is this?'

'This is a friend,' she answered. Our voices were soft, almost whispering. No one outside of our alcove would be able to hear what we were saying. Her friend wasn't reassured.

'One who is aware.'

Now that was cryptic. Aware of what? If she meant the Establishment and our quest, then it followed that this guy obviously did as well. Otherwise, her words would be meaningless to him.

That put him in a different light. I looked up and studied the guy in more detail. He was average in every way. A grey mouse. The kind I would never notice in my past life. His fidgeting told me that was not his usual haunt. The constant glances he sent to Aaliyah and the nervous tremor in his hand around the glass compounded that conclusion. There was also something else there. A reverence. No, admiration. Maybe even love.

'He is not what he seems.' The guy was observant. I'll give him that.

Aaliyah turned back to me. 'What did you mean, you came here for me.'

I glanced at her companion, then back to her, expecting some kind of introduction, but she just nodded. I shrugged my indifference. On the inside I was worried.

'I came here to tell you something,' I continued. She nodded me onwards. 'Last time. When I left that storage room, I saw someone we knew. Someone I'd never expected to see here.'

'Who?'

She was obviously comfortable with names in front of her companion.

'Ibrahim.'

'Fuck.' That said it all.

'There's more.' I cautioned. 'He's in a position of power here. He was dressed in black with guilt edging and wore a curved sword.'

'The gold thread,' she asked. 'Was that in any specific pattern?'

'I didn't really look that closely,' I had to admit. 'I was too busy hiding, once I got my body to move.'

'Understandable.'

She took a sip from her drink.

'How did people act around him?' Worry creases became more pronounced on her forehead.

'With a lot of reverence. Fear even. He is obviously someone with authority.'

'This is bad.' She continued. 'Very bad. By the sound of your description, I think he's in Bashir's inner circle.'

'If that is so, then why hasn't Bashir arrested you?' the companion asked. He was evidently party to what had happened on Earth.

'That's what's worrying me,' she agreed.

'Maybe he's lost some of his memories,' I suggested. 'The big man had the same after reincarnation.'

'Could be. But I'm going to have to be very careful.'

'What worries me most,' I added. 'Is that he's in such a high position even though you took his ticket-to-heaven. I'd expected him to be a grunt once reincarnated.'

Aaliyah nodded. 'Somehow, he must have stood out. Maybe someone recognised him in the holding pens, or he managed to get a message out. He knew Bashir. He met him the one time my brother came to that dimension. This is not looking good. Either he's a volcano waiting to explode, or he and my brother are brooding on a plan.'

I nodded and drank heavily from my glass. Both options were lousy. Whatever was happening, Ibrahim was bad news.

I pushed the chair back and—fully in my role—struggled to my feet. 'Time for me to go.'

'Thanks.' Aaliyah whispered.

'I owed you. Big time. Least I could do.' I waved it off.

'I'm aware of the danger you faced by coming here,' she added.

We left it at that. Both uncomfortable with friendliness. It wasn't what we did.

I made my way to the door on pretended shaky legs, not looking back at either Aaliyah or the bar keeper. I'd done what I come here for. Now I had to get the hell out of Dodge.


TWO HOURS LATER, I was back on Earth. I'd shed my makeup and the smelly cloths, taken a shower and finally allowed myself a deep sigh of relief.

'Thank god you're okay.' Ebony hugged me. 'We were worried.'

'You were gone for almost two days.' Jonah chimed in.

'She didn't show up at the bar until a few hours ago, and I had no idea where else to find her.'

'How did she react?' Jonah was still apprehensive.

'Surprised. And worried. She thinks he's in Bashir's inner circle.'

'Not a good development.'

I agreed wholeheartedly. 'Understatement of the year.'

'Ebony looked as concerned as I felt. 'Does she think he might have amnesia?'

'I don't know. She and the guy with her don't trust him.'

Jonah picked up on the companion. 'There was a guy with her?' I nodded. 'And he knows about what we're doing?'

'Yes. She had no secrets from him.'

'Who is he?' Ebony challenged.

'She didn't say. But he's not any direct family, or I would have recognised him. They seemed like old friends. Comfortable in each other's company, the kind that comes from a long relationship and trust.'

'She knows what she's doing,' Jonah concluded. 'Thanks Gabe. I appreciate it.'

I smiled. More wasn't needed.

## Chapter Forty-Six

'INCOMING!'

Ebony's shout filled the room and was enhanced by the shrill siren that accompanied a teleportation warning.

Jonah sprang up, the ever-present axe already in his hand.

The book I was reading clattered to the floor as I pushed myself out of the easy chair and sprinted to the side table where my weapons were.

Incoming was bad news. We were all here, none of our few allies had announced their arrival, so the obvious conclusion was that whoever was transporting to our lair was unwanted and most likely an enemy.

The soft whirring sound intensified, and a blurring image appeared in the centre of the vast room. The contours were hazy at first and made it difficult to determine either friend or foe. Then the process intensified, and I made out Aaliyah's shape. I was instantly concerned and glanced sideways at an equally puzzled Jonah. Aaliyah never surprised us like this.

Her form solidified and it became obvious why this visit was different. Pools of purple blood appeared beneath her huddled form.

We both rushed to her as soon as the whirring stopped. Jonah beat me to it and caught her as she collapsed into his arms. He picked Aaliyah up effortlessly and brought her to the sofa where he lay her down carefully. Ebony rushed over with clean towels and cloths from the kitchen. I joined them.

Aaliyah was conscious but in great pain. Her creased brow, the tightness of her lips, her closed eyes and the sweat on her brow confirmed my conclusion; that she was in a really bad state.

Ebony walked to the side of the room, mobile in hand and punched in the speed dial for our medic. 'Get here, stat!' I heard her say. She moved back to the kitchen and filled a bowl with water which she put on the table next to the sofa.

She pushed a worried Jonah to the side and with the wet cloth wiped the blood and grime from Aaliyah's forehead. It came back deep purple. She rinsed it in the bowl again and continued her work.

The familiar tingles were present at the base of my spine. The irritating voice in the back of my mind screamed that whatever had happened to Aaliyah was bad, not just for her, but for all of us. Ibrahim came to mind again. But if this was his doing, why now?

I waited with my hundreds of questions until Aaliyah slowly opened her eyes.

Her body tensed and she tried to sit up, shock etched in her features.

'Easy, easy,' Ebony said softly, holding her down. 'You're with friends. It's okay now, Aaliyah. You made it here.'

Her eyes open to the max. Aaliyah stared at Ebony, slowly turned her head to Jonah, then to me. Realisation dawned on her, and she let out her pent-up breath. Her tense muscles relaxed, and she let herself be pushed back into the plush cushions of the sofa. She closed her eyes tightly as the pain once again announced its presence, all adrenaline now depleted.

Five minutes later, there was a knock at the door and Jonah moved to let Doctor Patil in. He rushed over to the sofa and pushed us away. We gladly made room for him and watched as he proceeded to take control of the situation.

'More clean water, please,' he ordered, without looking up from his tasks. He pulled his old-fashioned doctor's bag towards him and opened it. Rummaging around in the contents, he brought out a collection of syringes, small bottles of liquids and a stethoscope.

Not for the first time, I was thankful for Ebony's team.

We hovered around the sofa while he did his initial checks, then gave Aaliyah an injection with what I expect was a painkiller or maybe a light sedative. Her body relaxed and the tightness of her features softened. The bleeding abated slowly, the edges of the many cuts slowly knitting back together. Colour started to come back into her features, and I let out a sigh of relief.

'She'll be all right,' Doctor Patil announced. 'No major damage as far as I can see, but I do want to see her in the clinic and do a full examination as soon as possible. She's lost a lot of blood.'

'Will do, doctor,' Ebony answered. 'Thanks for getting here so quickly. We'll organise transportation and see you there.' Her friendly dismissal urged the good doctor to leave us. He—like so many of our helpers—was here on a need-to-know basis.

Doctor Patil gathered his things and left, pulling the door closed behind him.

Ebony keyed some commands in the computer and reset the warnings and alarms she had in place. When she came back to us, Aaliyah pushed herself up into a sitting position. The bleeding may have stopped, the pain hadn't. She soldiered through it, sweat again on her forehead, and sat up.

'What happened?' I asked apprehensively. The tingles intensified exponentially and moved up my spine. Jonah's creased brow and dark eyes mirrored my foreboding.

'My father is dead.' Tears congealed at the edge of her eyes and slowly made their way down her cheeks.

Jonah glanced at me, concern growing. He took her hand in support.

'How?' I asked.

'They murdered him.' Her voice faltered.

I didn't want to rush her, but I was desperate to know what had happened. Jonah squeezed her hand to urge her onwards. She looked up, first to him, then to me. The anguish in her features touched me. It also intensified the block of concrete that had taken up residence in my gut. Whatever it was. It was bad. Very, very bad.

'Bashir, my brother. Him and his thugs, they attacked our home and corralled the whole family together. I tried to stop them. I did.' Her cries broke my heart. 'Nothing helped. There were too many of them. Too many.' Jonah pulled her into his arms, and she sobbed hysterically against his chest.

My mind worked in overdrive. Bashir had taken over? He'd killed his father? Surely that wasn't right. He was basically a coward. There was no way in Hell he would have the cojones to do that on his own. Never mind his rag-tag group of thugs, they were no different. All mouth and no spine.

There had to be more. This was bad enough. But my gut told me it would get a whole lot worse very quickly.

I glanced at my partners and the apprehension I saw in their eyes compounded the sense of foreboding that shot sharp stabs of pain into my brain.

Aaliyah stopped crying. She reluctantly pushed herself backwards, out of Jonah's embrace and sat up straight. She sniffed loudly and angrily wiped the tears from her cheek.

She looked up at us, daring someone to say something about her temporary lack of control. We abstained.

She took a deep breath and stared me right in the eye. 'Bashir had backing.'

I swallowed hard and nodded her onwards. I didn't want to hear what she was going to say, but I had to.

'Your brother and your father came into the room where they were holding us.'

The bottom dropped out of my world.

I'd known. Of course I had.

He would need support and who better to get it from, than the competition. I flinched under Aaliyah's hard stare. Anger grew and replaced the anticipation of earlier.

'Did they kill your father?' I had to ask. I had to know.

She shook her head. 'No. They didn't actually do the dirty work. They just encouraged Bashir to. So that makes them just as accountable.'

I nodded. 'More,' I answered. 'They probably engineered the whole thing.'

Her turn to nod.

'What happened?' Jonah asked her. She turned to him, and I felt the heat of her hatred leave me for the moment. I had no illusions. She saw me as the enemy. It was, after all, my family.

'His father.' She pointed to me. 'He pushed Bashir to confront my father. Bashir demanded that dad relinquish all control of the family and the business to him. When my father refused, he panicked.'

I saw it all in my mind's eye. Bashir crumbling, then my own father and Michael urging him onwards.

'He demanded it again. Father refused for a second time. Michael said something like "make him" and Bashir turned to one of the guards. He shouted that he was the new leader, and that my father would relinquish control, or he would hurt the family.' She swallowed hard. Her anger holding back the tears that threatened to push through her hard facade.

'My father refused. Bashir grabbed the guard's sword and hefted it above his head. He ordered my father to relinquish control again. When he shook his head, Bashir brought the sword down and…and…almost severed my father's head from his body.'

She deflated again; all energy seeped from her body.

She continued. 'We were shocked into silence. Then my mother started to scream. Bashir looked as shocked as we were. He stared at the bloody sword in his hand, then threw it away in horror. He turned towards your father who urged him onwards.'

'You are now the head of the family, he said to Bashir. It broke my brother out of his stupor. He grabbed our mother and pulled her violently from my father's dead body. She screamed and flailed at him. He struck her and she fell over. I don't know if she's still alive. At the least, she was knocked unconscious. That was the moment the rest of the family came into action. My siblings attacked Bashir and his men.

I joined in. I know I killed at least one of them, but there were too many. Michael and your father stood to the side, not partaking in the fight, just observing with a wicked smile on their faces. They were enjoying it. I know they were.'

'I fought. We all did. But it went downhill quickly. I saw bodies on the ground. Lots of blood. I was wounded myself. I knew I couldn't win. The only thing that awaited me there was my own death, and that wouldn't help anyone. Just before they overpowered me, I managed to run out of the room, through to the courtyard and I teleported here.'

The room was silent.

I didn't know what to say. Words would fall short on the emotions we were all feeling now. My own were governed by equal parts rage and shame. Shame for my family and their part in this patricide. Rage because I hadn't been there to stop this from happening.

That I wouldn't have been able to, was of little solace. I should have been there. I should have at least tried. Instead, Arand, and possibly more of his family, were dead.

And mine was to blame.

THE DOMINION SERIES

TO HELL
& BACK

*USA TODAY* BESTSELLING AUTHOR
MONIQUE SINGLETON

vinci-books.com/hellandback

**The big man is dying—again.**

He refuses to be reincarnated, but we need him. My father's slave trade threatens Earth's survival, and we're the only ones who can stop it. But with The Establishment closing in, staying alive long enough to save two worlds may be the toughest challenge yet.

Turn the page for a free preview…

## To Hell and Back: Chapter One

HE'S GETTING WORSE. Much worse.

Not just physically, but mentally too. Jonah is paranoid. Couple that with a two-hundred-and-forty-pound physique, immense strength and a violent nature, and you have a disaster waiting to happen.

We're all tiptoeing around him, walking on eggshells to avoid him blowing up. Last time that happened—two days ago—three of Ebony's people ended up visiting doctor Patil. One came back with a cast on his arm. The other two made do with stitches.

Other days Jonah's depressed to a point where we fear for his life.

The situation is taking its toll on all of us, but most of all on Ebony. Jonah has distanced himself from everyone who cares for him including her, and it's breaking her heart.

She buries herself in work, as expected, but I can see it hurts.

The blueprints Aaliyah gave me are coming to life in the

workshop: a mini re-incarnation machine. It is a completely unheard-of technology in this dimension, but common in mine. Finally, it will be used for good, if we can convince Jonah to go ahead with our plan. And that's a big "if".

Reuniting him with his old body is the only way to save him, but the outcome of the procedure is uncertain. His human body is in cryostasis, a relatively new technique here. Human medicine is able to freeze bodies but has yet to bring anyone back from the dead. Add that Jonah's essence has already been re-incarnated once before into his current —declining—alien form, and we have no way of knowing whether it can survive another procedure.

And then there's Jonah himself.

For this to work, he must want to live.

Only his tenacity will see him through. Re-incarnation is an invasive procedure, painful and disorienting. If he lacks the resolve, then all this has been for nothing.

We don't have much time. Jonah's alien body is failing rapidly.

His blackouts are more frequent and protracted, leaving him disoriented and volatile. One of his two hearts functions on less than half-strength. We think he can live on only the second one, but the body was never designed for that. Our two hearts complement each other fully. The strain on the remaining heart is already exceptionally high and it's just a matter of time before that one gives up as well. Especially because Jonah refuses to slow down.

He complains about voices in his head that are driving him mad. And he berates me constantly for bringing him back in this new body.

In general, he hates his life.

And me.

We're running on borrowed time.

And at present, Jonah is nowhere near ready for the only thing that will save him.

## To Hell and Back: Chapter Two

WE WERE GATHERED TOGETHER at the dinner table. Always a difficult time.

We had to face each other and make small talk. In the past weeks, I'd found reasons not to be there, but today Ebony had specifically asked me to come.

'You have to go through this, Gabriel. You can't keep avoiding Aaliyah,' she tried to convince me.

I shrugged. 'I was doing a good job with it.' I attempted to make light of the situation.

She shook her head.

I guess that was a negative then. Bummer.

'She doesn't want me there,' I tried. Ebony stayed silent. 'Really, she doesn't.'

Still no answer.

I gave in. 'Okay. I'll be there.'

She smiled, kissed me on the cheek and turned to leave my quarters. 'Six o'clock, Gabe. No excuses.'

I'D MADE it on time, and it took all of five minutes before Aaliyah went for my throat. Virtually, but her words hurt me almost as much as her knife could. I felt guilty already. I didn't need her to compound the emotion.

'That's not fair, Aaliyah.' Jonah's loud voice stopped her tirade. She turned to face him, temporarily freeing me from the onslaught.

'He's not the one who killed your father.'

'It's his fault,' she shouted at the big man. 'He started this stupid quest and because of that my father is dead.'

'Actually, I started it. Gabe joined me. Not that it matters. From what I know, it was just a matter of time,' Jonah answered. 'Your families have been at each other's throats for centuries. We didn't cause this. It would have happened anyway.'

I waited. Not wanting to divert Aaliyah's attention back to me.

'Besides,' the big man continued. 'It wasn't Gabriel who killed him. It was Bashir.'

'Brainwashed by his father,' she pointed to me with an outstretched arm, her glare sending new shivers up and down my spine.

Jonah shrugged. 'Maybe. But it still wasn't Gabriel.'

She crossed her arms in front of her chest and stared at Jonah, her eyes shooting fire. 'Why are you protecting him?'

'Because he doesn't deserve this.'

I was as surprised as Aaliyah. I'd felt the brunt of Jonah's rage in the past weeks, and this was completely out of character.

'He's sacrificed everything to bring his dad down. He has no home. No family. He killed his brother for wounding me. He risked his life for every single one of us here, including you.'

Aaliyah was silenced. She looked at Jonah from under her eyebrows, sulking.

'He's the reason we're all here. That we're doing this. So how about we give him some slack for a change. He can't help who his dad is any more than you could.'

Jonah sat down and left it to us.

'Jonah's right,' Ebony chimed in.

Aaliyah reluctantly nodded ever so slightly.

'Maybe we should stop referring to our real enemy as "Gabriel's Father" all the time,' Jonah suggested.

He looked up at me. 'What's his name? No way I'm calling him "God" or anything like that.'

I smiled despite the situation. 'His given name in Cal-Tan, it's an old name in our dimension.'

'Not anything biblical?'

'No, it originates from before we ever came in contact with your religions.'

'Well, Cal-Tan it is then,' Jonah stated resolutely.

I was swamped with feelings of gratitude for my big friend.

I felt relief. I hoped it would distance my father from me and let me relax a bit. Jonah was right. It had felt like a personal attack every time someone referred to him as my father. My name always came first. It was depressing, and infuriating. It wasn't my fault we were related.

I despised the man, maybe more than anyone here, with the exception of Aaliyah. He'd constantly made my life a living hell. First with his never-ending manipulations and denigration tactics, and now with his relentless pursuit of me and my strange group of friends.

I needed distance, and hopefully this would give it to me.

'Now that's out of the way,' Jonah brought us back to the present in his weirdly practical way. 'Let's eat.'

His appetite was legendary, and today was no exception.

We all helped ourselves to the great meal Sly, the cook-come-bodyguard, had prepared. The man was an accomplished chef, and I enjoyed his food every single time.

We ate in relative silence. Mainly because of the good food, but still partly due to the argument and the tentative status-quo that was in effect. I glanced up from under my eyebrows at Aaliyah. She was pushing her food around on the plate, not eating like the rest of us. I felt for her. She'd been party to the brutal murder of her father. Even though she didn't agree with his practices, she'd loved the man deeply.

It showed.

Not for the first time, I wished I could turn back time.

Not one of my talents.

Regrettably.

# To Hell and Back: Chapter Three

'WE NEED to determine our next steps,' I broached the subject carefully.

After-dinner banter was over. It was time to get down to business.

We were all seated at the big round table in the dining area that doubled as an extra meeting room. The light outside was waning and subdued lamps around the perimeter offered enough illumination to be able to read the documents on electronic devices that invariably followed every meeting. The blinds were drawn and only feint pinpricks of moving headlights showed we were in a populated area. The triple glass held out any sounds.

I sat between Jonah and Ebony, I thought between friends would be comfortable, whereas the other side of the table with Aaliyah still noticeably cooler. She was coming around millimetre by millimetre, but the status quo was still very fragile.

I'd calculated badly, the air between Jonah and Ebs was almost as loaded as between Aaliyah and me, though this time it wasn't the result of anything I'd done. They were going through a difficult patch in their relationship, mainly due to Jonah's difficult disposition. He was never easy to live with, now he was downright impossible. They no longer shared a bedroom, another bad sign.

'What are our options?' Ebony asked.

Good question. We didn't have many. Not anymore.

'We've exhausted the Islamic route,' I answered.

'Unless we go to another Islamic community somewhere?' Jonah suggested to my dismay, though he might have a point there.

'What if the mosque shared the information with others?' I asked.

'We have no way of knowing,' Aaliyah answered. 'We must assume they have.'

'The Christian side is actively hunting us, so I don't think we have much leeway there.' Ebony pointed out.

'Unless we can use some assets we already have.' Jonah joined the conversation.

'You have any in mind?' Aaliyah sat close by, not touching him, but still nearby. I expect it was the feeling of safety the big man gave her. No matter that he was as unstable as ever. He still exhumed a strength she needed.

'Benedict?' I asked.

Jonah shrugged. 'Maybe'

'Who's Benedict?' Aaliyah asked him.

Jonah filled her in with a brief history of our dealings with the archbishop.

'Sounds like an asset.'

'Yes, but one we don't want to endanger. Not while he may be our only way into the Inner Circle of the Establishment.'

'Any success on the data side?' I asked Ebony.

'Some. I've picked up a financial stream that looks promising. If I can block that, or even better divert it, then it will be a major blow to the Ventus Dei.'

'Then what?'

'Do you have any contacts we could approach?' Jonah asked Aaliyah. 'Anyone?'

'I'd have to think,' she replied. 'Most have been lost now with the change of power, but there have always been people like me who opposed the direction Bashir wanted. Problem is most of them are still back in my dimension.'

'Is there any way you can contact them?' I added. 'Without endangering them or yourself.'

She glared at me. Still not happy with my presence. Then her eyes softened, and she let go of some of her anger. 'I'm afraid Bashir may be monitoring all communications.'

'I would, if I were him,' I agreed.

She nodded.

Okay, another dead end then.

'If we could find a way, 'Ebony suggested. 'Would you be open to it?'

'Maybe.'

**Grab your copy...**
**vinci-books.com/hellandback**